A Race Against Death

A Race Against Death

A Lenny Moss Mystery

Timothy Sheard

Five Star • Waterville, Maine

First Edition
First Printing: August 2006

Published in 2006 in conjunction with Tekno Books
and Ed Gorman.

Set in 11 pt. Plantin by Christina S. Huff.

Printed in the United States on permanent paper.

Library of Congress Cataloging-in-Publication Data

Sheard, Timothy.
    A race against death : a Lenny Moss mystery / Timothy Sheard.
—1st ed.
        p. cm.
    ISBN 1-59414-463-X (hc : alk. paper)
    1. Philadelphia (Pa.)—Fiction.   2. Hospitals—Staff—Fiction.
I. Title.
PS3569.H3913R33 2006
    813′.6—dc22   2006000062

For my dear wife, Mary
"Hands off Poland!"

Chapter One

Nurse Gary Tuttle, seated at the foot of the bed, was writing his first note of the morning when he heard his patient mutter "I'm a dead man for sure." Looking up, Gary saw a sour look on Rupert Darling's face.

"It's no fun being sick, is it?" said Gary, offering a sympathetic look.

"You can't fool me," Darling said. "I know these doctors like to experiment on you, and when you die they cut you open to see where they screwed up." He scratched his chest with long, bony fingers and looked with despair at the other patients in the Intensive Care Unit.

Gary knew Darling had put off coming to the hospital until he lost the feeling in his legs. Unable to walk, he finally called the paramedics, who wrapped him in a shabby blanket and brought him to James Madison University Hospital.

Tests revealed a progressive paralysis that might be permanent or might go away on its own, the course was wholly unpredictable. Darling took the uncertainty of the prognosis as proof that the doctors were idiots and that his life was in greater danger from them than from any disease.

While the patient muttered complaints, a housekeeper mopped the floor a few feet away, and the stinging odor of bleach tickled the young nurse's nose. The soft *sssh-ssssh* of a ventilator filled the room with its gentle rhythm. Gary closed his eyes and tried to imagine how the blind navigated through the world by their other senses. He was a sandy-haired fellow just a few pounds over his ideal weight, dressed in a green scrub suit. Rimless glasses framed sleepy blue eyes and a gentle countenance.

"You are perhaps not getting enough sleep, Mr. Tuttle?" said a puzzled voice in the darkness.

Gary opened his eyes, saw Dr. Samir Singh, the ICU attending physician, watching him with a bemused look on his face while a gaggle of residents and medical students stood by. The nurse felt his face begin to color in embarrassment.

"I'm sorry, Dr. Singh, I was just . . . listening."

"An excellent skill to develop," said the physician, speaking with a polished British accent that reflected his London training. He stepped to the bedside. "Good morning, Mr. Darling. How are you today?"

"Lousy! I don't want you draining all my blood and replacing it with some synthetic crap. I know how you doctors operate!"

Dr. Singh turned to his team. "Mr. Darling is under the misperception that the plasmapheresis treatment we are planning is an experimental procedure." To Gary he said, "Tell me please, what is the level of the patient's loss of sensation?"

"I, uh, haven't checked that yet," said Gary, realizing he hadn't finished his neurological exam.

"It is very important to assess the level of the paralysis every four hours," said Singh. "May I have a Q-tip, please?"

Gary pulled a Q-tip from a bedside cart and handed it to the physician. Singh broke off the end of the wooden stick, leaving a tip as sharp as a splinter.

"In the past we used a needle to test for the sensation of sharp," he explained. "But with the advent of HIV, a needle

8

used to prick the skin becomes a potential source of exposure for the physician."

Beginning at the chest he alternately jabbed the patient with the sharp end and pressed gently with the cotton-padded tip. "Is that sharp or dull?" he asked. When the doctor reached the groin, Darling found it difficult to distinguish the sensations. At the thigh the patient, frustrated, gave up answering.

"Note that the paralysis is symmetrical and ascending. When it approaches the level of the cervical spine, there will be loss of enervation to the diaphragm. At that point we will have to—"

"*Attention! Attention! Code Blue, Intensive Care Unit, third floor.*"

The physician froze in place at the sound of the hospital operator in the loudspeaker overhead. Perplexed, he looked up and down the ICU, but saw nobody rushing to a bedside.

"The operator must mean the *CCU*," said Dr. Singh. "Nobody is coding in our—"

Whoosh! The automatic doors to the unit opened as a stretcher came hurtling through.

"She's brady'd down!" yelled a nurse who was pushing the stretcher. "I called a code from the phone in the elevator!" He squeezed an ambu bag connected to oxygen with one hand while guiding the stretcher with the other. A young African-American woman lay motionless on the stretcher while a woman in a white lab coat pressed vigorously on the patient's chest.

With nurses and physicians rushing to assist, Dr. Singh said, "I was led to believe that this patient was going directly from the Emergency Room to the OR."

The ER nurse grabbed a fistful of sheet. "They told me she was coming to the ICU to be tanked up first."

After they moved the lifeless figure to the bed, the charge nurse told Gary, "I wasn't expecting this admission for a couple of hours. Can you handle a second patient?"

"Uh, I guess so," he said, feeling a knot in his belly tighten at the thought of caring for a patient in cardiac arrest.

The charge nurse saw the worry on his face. "Relax. I wouldn't give you a train wreck your second week of orientation. You'll pick up Dillie's pneumonia; she can take the admission."

"Okay," said Gary, feeling the knot begin to loosen.

Dr. Singh asked the Emergency Room nurse, "What medications have you given her?"

"One amp of atropine and one epi."

"Stop CPR, feel for a pulse."

The woman in the lab coat took her hands away from the patient's chest and felt at the groin. In the space between the patient's legs a pool of bright red blood glistened beneath the harsh fluorescent light.

"She's got a pulse!" the woman announced. "It's thready, but palpable."

Singh turned to Dillie. "Run a liter of normal saline in under pressure." While Dillie was preparing the intravenous fluids, Singh asked the woman in the lab coat, "Why hasn't the OB team taken this patient to the OR, Doctor . . . ?"

"I'm a fourth-year student," she said. "Kate Palmer. The ER Attending told me that Doctor Odom was reluctant to accept the admission onto his service."

"What do you mean 'reluctant'? This is his patient, is it not? Dr. Odom performed the abortion on her four days ago. Is that not correct?"

"She was his patient last Saturday, yes, but I understand he told the ER that she should be on the Infectious Disease Service, so we paged ID. They haven't answered yet."

Perplexed, Singh said, "This patient's infection is due to remnants of the fetus adhering to her uterine wall. Dr. Odom *must* take her to surgery and remove the source of the infection before ID can help her. It is her only chance of survival."

Noting that the first unit of blood was nearly completed, he told the charge nurse, "Hang two more units of blood, please."

"I'll send the aide right away," she said, hastily scribbling numbers and a name on a pair of blood bank requests.

"Tell them also to thaw two units of frozen plasma in the microwave right away."

Dillie informed Dr. Singh that the patient's temperature was one hundred and four degrees. She hurried to the supply closet for the hypothermia blanket.

Feeling his frustration mount, the attending physician turned to his medical resident. "Page Dr. Odom and tell him he *must* come and see the patient right away. Page him STAT. And page Infectious Disease as well."

"Got it," said the resident, hurrying to the phone to make the calls.

Dr. Singh studied the patient, worry dragging his handsome features down. He watched the young woman gasp for breath like a fish out of water. Despite the one hundred percent oxygen being forced into her lungs, she was experiencing severe air hunger—a grave sign.

The resident returned to the bedside. "OB said they're doing an emergency C-section. They'll be up as soon as they're through."

As Dillie pulled back the top sheet in order to put the cooling blanket in place, she saw a stream of bright red blood pour out of the patient's vagina. "The blood is a river," she said to Singh, her face grim.

"She has perforated her uterus. She must have the surgery

right away." Singh watched the blood pressure reading on the monitor slowly fall. He turned to the surgery resident.

"Have you ever done an exploratory laporotomy?"

The young resident, heavily muscled and darkly handsome, hesitated, knowing what was coming.

"I've *assisted* with one. I've never actually *done* one."

"You may have to begin the procedure; it is the only way to control her bleeding."

"You mean, open her abdomen? Here in the unit?"

"Yes," said Singh, his face deadly serious. "She is losing blood faster than we can replace it. If you can clamp off the uterine artery it will give us time to stabilize her and transport her to the OR. Dr. Odom can complete the hysterectomy in a more controlled setting."

He asked Dillie to bring a cut-down tray. As the pool of blood between the young woman's legs grew, her blood pressure continued to fall.

Chapter Two

Dr. Singh looked with growing alarm at the young woman's falling blood pressure and at the blood pooling in the bed. He was worried even more by the patient's oxygen saturation, which was only eighty-five—too low to sustain the vital organs, especially the brain. He glanced at the doors to the ICU, looking for the obstetrics team to come take her to surgery, but there was no sign of them.

Handing the young surgical resident a sterile gown and a pair of gloves, Singh began to don similar garments. Dillie peeled open the cut-down tray and set it on the bedside table, exposing the shiny, stainless steel instruments. Once gowned, the young surgery resident's voice cracked from anxiety as he instructed the nurse to pour betadine into a bowl. He cleared his throat, dipped a wad of sterile gauze into the antiseptic, and began to wipe the abdomen with a trembling hand.

"First try to find the perforation," Singh told him. "If you cannot locate the bleeding site, clamp off the uterine artery."

The resident selected a scalpel from the tray. Holding it above the patient's abdomen, he went over in his mind the layers that he would be cutting through, anticipating the bleeding that would follow the incision. If the young woman even had enough blood left to ooze from a fresh wound.

As he slowly brought the scalpel down to the skin to make

the first cut, the cardiac monitor alarm sounded, startling him. He looked up.

The heart was flat line.

"Begin CPR," said Singh, his voice calm and businesslike.

The resident gratefully put down the scalpel, moved his gloved hands to the chest, and began the compressions. With each compression another rivulet of blood was expelled from the vagina. When the stream of blood spilled onto the floor, Dillie threw towels over the pool to try and keep people from stepping in it amidst all the confusion and excitement.

Crystal, the charge nurse, sent the nurse's aide running to the Blood Bank for more blood and plasma. She called to Gary to mix another bag of epinephrine, reminding him of the concentration. He was happy to be of help, having felt useless during the initial emergency.

After administering adrenalin and atropine, Dr. Singh said, "Stop CPR, feel for a pulse." The resident froze, his hands hovering above the young woman's bare chest, while another resident felt for a pulse. The heart monitor still showed a flat line, the most difficult of all arrhythmias to correct.

"Resume CPR," said Singh. "Give three more amps of epinephrine, an amp of bicarb, and hang another unit of blood."

Kate Palmer, frustrated at being pushed away from the patient by the residents, made her way to the head of the bed. Taking a penlight from her lab coat pocket, she pried open the patient's eyelid and shined the light into it. The pupil was enormous and nonreactive. The other eye's pupil was equally fixed and dilated. The windows to her soul were broken; the spirit had fled.

Dr. Singh saw the look on the medical student's face and

knew at once what she had found. He stepped back from the bed and surveyed the scene. Looking at his watch, he noted that they had been working on the patient for thirty-five minutes without restoring a pulse. The death of the brain convinced him that further efforts would be futile.

"You may stop," he said, his words laden with sadness and finality. "Thank you."

The sadness in his voice was matched by the sorrow in his eyes. The others looked equally dispirited. Nobody spoke as they peeled off their gloves and dropped them in the trash bucket on their way out of the cubicle.

Turning away from the bed, Singh reflected on the fact that the dead woman had no underlying medical problems, having reviewed her history when his team examined her in the Emergency Room. She was not a diabetic. Did not have lupus or sickle cell. Her only significant history was the abortion that had been performed four days ago.

He couldn't understand why Dr. Odom had failed to take the patient from the Emergency Department directly to the OR.

On Seven South, Lenny Moss lifted a bag of trash from a patient's trash receptacle and turned it around, looking for hazardous material. Seeing nothing dangerous, he swung the bag into the wheeled cart, along with the rest of the trash. He was a nondescript man in a blue custodian's uniform, not very tall, with coarse features and a face that would win no beauty contest. His face showed a five o'clock shadow, though it was only eight-thirty in the morning.

As he walked by the tiny pantry, he saw his housekeeping partner Betty stirring a large pitcher. Betty was a middle-aged woman, with gray hair, bow legs, and an unrelenting optimism.

"Hey, Boop," said Lenny, sticking his head into the pantry. "What are you cooking up?"

"Well, dear heart," said Betty. "Since the Lord has seen fit to visit this heat wave upon us, I'm making us some lemonade. Moose brought a bag of lemons and a pound of sugar."

She vigorously stirred the pitcher, added more sugar, then poured herself a cup and sipped it. "Mmm-ah," she said, smacking her lips. "Perfect." She poured a cup for Lenny.

"This is great," said Lenny, delighted by the sharp flavor. His blue custodian's shirt was already wet from perspiration, as were his coarse black hair and thick eyebrows. He took off black-framed glasses and wiped his face with a paper towel.

"I'm afraid some of my coworkers will be heading out for a cold beer come lunchtime," he said.

"Beer is a mighty temptation with heat like this," she said. "Did you go around with the thermometer today?"

"Not yet. I checked several sites yesterday. I got a reading of a hundred and one in Central Sterile. The laundry hit one-ten."

"Lord have mercy! Can't the union do nothing about it?" She dumped more ice cubes into the pitcher and stirred.

"I filed a grievance with the hospital over unsafe working conditions," said Lenny. "Engineering claims they have a new condenser unit they're gonna put on line today. Maybe tomorrow."

"Huh! It'd take a miracle to get *this* old place running like it should." Betty put the pitcher and a sleeve of cups on her housekeeping cart and pushed it into the hall. A carved marble figure of Jesus on the cross sat among the rags and spray bottles of cleaner.

At the nursing station she gave a cup of lemonade to Mai

Loo, a slim, pretty Filipino nurse with long black hair and full scarlet lips. Mai Loo took it gratefully, thanking Betty for her thoughtfulness.

The nurse sipped her lemonade as she checked a chart with doctor's orders. Her lipstick left a scarlet stain in the shape of her lips on the Styrofoam cup. Signing the order sheet, Mai Loo felt eyes staring at her. She looked up, saw one of the hospital messengers staring at her over the OUT box. His dark eyes and blank, expressionless face made her shudder with fear.

She closed the chart and went into the medication room behind the station to get away from the messenger, who continued on his rounds.

Noting the interaction, Betty thought of the birds and the bees. She couldn't blame Maurice, the messenger, for looking a little too long at the girl; she *was* awfully pretty. As Betty made her way along the corridor, she softly hummed, "Bringing in the sheaths . . ."

Lenny emerged from room 712 with a bag of trash in either hand. Hoisting the bag to drop it in the cart, he felt a sharp pain in his leg. Looking down, he saw an intravenous needle sticking out of the bag.

"Shit," he muttered. "Look at this, Boop. Another fricking needle in the trash!"

He ripped open the bag, pulled out the needle and held it up to the light. Betty inspected it with him. Although the shiny steel needle had no blood on the outside, they knew it could easily have been used to inject a patient.

"You got to go to Employee Health and let them check you out," she said.

"Aw, Boop. They're gonna ask me to take that HIV medicine."

"Don't be a stubborn old mule. If the doctor tells you to

17

take the AIDS medicine you take it. It's better to be safe. You know that."

"I know," said Lenny. "I just wish I knew if the needle was contaminated."

"Well, you're a detective, sure as I'm standing here," said Betty, wagging a bony finger at him. "If there's anybody in James Madison Hospital can figure out if a needle was stuck in somebody's behind, it's Lenny Moss."

Chapter Three

Carrying the needle that had stuck him in the leg, Lenny walked to the nursing station. He asked Mai Loo if either of the patients in room 712 had received injections. The nurse opened her medication book and ran her finger down the column.

"No, I don't think so, Lenny. I didn't give them anything by injection. There's no record of the night nurse doing it, either."

"Well, somebody used a needle in there, and I'd really like to know if it's dirty."

The young nurse screwed up her face. "Let's look in the chart. Maybe one of them had some kind of procedure last night."

She pulled the two charts from the rack, opened each one, and read the doctor's and nurse's notes for the last twenty-four hours.

"I'm sorry," she said. "I don't see anything that needed a needle."

"Damn! Do either of the patients have any disease I should know about?"

Mai Loo hesitated. "You mean, like HIV?"

"Yeah, like HIV."

"That's confidential information. I can't tell you."

"But I was stuck with a needle!"

"Do you want me to lose my license? The only people who

are allowed to know the patient's condition are the ones who take care of him."

"Great. So they could have AIDS or hepatitis and nobody's going to let me in on it."

"It's not like that, Lenny. If you go to Employee Health, the HIV counselor will come review the patient's medical history. If either one of them has a communicable disease, they'll tell you."

"They will?"

"Of course. Go see Employee Health."

Lenny called his supervisor and told him what happened. After filling out an Incident Report, he made his way to the Employee Health Clinic. Without knowing if the needle was contaminated, he doubted that they would be able to tell him anything he didn't already know. But as a union steward he knew better than anyone else that if he came down with AIDS and he hadn't followed the hospital protocols for a work injury, workmen's compensation would refuse to pay his benefits.

Dr. Leslie Odom, an attending physician on the Obstetrics-Gynecology service, advanced on the ICU nursing station, his phalanx of residents, interns and medical students guarding his flanks and rear. He was a short, trim man dressed in an expensive pinstriped suit, silk shirt, and a tie of understated elegance. Seeing Dr. Singh writing in a chart, he said, "Good morning. I was in the OR when I heard the code being called. Was it the young woman from the ER with sepsis?"

Looking up, Singh concealed his anger beneath a neutral demeanor.

"Yes, it was she. I am very sorry to report, Charyse Desir has expired."

"That is regrettable," said Odom, keeping a perfect poker face.

"I believe she was a patient of yours recently."

"The removal of her products of conception was without complications. I have no reason to believe that this admission is related to the procedure."

Singh had to call on all of his training as a Buddhist and as a critical care physician in order to remain calm. "The etiology of her infection and her hemorrhage is most certainly related to the abortion. Why else would a young, otherwise healthy woman develop overwhelming sepsis and massive vaginal bleeding?"

"I have only a cursory knowledge of her medical history," said Odom. "No doubt she had other risk factors for an infection."

"What sort of risk factors?"

"She is young. Black. Unwed. Who knows what sexual partners she may have had, before or after the procedure. She may have used illicit drugs. There are many possible explanations for an infection."

Singh felt his patience stretch to the breaking point. "Whatever the source of her bleeding, I fail to understand why you did not take her directly from the ER to the Operating Room. Surgery was her only chance for survival."

"My information from the Emergency Room physician was that the patient was stable. I was unaware of any urgency."

"But my resident paged you STAT," said Singh.

"And my resident informed you that I was doing an emergency C-section. I came as soon as the baby was delivered and the mother stabilized. It was you who failed to inform me of the patient's critical condition."

Before Singh could respond, Odom turned and led his group out of the ICU.

The frustrated ICU Attending went back to the dead woman's chart. He removed the death certificate from the front and began filling in the form. Under Cause of Death he wrote: *Septic & Hemorrhagic Shock,* leaving it to the pathologist in the Medical Examiner's office to determine that the woman's tragic death was due to a badly executed abortion.

Unnoticed where he sat at the nursing station, Gary Tuttle had listened to the dispute in silent horror.

Stepping into the Employee Health Office, Lenny noted a fresh coat of paint on the walls and bright, new ceiling tiles. Even the old broken chairs had been replaced by new curvaceous plastic seats with thick padding.

As he stepped up to the nurse's desk, he said, "Wow. Margie, you've done a great job fixing this place up. Who's your decorator?"

"Harry Potter," said Margie, a stout, graying nurse with a furry upper lip and a perpetual frown. "But it's still as hot as a Swedish sauna in Texas."

"Engineering says they'll have the AC upgrade completed any day now."

"Fat chance!" Margie wiped her face with a towel. "I think they're secretly filming some sort of survivor show for TV."

Lenny held out the needle from the trash.

Margie shook her head. "How many times have you been stuck?"

"This is the second time this year."

"Only two? There are some guys in housekeeping been stuck four, five times."

"I'm usually careful. Listen, can you tell me if it was used on a patient?"

"The best I can do is flush it with sterile water and see if it has blood in it."

"Let's do it," said Lenny.

The old nurse shuffled back to a little cubicle with a door like a lavatory stall. She drew up some sterile water into a syringe, attached the syringe to the offending needle, then squirted the water into a specimen cup. She submerged a test strip in the water, took it out, and held it up to the light.

"There's no sign it had any blood in it," she said. "See? The strip isn't registering any hemoglobin." She poured the water in the sink. "It could have been used to give an injection. There's usually no blood in that case."

"Fricking great," said Lenny. "What are my chances of getting AIDS if it was?"

"The chance of sero-conversion for a hollow-bore needle that doesn't contain frank blood is less than a tenth of one percent."

"But it's not zero," said Lenny.

"No, not zero," she said, dropping the needle and syringe into a sharps container. "Fill out the Exposure Form and leave it with me. I'm going to draw your blood to document that you don't have HIV antibodies at the time of the incident. Later on, when you're dying of AIDS, the hospital will have to pay your hospital bills."

"I want them to cover the funeral, too," said Lenny.

"The funeral's a tougher case to win, but it's worth a shot." She smiled angelically as she assembled the blood-drawing equipment. "Do you want to take a three-week course of the antiviral cocktail?"

"I don't know," said Lenny. "I defended a guy in Maintenance who got really sick from it. The hospital didn't want to pay his sick leave; he had to use up his own time."

"There *are* serious side effects." She deftly stuck Lenny's vein with a needle and drew a tube of blood. "It's entirely up to you."

"The needle came out of room 712. If I knew one of the patients had AIDS, it would help me decide what to do."

"Hmm," said Margie, watching his blood fill the tube. "I'll ask the HIV counselor to review the patients' histories. But unless she's sure that one of them is the source patient, she won't ask for permission to test them."

"You need permission to test somebody for HIV?"

"In Pennsylvania you do. It's the only blood test that requires written consent. It's stupid, but it's the law."

"Liability," said Lenny.

"The lawyers rule the world," said Margie. "But you know that."

Chapter Four

Gary stuck his head through the curtains surrounding the bed and saw that Dillie was gently bathing the slim, naked body of Charyse Desir. But for the swollen abdomen, she looked small enough to be a child. He estimated she was probably not much over twenty years old. The linen in the hamper was crimson and heavy with blood, the housekeeper having already mopped up the pool of blood from the floor.

"Can I help any, Dillie?" he asked. As a new nurse he was assigned to the most stable patient, and so had the most free time.

"No thank you, Gary. The aide and I are okay. She's small."

He watched Dillie gently wipe dried blood from the lips and nose, then carefully suction out blood that was pooled deep in the throat.

Gary reflected on Dillie's unflappable demeanor. In the two weeks he had been in orientation, he had never seen the burly woman get emotional or hesitate for a second. He worried that, being a softhearted guy, he would never become as cool and fearless as she.

He marveled when a veteran nurse reported suctioning "malodorous material from the retro-pharyngeal area," or asking a physician to address "a drop in preload and a need to restore volume." Having worked on the wards for four years, Gary thought that he was a pretty good nurse, but a few days in the ICU made him realize that he was a puppy compared with the critical care nurses.

Returning to his own patient, Gary checked Mr. Darling's vital signs, noting that the man was unusually quiet. The nurse suspected that the young girl's death had reinforced the man's fear of dying. A fear he was reluctant to express.

Gary was examining an ECG strip that the monitor had printed out, unable to make sense of it, when the charge nurse came up to him.

"Motion artifact," she told him nonchalantly, and tossed the strip in the garbage. Then she told Gary to take his lunch break. So he went to lunch.

Maurice, the tall, gaunt messenger who had watched Mai Loo drinking lemonade, approached the Seven South nursing station. Casting his gaze around the ward, he saw only a lone physician at the nursing station writing in a chart. Maurice looked through the glass window into the medication room, saw that it was empty.

Stepping behind the nursing station, he looked into the trash receptacle beneath the desk. A Styrofoam cup with a deep red lipstick stain was bobbing on top of the paper trash. The color and the shape of the lipstick were familiar. He reached down, pulled up the clear plastic liner, and stepped back around the station. He tied off the liner and placed it on the bottom of his messenger's cart. Then he looked back at the station. The solitary physician had noticed nothing.

As Maurice hurried off the unit, Betty stood in the doorway of a patient's room halfway down the hall watching him. She had seen him take the trash liner from behind the nursing station. He was a strange bird, all right. All those crazy stories about him. That he'd been institutionalized. In prison. Homeless. She wondered what in the world he would want with their garbage, and she worried that his puppy love might be of the rabid type.

Lenny carried his iced coffee and sandwich to a table in the cafeteria, where Gary Tuttle was seated with several hospital workers, their uniforms a rainbow of colors. As he pulled out a chair, Lenny said, "Hey, Tuttle, how are things going in the ICU? You look like a doctor in your scrubs and lab coat."

"I feel like a little kid in school, I have so much to learn. But the staff is very supportive. They only assign me to stable patients."

"You're working in a rough place," said Moose, a tall, muscular man who worked in the cafeteria. "Most of them patients are too sick to even eat. They have to feed 'em liquid food through a tube."

Moose pointed at the sandwich Lenny had in his hand. "I see you moved up from peanut butter and jelly to ham and cheese. Somebody must be teaching you how to cook."

"It's too hot for anything but sandwiches," said Lenny. "I don't want to boil a hot dog when I get home."

"Speaking of hot," said Moose, "what's with the fricking air-conditioning? We're dying down the kitchen. You could fry an egg on the worktable, that's how hot it's getting."

"I filed a grievance for unsafe working conditions," said Lenny. "The head of Engineering swears he'll have the system upgraded today or tomorrow."

"They been saying that ever since the heat wave started," said Moose. He took a stab at his tuna fish salad. "How come you're so late getting down to lunch?"

"I had to go to Employee Health," said Lenny.

"The heat get to you?" asked Moose.

"No, I got stuck with a needle. In the leg."

"That's terrible," said Gary. "Do you know if the needle was used on a patient?"

"No, I don't, and that's got me even more pissed off. I asked Mai Loo about it. She said the two patients in the room didn't have any medications that would be injected. There's no telling where the needle came from."

"Did they start you on antiviral therapy?" asked Gary.

"I don't think I'm gonna take it. There wasn't any blood in the needle. Margie checked it."

Gary leaned forward, an earnest look on his soft features. "Lenny, please seriously consider taking the HIV prophylaxis."

"Why, Tuttle. Are you worried about me?" Lenny feigned a look of surprise. But Gary just stared back at him, and the young nurse wasn't smiling.

Gary put a hand on Lenny's arm and looked him in the eye. "I want you to promise me, if you find any indication that the needle that stuck you was contaminated, don't wait for them to test the patient. Take the AIDS cocktail."

Lenny abandoned his jocular face and adopted an equally serious tone. "I will, Tuttle. Honestly. The HIV counselor is going to check out the two patients in the room. I'll take the drugs if one of them looks like he has AIDS."

"Or has any risk factors!" Gary added.

"Yeah, that, too," said Lenny.

Moose picked up his tray. "I got to get back on the line. You gonna come jogging with me Saturday?"

"I heard on K-Y-W it's gonna rain this weekend," said Lenny.

"Clear and hot, weatherman said."

"Aw, Moose. It's not healthy to exercise in this heat."

"The heat'll sweat out all your troubles. Trust me."

Lenny manufactured a big sigh. "All right. But if I die from heat stroke, it'll be on your conscience."

"Heh, heh. If you get dizzy I'll throw your sorry ass in Wissahickon Creek. You can chill out with the fishes."

Turning back to Gary, Lenny saw that the young nurse was staring at his food without touching it. "What's the matter—heat got you down?"

Gary looked behind him, saw that nobody was near their table. In a low voice he said, "This morning we had a young woman admitted to the unit who coded and died an hour after she arrived. It was terrible." He put down his fork and pushed the salad away.

"No wonder you look so down. What was it, a drug overdose? A shooting?"

"She apparently developed an infection after going for an abortion. We couldn't pump blood in fast enough, she was bleeding so heavily."

"Some kitchen butcher did it, eh?" said Lenny.

"That's what's so weird. She had the abortion right here at James Madison. Dr. Singh wanted her to go for emergency surgery, but for some reason the OB doctor didn't take her."

"What's a life worth these days?" said Lenny. He got up from his chair. "I'm getting a cup of iced coffee. You want something?"

Gary shook his head. "This heat is giving me a royal headache."

"You and everyone else in this fricking place," Lenny said.

Tyrell Hardy stood in the middle of the Intensive Care Unit. He looked up and down, saw one of the beds surrounded by curtains, figured it had to be Charyse's bed.

He took a step toward the curtains and stopped, unsure of whether to go through. He was a compact, dark-skinned young man with a shaved head, a long scar along the side of his neck, and a diamond-like earring in his right ear. He had black grease stains on his dark blue work clothes and cuts and scars on his hands and arms.

Crystal, the charge nurse, saw him from the nursing station and approached.

"Can I help you?" she asked, eyeing with suspicion the young black man in work clothes.

"Uh, maybe. Yeah. I'm a close personal friend of Charyse Desir. I heard that . . . that she died. Is that right?"

Stepping closer to the young man, she saw from his ID badge that he worked in the hospital machine shop. Recognizing a fellow employee, her face softened.

"Were you very close to her?" she asked gently.

"Yeah, you could say that. We were gonna get married."

"I'm so sorry," said Crystal. "We worked very hard to save her, but we couldn't."

"What happened?"

"I really can't say much about it. I can only release confidential information to the immediate family, and even there it's up to the physician to explain things."

"Yeah, I know how it is."

"I can let you view the body, if you wish."

Tyrell bit his lower lip, stared at the drawn curtain around the bed.

"Does she look bad?"

"Not really. Still, if you'd rather not."

"No, I do. I want to see her."

Crystal poked her head through the curtains, saw that Dillie had finished the postmortem care and was straightening out the bedside. "There's someone here to view the body," she said. When Dillie nodded an okay, Crystal gestured to Tyrell to come through.

The body was neatly composed, with hands folded over the abdomen, hair brushed and tied back, face and throat exposed. The rest of the body was wrapped in a plastic shroud and concealed by a crisp white sheet, trim and squared at the corners military fashion.

Tyrell approached the body, his mouth open in shock, his hands hanging at his side. Though he wanted to touch her, he was afraid to reach out, fearing she was cold.

"It's a hard to see her like this, isn't it?" said Crystal.

He nodded his head dumbly, a zombie in a trance.

"Were you together a long time?"

"We go back a long old while," he said. He looked into the nurse's face, searching for an explanation. "It was the abortion, wasn't it? Made her sick. Killed her."

Although Crystal told him that it was up to the Medical Examiner to determine the cause of death, Tyrell knew what was what. It was a story old as slavery. Charyse was just a poor black girl from North Philly. They would never butcher a white woman from the Main Line like they butchered his Charyse.

Even seeing her still and pale, he couldn't believe she was dead. It had been hard enough to accept her story about getting rid of the baby. That news freaked him out. It made no sense. Even if the baby wasn't *his*, there was no reason to *kill it*. He would have raised it like his own. Tyrell hadn't cared about who the father was so long as Charyse came back to him.

Her being dead, never coming back, never giving him a second chance—it was all beyond belief. A nightmare that wouldn't let him wake up.

Tyrell turned, pushed out through the curtains and stalked off the unit, his face locked in fury. He had only one thought in his mind: to find the doctor who had done this to his girl. He would find that bastard and he would have his revenge. It was the only way to get justice in the white man's world.

Gary returned from lunch just as Tyrell was stalking out of the ICU. The nurse saw the young man's face twisted in anger. Waves of emotion seemed to radiate out from him as he passed.

At the station Gary asked Crystal who the young man was.

"The boyfriend," she said. "He works here."

Gary recalled a lecture on death and dying from nursing school. The first stage was anger. It took time to get beyond the anger to the other stages. Bargaining. Grief. Acceptance. Gary understood that some people who suffered a loss never got past their anger. He worried that Tyrell was that kind of person.

A few moments after Charyse Desir's body was wrapped in the shroud and tagged, Regis Devoe, the young morgue attendant, wheeled a battered gurney with the canvas cover into the ICU. Knowing that Dillie had gone to lunch, Gary led the young morgue attendant to the bed with the curtain drawn around it. He parted the curtains for Regis, then followed him to the bedside.

In the white plastic shroud sealed with nursing tape, the figure looked like a lumpy, badly wrapped Christmas gift. Gary double-checked the name tag taped to the body. It read, CHARYSE DESIR. Not that he had any doubt who it was, but the check was a reflex. A year ago someone put an incorrect name tag on a body. The family made a stink when the funeral home displayed the wrong body in its viewing room. Better to be sure, even with the dead ones.

"I'll help you with her," said Gary, crossing to the opposite side of the bed.

"That's okay," said Regis. "She's not much more than a wrinkle in the sheets." He slid the body across to the gurney on a sheet, then he attached a battered canvas canopy that hid the contents from other patients and family members.

Gary drew back the curtains and watched as Regis slowly wheeled the stretcher away. He felt a familiar mantle of sadness settle on his shoulders. A quip his old nursing instructor had made in his first year at school came to mind: "Never get in bed with the patient." Over the years he tried to keep that professional distance, but sometimes he couldn't remain detached; his heart was too tender.

Even though he never had a chance to talk to Charyse Desir or know her in any way, he felt deeply troubled by her death. Like Dr. Singh, he could not understand why Dr. Odom didn't rush her to the operating room and repair or remove her bleeding uterus.

But there was so much about medical care that he didn't understand.

Chapter Five

Returning to Seven South, Lenny spotted a slim female figure pushing a big x-ray machine around the corner. He smiled. For a moment the heat wave and the faulty air-conditioning were forgotten. He saw only Patience Sinclair, slim and pretty, with her pug nose and pointy chin, her full lips and shapely legs, and her smooth mocha skin.

In addition to her lovely form, he saw the mother of two sweet children. He couldn't say why, but knowing that she had given birth made her even sexier to him. Sometimes he felt a bit like a baby yearning for his mother's breast, except the breast was the prelude to so much more.

"Hi," he called out, catching up with her.

"Hi, Lenny," she said, her face lighting up in a sparkling smile. There were beads of sweat on her forehead, and her scrub suit was damp with perspiration. Her smile turned into a frown and she thumped him in the chest.

"Are they gonna fix the air-conditioning in this rat hole, or do we all have to pass out from the heat?"

"Hey, don't jump on my ass. I've filed a grievance. I can't upgrade the system, too."

"I know, I'm sorry. Working in this heat is making me cranky."

She stepped closer to him and took his hand. "I know the heat's got you beat, too. Look at you, you're drenched in sweat."

He leaned closer to her and lowered his voice. "Listen, can you step out onto the stairwell for a sec. There's something I want to discuss—"

"*No,* I am *not* going out on the stairs to make out with you, Lenny. That's for *teenagers.* "

"Yeah, but—"

"I can't afford to lose my job just because you're so damn horny!"

Lenny looked crestfallen. Seeing the look on his face, she touched his cheek gently. "We're still going to the zoo on Saturday, aren't we?"

"You don't think it'll be too hot?"

"If it hits a hundred, we'll take the kids to an air-conditioned restaurant." She pressed the lever on her x-ray machine. "I have a portable to do; I'll see you later."

"Bye!"

He watched her slim figure move away, mindful of his incredible good fortune to have such a sweet, loving woman in his life. He didn't quite understand what she saw in him, other than his relation with her children, which was playful to the point of The Three Stooges. He couldn't believe that she found anything sexy in his pale, blotchy skin, broad nose, and coarse features.

He decided not to think too hard on the issue. Thinking would just throw a monkey wrench in their affair just when they were talking about making the relationship permanent.

Mai Loo picked up the ringing phone at the Seven South nursing station, heard the voice of her friend, Dillie.

"Can you get away for lunch?"

"Oh, I'm so busy," said Mai Loo. "I don't think so."

"You must come away," said Dillie. "Something terrible happened in my unit. I need to tell you."

"What is it? What happened?"

"Meet me in the cafeteria in five minutes."

Mai Loo hung up the phone, wondering what event could worry her friend with the iron will. She asked the other nurse to cover for her, locked up her medication cart, and hurried off the ward.

Lenny watched Mai Loo going to the elevator. He pushed the dry mop along the floor, not wanting to add to the humidity on the ward with a wet mop and bucket. The big pedestal fan he'd placed in the hallway gently stirred papers at the nursing station. In the rooms the patients lay quietly in their sweat-stained beds. Even the page operator sounded listless in the loudspeakers overhead.

A young black woman stepped up to him and held out her hand. "Hi, I'm Cody. I'm the HIV counselor. You must be the famous Lenny Moss." She had a wide smile that sparkled with gold caps on several teeth.

"Nice to meet you," said Lenny, taking her hand. It was warm and dry, with a firm grip. "I don't know about being famous. Mostly, I'm in trouble with Joe West."

"That's one bad boy I try to stay away from," said Cody, smiling again.

"Listen, it's pretty hot, do you want some lemonade? There's some in the fridge."

"Great!" she said. "This heat's about to make me pass out!"

They walked to the little pantry across from the nursing station.

"I heard from Margie in Employee Health that you were stuck with a needle from a patient's room, but you don't know if the needle was used on a patient. Is that right?"

"Yeah, that's the problem," he said, dropping ice cubes into two cups and pouring them each a glass of lemonade. "If

I *did* know it was stuck in a patient, you could find out if he has HIV, couldn't you?"

"Most patients are pretty good about giving consent to be tested when they hear it's to help out a hospital employee. But you can't force them to be tested; it's their right to refuse."

"I got you," said Lenny. He drank some lemonade and pondered the situation.

Cody took a long pull on her lemonade. "Man, the only thing better than a cold lemonade on a hot day is a warm husband waiting at home." She dipped a finger in the cup, enjoying the cold. "You want to take the HIV prophylactic course?"

"I don't know. I don't think so. I mean, I don't even know it was a dirty needle. Margie didn't find any blood in it."

"That is encouraging," said Cody. "But I got to tell you, you want to decide today. The best way to prevent HIV infection is to take the antiviral meds within hours of the exposure. The virus begins to replicate the second it enters the bloodstream. It divides—" she snapped her fingers together "—like that! The first few hours can be critical."

Lenny rubbed his chin, felt the stubble, despite his having shaved with a new razor blade that morning. After a moment's reflection he said, "If you looked in the patients' charts and they didn't look like they had AIDS, that would help. Don't you think?"

"It would if I knew one of them was the source patient," said Cody.

"It's got to be," said Lenny. "Why else would the needle be in their room?"

"You're right. It would be crazy to bring a dirty needle from another area and throw it in the trash on your ward."

"Well," said Lenny, offering to refill her cup of lemonade, "can you at least tell me if they have any signs of having AIDS?"

"Yeah, I can do that." She looked at Lenny with sympathy and regret. "But if you can't determine that the needle was exposed to a patient, I can't help you."

While Cody went to the nursing station to examine the two patients' charts, Lenny returned to his sweeping. He stood a moment in the middle of the floor and let the breeze from the pedestal fan cool his skin. Something that Cody had said was troubling him: *nobody would be crazy enough to bring a dirty needle to his ward from another area.*

Or would they?

Chapter Six

Dr. Fingers stepped out of his office and found Regis, who was cleaning instruments used in the autopsies. The young man sported iPod ear buds and was bobbing to the music.

As he approached Regis, the physician reflected on his assistant's work history. It had not been stellar. When he had worked in the laundry, Regis had had more than his share of disciplinary letters and suspensions. Since transferring to the morgue, he had not been in trouble once.

Regis's good work habits reinforced the doctor's belief in the potential of the angriest of young men finding a place to apply their energies. He made a silent promise to one day tell Regis about some of the risky behavior he had pursued before starting medical school.

Dr. Fingers tapped Regis on the shoulder, waited while the young man turned off his music.

"The Medical Examiner has given me permission to do the postmortem on that septic abortion from the ICU. Can you stay an extra hour or two and get the body ready?"

"Sure thing, doc. You expecting a big crowd?"

"Oh, I shouldn't think so."

"Okay, I'll have her set up."

As soon as the pathologist had gone into his office, Regis took out his cell phone and called home. The answering machine was on. *She's probably napping with the baby,* he thought. He pictured his wife, Salina, curled up on the sofa while the baby lay in her crib. She would have the air-conditioning on high. One thing his wife hated was to sleep in a hot room. She was always taking off her nightgown during the night and complaining that the room was too hot.

As was she. Boiling with anger one time, overflowing with passion the other. That was his Salina, the best thing that ever happened to him.

He left a message that he would be staying over a couple of hours and hung up.

Coming out of a patient bathroom he had just cleaned, Lenny almost ran into a six-foot fireplug dressed in a sharply pressed navy blue suit. Joe West, Chief of Hospital Security, was standing in the room like a robo cop on steroids.

West looked cool and crisp in his navy blue suit, starched white shirt and mirrored black shoes. He never seemed to sweat, not even in the current heat wave, reinforcing Lenny's frequent assertion that the bastard was actually one of the living dead.

"Your people are taking too much time on their breaks. I don't care how hot it is; there's no excuse for ducking work."

"This isn't the French Foreign Legion," said Lenny. "Nobody signed on for desert duty."

"You're not funny, Moss."

"Give me a break. The whole staff is dying in this heat. Nadia Gonzalez had to go to the emergency room; her ankles were all swollen up."

"I won't have anybody stealing company time. Besides that, I know a lot of our employees have been consuming alcoholic beverages on their lunch break. That's against hospital regulations. Tell them to cut it out or I'll start taking urine samples."

"The contract doesn't say anything about drinking when

off duty," said Lenny. "It only specifies drinking while *on* duty or showing up drunk."

"I can smell the beer and wine coolers on their breath."

"That's your cheap cologne you're smelling. And if you try to order urine tests I'll file a grievance for unfair labor practice."

"You can whine to the feds all you want," said West. "The next one I catch drinking will be terminated forthwith." West turned and stalked out of the room.

Lenny turned off the light in the bathroom, collected his bucket and rags and stepped into the hall. He looked to the right and left, not surprised that West was already out of sight. That was one of the security chief's tricks. He was always appearing and disappearing without warning. It added to his hard-ass mystique.

A few moments after Joe West left Seven South, Moose came onto the ward and began collecting the lunch trays.

"Nobody's doing much cooking down there today, it's way too hot," he said. "We're only sending up cold soups and fruit salads and cottage cheese. Man, I haven't sweated so much since I was in the ring going twelve rounds."

"I'll take a reading down in your department and add it to my grievance," said Lenny.

"Something better change soon. Most of the milk's gone sour and it's not even past the expiration date."

Lenny told his friend about West's threat to test anyone seen drinking on their break. "West has snitches everywhere," said Lenny.

"He can't make somebody pee in no cup, can he?" said Moose.

"Not as far as the union's concerned, but it's a gray area. Remember, security *does* have police powers on hospital property."

"Shit. If those bastards want to test my urine, they're gonna have a fight on their hands." Moose slid a pair of lunch trays into the cart. "And I'm gonna land my first punch in the middle of Joe West's face."

Nurse Gary Tuttle watched while a redheaded Respiratory Therapist with a splash of freckles across her nose handed a mouthpiece to his patient and said, "Okay, Mr. Darling, I want you to take a deep breath, as big as you can, and then blow out as hard as you can."

"Yeah, yeah," said Darling. He filled his lungs, wrapped his mouth around the instrument and blew as hard as he could, his face turning red from the effort. The gauge on the therapist's instrument jumped halfway around the dial, then returned to zero.

"The numbers are pretty good," she told him, entering the reading in the patient's flow sheet. "You may dodge the ventilator after all." She pointed to the machine beside the bed, set up in case the patient's paralysis rose to the level of his diaphragm.

"I better," said Darling. "I see guys go on that machine, they don't make it off alive."

When the therapist left, Darling beckoned to Gary. "Get me my cards out of the drawer, will you?"

Gary hunted through the bedside cabinet, searching among old socks, hair cream, cologne and several magazines with cover photos of busty, lascivious women. He finally found a beat-up, old deck with nude women on the backs.

"See these cards? I got them in Hong Kong. They're a hundred percent waterproof."

He divided the deck in two. Although old and worn, the cards still made a crisp snap as he shuffled them with his big hands.

"I've played poker on every continent and every ocean on this earth. I was in the Merchant Marine, see? And I always carried my lucky cards."

He cut the deck, trimmed the stack, looked up at Gary with a twinkle in his eye.

"Got time for a hand of gin?"

"As soon as I write my notes and add up my I-and-Os, I can play one hand," said Gary. "But I'm not playing for money."

"It's a child's game if there's no wager," said Darling, starting a hand of solitaire with a snap of the cards.

Gary went to the nursing station to update his nursing note in his patient's chart. He found a young physician with dreadlocks rooting around the desk.

"Can I help you, doctor?"

"Oh, yes. I'm looking for the chart on the young woman who coded this morning."

"It may have gone to Medical Records," said Gary. "No. Here it is in the mail basket."

"Thank you. I just need to check that I stamped my name on the H & P."

Gary watched as the physician found a quiet spot at the end of the station, opened the chart, now just a pile of papers in a manila folder, and began looking over the records. After making a brief notation in the chart, he returned it to the mail basket and quietly left.

As the physician strode out of the unit, Crystal, the charge nurse, said to Gary, "What did that med student want with Charyse Desir's chart?"

"Med student? I thought he was a physician."

"Not for another year, although the fourth-year students can write orders on some of their rotations if they're co-signed by a resident."

"He said he had to check to see that he stamped his name in his progress note."

"Ha! He was probably covering for one of the Attendings. They never write their discharge summary on time."

Returning to his patient, Gary wondered if the medical student had cared for Charyse in the Emergency Room. *It's probably not important,* he thought, and went back to Mr. Darling's bed for a hand of gin rummy.

Chapter Seven

Lincoln Jones found Cleopatra outside the assembly room where the medical students' association was meeting. When he approached Cleopatra, he saw right away that she was in one of her moods. He could tell by her set jaw and quick jabbing hand gestures as she spoke to a pair of lower level students.

He loved her high cheekbones, her smooth, deep brown skin, and her dark eyes that flashed with passion. She carried herself erect, head back, chin out: his proud African princess. But watch out for her royal wrath when she didn't get what she wanted.

"We have to rip the heart out of this racist butcher," she was telling the junior black students. "I don't give a damn if it tears the hospital apart, I'm not accepting a whitewash by the Medical Board. They're going to have to cut Leslie Odom loose or go down with him . . . Oh, hi, Lincoln." She turned to her fiancé. "Did you find the chart?"

"Yes. It was in the ICU."

"Was the record of the abortion from Saturday with it?"

"Yes. There's no doubt her infection was a complication of the procedure. But I couldn't find a way to make a copy—"

"That was the whole idea! You were supposed to copy the record of the abortion!"

"There were nurses watching me. I was in the middle of the ICU. The best I could do was make notes."

"Notes cannot be quoted in a press release."

"Maybe not. But the death is a matter of record; they can't hide that."

She gave him a withering look. "I *have* to have a copy. We can't expose Odom's racist acts without the clinical record." Turning to the other students, she said, "This was a lynching. When we put together Charyse Desir's death with the injuries to the other pregnant women, the evidence against the hospital will be overwhelming."

Pulling open the door to the meeting room, she said, "The student meeting is starting. I'm going to condemn the hospital, even without the copy of the chart."

Cleopatra marched into the room, followed by Lincoln and several other students. She took a seat on the side, where she could see the entire audience, while keeping an eye on the student president standing at a podium.

After the president of the student association passed out a sign-in sheet and made a handful of announcements, he asked if anyone had any problems with their schedules. Before he'd finished his question Cleopatra jumped up. Turning a fierce gaze on the president, she began speaking without waiting for him to call on her.

"I have a motion to put before the student body," she said.

"Cleopatra," said the president, his voice strained with weariness. "I didn't call for motions. I just asked if anybody had any concerns about their programs or—"

"This is an issue of grave concern to every student of color, and I will not be silenced when black women are being butchered and killed."

"Cleopatra, we have a student steering committee. You know that's the appropriate venue for bringing concerns about medical practice. We have classes and placement issues that need to be addressed—"

"James Madison Hospital condones and supports genocide! I am here to enlist the aid of the student body to put an
end to this vile practice!"

The student president gave up and took a seat, knowing he
would have to wait and hear her out. Striding to the podium,
Cleopatra cast a fierce gaze across the audience. She estimated there were well over fifty students present. Nearly a
third of the entire class.

"Brothers and sisters, in America's long, oppressive treatment of people of color, racist health care has been one of its
most shameful and criminal institutions. Here at James Madison University Hospital we have an attending physician on
staff who is practicing the worst kind of gutter racism. Dr.
Leslie Odom, a *full professor of Obstetrics and Gynecology,* is
performing the type of kitchen-table abortions that poor
black women have suffered for decades. His abuse is causing
them to be infected at alarming rates. In some cases the
women have been left sterile from the infection.

"His *method* of aborting these infants is *barbaric.* His attitude toward the women is *racist* to the core. And the hospital
is well aware of his genocidal methods but does *nothing.*
M-SOC, the Medical Students of Color, has drafted a resolution condemning this racist doctor and demanding that his
privileges be suspended immediately. We call on the student
association to approve this resolution unanimously."

A white male student in the front row called out, "Come
on, Cleopatra. Don't blame the doctor if women want to
abort their babies!"

"I am not condemning the doctor for performing abortions in and of themselves," said Cleopatra, "although I do
believe that aborting children of color is an effort to reduce
the African-American population in this country."

Murmurs of disagreement broke out around the room.

"But today, after years of racist practice, we see the inevitable outcome of his arrogance and indifference. After refusing to help a woman who became infected from his brutal methods, a young African-American woman has died."

The crowd of medical students, restless and murmuring a few moments before, became silent at the news of the fatality. Even a first-year student knew that a healthy woman does not die from a routine procedure unless somebody screwed up.

In the morgue Regis Devoe had the instruments laid out just the way Dr. Fingers liked them. There was the circular saw for splitting the breastbone and the skull, the scalpels and pruning shears for dissecting the organs and tough connective tissue, and the old butcher's scale. A waterproof gown, mask and extra long latex gloves awaited the pathologist.

Fingers entered the room and nodded to his assistant. He was a large, stoop-shouldered man wearing a long, clear plastic gown. He had dark, greasy hair streaked with gray and salted with dandruff, and a tie that was spotted and wrinkled. Regis often wished the man would find a wife to clean up his act.

Seeing only two residents waiting to watch the autopsy, he said to Regis, "It looks like she won't be drawing much of a crowd."

After splitting the breastbone with the saw and slicing neatly through the abdominal wall with a scalpel, Dr. Fingers pried open the rib cage and the abdominal cavity, making one great yawning cavern.

He attached clamps to the edges of the abdominal wounds and pulled them apart, using additional clamps to hold the wound open. Then he directed the spotlight into the wound and inspected each organ.

"The kidneys have multiple scattered petechiae. I expect

to find clots in the glomerular loops." He ran his finger over the bowel. "The colon is dusky, but without signs of obstruction or ischemia." He ran his fingers over one of the lungs, now lying in the chest as limp as a jellyfish on land. "There is fluid and exudates in the alveoli consistent with pulmonary edema."

Looking at Regis, he said, "I want to dissect the uterus first. Let's get it out."

Cleopatra cast burning eyes on the medical students seated before her.

"The death I am speaking of is a direct result of Doctor Leslie Odom's *method* of aborting babies. He uses a *vacuum* to rip the fetus and the placenta from the uterine wall, and he does it late in the pregnancy, long after that method is safe to use."

"What should he be doing, giving them RU-four-eighty-six?" asked a white student who did not want to be intimidated by Cleopatra's accusations.

"No, RU-four-eighty-six is equally inappropriate for late-term abortions. The only safe way to perform second-trimester abortions is to induce labor, preferably with a hypertonic saline solution instilled into the uterus. Odom *never* induces labor."

"Why not?" called out a black student.

"The vacuum abortions take minutes to perform; labor takes hours."

"So he's fast," said a white student. "So what?"

"His procedure produces extremely high rates of infection. We have the statistics," she said, holding up a folder. "His infection rate is eight times the rate of other physician's D&Cs. We demand that the student association condemn this racist butcher."

The student president stood up and came to Cleopatra's side. "I am against unsafe medical practice regardless of who is performing it or who is receiving it. Since you say that you have reports that need to be addressed, I'm going to refer this issue to the steering committee for immediate review."

"We don't need a review, we need to stop him from his barbaric practice."

"I fully support your concerns," the president said. "And I'm sure we all support your desire for safe medical practice for all our patients. If your observations are correct, I will personally give the report to the Chief of Staff, Doctor Slocum, and ask him to intervene in the matter."

"This will not be swept under the rug," said Cleopatra. "I will not—"

"Nobody is sweeping away anything. You have my word that the student association will look at your report carefully, and will follow up if we find the facts merit a report."

Seeing that she had won as much as she was going to, Cleopatra turned the microphone back to the president. She walked out of the meeting room without waiting for a motion to adjourn.

As the meeting ended, Jennifer Mason leaned over to her friend Kate and said, "God, that woman is always angry about something. Who does she think she's kidding with her Third World chic? I saw that outfit at Lord and Taylor's."

Kate Palmer found the anger she had felt while trying to save Charyse Desir in the ICU bubbling up, stoked by the new charges against Dr. Odom.

"She's right," said Kate. "Odom is a racist."

"People die in the hospital all the time. It doesn't prove there was malpractice."

"You didn't see her, Jenny." Kate stood up as the other students filed out of the room.

"You're not going to get involved, are you?" asked Jennifer.

"I want to talk to Cleopatra."

"Oh, God. Don't get thrown out of school in your last year!"

But Kate was recalling the blood that poured out from the dying woman's uterus faster than the nurses could replace it. The small, helpless figure unconscious from shock. Had she felt Kate's hands pressing on her sternum, trying to squeeze life from her failing heart? Had she heard the voices calling for medications and preparing to open her abdomen? With a shiver Kate recalled that, as you die, hearing was the last sense to be lost.

Slicing neatly through the arteries, veins and connective tissues that held the uterus and ovaries in place, Dr. Fingers gently picked up the organ like a mother cat picking up a kitten by the back of its neck.

He laid the organ on the stainless steel table and opened it with a scalpel, spreading the muscle so that the inner lining was exposed. "More light, please," he said.

Regis directed a spotlight on the organ.

The pathologist dictated into a microphone, "I see multiple areas of hemorrhage. The organ is dusky; it is not pink. There is mucosal sloughing and extensive muscle necrosis with suppuration—no doubt multiple infective abscesses." To Regis he said, "Let's collect some cultures."

As Regis handed him four plastic bottles, Fingers sliced around several lesions, dropping small sections of tissue into each culture bottle. He followed that with larger slices that went into jars of formaldehyde.

"Now I'd like a few slides, please," said Fingers.

The doctor sliced a narrow shred of tissue from a lesion

and slid it onto a slide. He continued until he had a half dozen slides.

"Give me the magnifying glass, please," he said. Receiving the big handheld lens, he bent low over the organ and slowly inspected the surface. "There are fetal remnants imbedded in the endometrium. It's that blasted vacuum abortion. It should never be used so late in the fetal development."

Taking up the scalpel, he cut away a thin slice of gray tissue and placed it on a slide.

"Let's project this one," he said.

Once Regis had the slide on the digital microscope, Fingers focused and adjusted the image on a large video display. He increased the magnification, moving the slide up and down.

"There!" he said. "Son of a bitch!"

"What is it?" asked Regis, new to pathology and not yet adept at interpreting the images of tissue samples.

"The price of sin, my friend," said Fingers, his face grim. "The price of sin."

Outside the student meeting room Kate spotted Cleopatra talking with several black and Hispanic students.

"Don't get in trouble again, Kate," said Jennifer. *"Please."*

"What makes you think I'll get in trouble?"

"I know you, Kate Palmer. You're one year away from graduating and becoming a doctor! You can't be thinking of throwing it all away over some stupid moral issue, can you?"

As much as Kate liked Jennifer—her friend since the first *week* of med school, when the beautiful blonde came up and told her they were destined to be kindred spirits—she was forever surprised at Jennifer's shallow thinking.

Kate approached Cleopatra, who stopped in mid-sentence and gave Kate a suspicious look.

"Yes?" said Cleopatra with an icy voice, her head tilted back in a look of disdain.

"I just wanted to tell you, I agree with what you were saying about Doctor Odom. I want to help."

"We have no need of assistance from *white* students from the suburbs," said Cleopatra.

"She's from South Philly," Jennifer put in.

Kate said, "I was assisting with Charyse Desir's case in the ER. I was in the unit when she coded. Odom never even came to examine her. It was disgusting."

Taking new interest, Cleopatra dropped some of her chilly demeanor. "Yes, we are investigating the incident."

"I was going to check her lab results when they came in. The cultures are pending. Do you want me to pass them on to you?"

Flashing a supercilious smile, Cleopatra said, "I am quite capable of downloading lab results. And interpreting them."

"But Cleopatra," said Lincoln, who had been standing to the side listening. "If Kate can help us, why not—"

"M-SOC will prepare a full report on the matter. All we ask of the white students is that they support us in the student council."

"Of course we'll support you," said Kate.

"Nothing more is required," said Cleopatra, who turned her back on Kate and Jennifer and led her fellow students away.

Jennifer poked her friend in the arm. "She sure blew you off."

"Yes, but I think Lincoln agrees with me. I'm going to keep in touch with him."

"I don't know why you always want to jump into these issues," said Jennifer as they walked down the corridor.

"You're jeopardizing your career before it even gets started."

"I guess it's because I'm from South Philly," said Kate. "We hate to see a murdering bastard running loose in our hospitals."

Chapter Eight

As Regis tried to make sense of the image on the video screen, Dr. Fingers reflected that he had seen many terrible sights in his career as hospital pathologist. He had seen organs choked off by invasive tumors. Brains bursting from hemorrhagic strokes. He had seen the waxy entangling matrix that produces Alzheimer's. Few were the findings that made him queasy. Fewer, still, the ones that made him afraid.

"Do you see the five small marks there in the middle of the specimen?" he asked, pointing to an area on the screen.

"Yeah . . ." said Regis.

"Think of it like a tiny fossil of an extinct species. You know how the footprint is left frozen in the mud and then hardens into stone?"

"Okay . . ."

"Those are the digits of a tiny hand adhering to the uterine wall. Odom's vacuum abortion tore the conceptus apart. The parts he left behind became the focus of infection."

Regis felt the same wave of fear that he had seen in his boss's face. "It's really grossed you out, hasn't it, doc?" he said.

"Yes, my friend. This one has really grossed me out."

Regis understood what Dr. Fingers meant when he spoke of the "wages of sin." He was not referring to the sex that resulted in pregnancy. He was referring to the kind of abortion that tore up the fetus and left pieces in the womb to become infected. Of callous care that resulted in unnecessary death.

By the end of shift, Lenny was cursing the heat and humidity. He had mopped the floor in the room of a patient with a stinking diarrhea dribbled along the floor. Lenny hated to add to the humidity, but the streaks and stains on the floor were unacceptable.

He placed the yellow caution sign in the doorway and turned on a fan to speed the drying. "Goddamn engineering," Lenny mumbled. "Supposed to have the AC fixed."

Rolling the bucket toward the dirty utility room, he stopped abruptly as he saw Kate Palmer walking toward him.

"Hi!" she said. "Heat got you beat?"

"Hey, look at you, you look like a real doctor!" Lenny eyed the bulging pockets of Kate's lab coat. He also saw that she was still the slim, pretty woman who helped him investigate the Randy Sparks murder two years before.

"Is this your last year?" he asked.

"It is. Next June I'll be a real physician."

"You must be excited," said Lenny.

"I'm more exhausted than anything else," said Kate with a laugh. "But it does look like they're actually going to let me practice medicine one day." She eyed the yellow caution sign and the mop and bucket. "I see you still have your job in housekeeping."

"Joe West hasn't fired me yet, but hope springs eternal." Seeing that the floor was nearly dry, he collapsed the yellow sign and set it against the wall. "How's your daughter . . . Sarah. Right? And your mom, is she still working at the Oak Lane Diner?"

"Sarah is ten, going on seventeen. She's a handful, but

she's great. And my mom is still waiting tables." Kate glanced over his shoulder to look down the hall, then lowered her voice. "Lenny, can we talk someplace private?"

"Sure, step into my office."

He led her down the hall to the housekeeping closet. The room was packed with cleaning supplies, a stepladder, and a pair of plastic buckets.

"I have matching furniture," he said, turning the buckets upside down. He settled onto one, offered her the other. "Are you okay?" Concern furrowed his dark brows.

"I'm fine. No, it's this issue that came up today at the Med Student monthly meeting."

"What was it?"

"There's a black caucus among the students called 'M-SOC' that's led by a rather militant woman, Cleopatra Edwards."

"I know about her," said Lenny.

"Really?"

"Sure. I see her pamphlets around the hospital. Some of the women in the union think she's another Winnie Mandela. What's she into?"

"Cleopatra accused one of the doctors at James Madison of practicing racist medicine. She thinks that the way he performs abortions on poor minority women from North Philadelphia borders on genocide."

"I didn't know she was a pro-lifer."

"She's not against abortions per se, she's against *his* abortions."

"What, she wants only black doctors doing abortions for black women?"

"No, that's not it. She claims that every Saturday this doctor performs ten, maybe fifteen vacuum abortions on poor women."

"Isn't that a social service?" asked Lenny.

"It would be if he performed them in a safe manner, but the vacuum leaves parts of the fetus behind in the uterus, and the tissue becomes a focus of infection. Some of the women even become sterile as a result. Cleopatra thinks he's doing it on purpose."

"She thinks he wants to *sterilize black women?*"

"That's exactly what she believes. I'd shrug it off as fanaticism, but I admitted one of his patients this morning, and she died. It was heartbreaking."

"Would that be the young woman who was brought up to the ICU from the ER?"

Kate leaned back and eyed Lenny, seeing the homely face with the large nose, the black arching eyebrows and thick glasses, and she wondered if there was anything that went on at James Madison that this harmless-looking custodian didn't know about.

"Does *everyone* in the hospital talk to you?" she asked.

"It sure feels that way," said Lenny, chuckling. "Sometimes I wish they'd all leave me alone."

"You're too good at your job. The union stuff, I mean. Anyway, the bottom line is, Charyse Desir bled to death from an infected uterus, and it should never have happened."

"That's terrible," said Lenny. "You're sure the infection was from the abortion?"

"That's the presumptive diagnosis. I'm waiting for the cultures to come back. They take two or three days."

Lenny stroked his stubbled chin. "It does sound like an abortion mill. And it probably is racist, unless he's treating poor white women from Kensington as well. But why are you telling *me* about it?"

Kate looked into Lenny's eyes, saw that guileless look of

his. When she hesitated answering his question, his look of perplexity turned to suspicion.

"Wait a minute! Are you talking about that son of a bitch Odom?"

"I'm afraid so," said Kate.

"He's one cold bastard. Remember when I broke into his locker in the OR changing room? He got me fired for that."

"Of course I remember. That little adventure almost got me kicked out of med school."

"You never said anything! Aw, Kate, I'm sorry."

She smiled, recalling how she had teamed up with Lenny and Moose and Gary to track down a killer. The memories summoned up the affection she had felt for Lenny at the time. She wondered why she hadn't said yes when he suggested they get together for dinner after they solved the case. There was med school, and her daughter . . . and one other issue she hadn't wanted to look at.

Kate's pretty face took on a grim cast. "Charyse Desir's death convinced me. I want to help M-SOC stop him. That's why I've come to you. You have to help prove that Odom is a murderer."

Lenny looked into Kate's eyes. He saw anger and conviction in her face; feelings he did not share at that moment.

"Come on, Kate. Investigating that bastard's medical practice is a job for the Risk Management people. Or the Department of Health—they investigate complaints against doctors. I wouldn't have any idea how to evaluate his practice."

"I can handle the medical stuff," said Kate. "I need you to dig up the evidence."

He stood and opened the door, feeling the room becoming suffocating. "No, this is nuts. I can't take on something like Odom's practice. I have a step-two grievance meeting tomorrow morning, and Joe West is threatening us over downing a couple of beers on the lunch hour."

"But Lenny, everybody talks to you. There's nobody else who can dig out the facts the way you can."

"Absolutely not." He stepped out into the hall. "I'm done with playing Sherlock Holmes."

Kate followed him into the corridor. Now it was her turn to put on the pleading look she had often seen on his face. "Lenny, I know this is asking a lot, but can't you just ask a few questions? Nose around a little? Very low profile."

"I'm sorry. I can't do it."

Her face hardened. She looked at her watch. "I have to get to lecture." Turning to go, she added, "If you won't investigate the bastard, I'll just have to do it myself!" She strode away, her white lab coat billowing behind as she walked past the pedestal fan.

As he watched her slim figure disappear through the double fire doors, Lenny felt a pang of regret for turning down his friend. He told himself that he really did have a full plate, with the heat wave and the workers falling out from exhaustion. The threats from Joe West about drinking on lunch breaks. There had to be a limit on what he could take on.

He was going to go home, have a cold shower and an even colder beer, sit in his air-conditioned bedroom, and not answer the phone for anyone.

Mai Loo was late getting off duty. Again. She wished that she could get out on time like the other nurses, but she always had so many things left to do by the time the next shift arrived: write up her nursing notes, clean up her med cart, double-check the doctors' orders. She didn't understand how the older girls finished on time, every day.

She passed through the main hospital entrance and

walked down the broad marble stairs. As she crossed to the employee parking lot she saw Dr. Odom walking toward her. Dillie had told her about the poor young woman who died in the ICU that morning. The thought made her heart pound in her chest and her throat constrict.

Drawing closer to the doctor, she glanced furtively at his deadpan face and cold, unblinking eyes. He seemed completely oblivious to her or to anyone else in the world.

As she looked into his indifferent face, a memory burst into her thoughts. She recalled an image and a sound that she had suppressed for years. The memory was as fresh and disturbing as if she had experienced it the day before.

She recalled a feeble sound coming from inside a dirty utility room. She had gone in to investigate. When she came out of the utility room, she had seen Odom watching her.

Now, as she came within a few feet of Dr. Odom, she felt that same sense of horror and of shame she had felt that day so long ago.

Mai Loo stepped in front of Odom. "God knows what you have done," she said in a trembling voice. "And I know."

He stared at her for a moment, his face a mask, his eyes indifferent and unfeeling. He was so close she could smell his cologne.

"Do not even consider resurrecting old stories," he told her, his voice flat and cold. "They will be your undoing."

Her fury melted away into a well of fear. Sinking into the well, her shoulders sagged, and she cast her eyes down at the ground. Odom walked past her. The click of his shoes faded. Feeling faint, Mai Loo hurried to her car, afraid to look back. Afraid of the blow that was sure to come crashing down on her.

Chapter Nine

Wilted and wrung out by the end of his shift, Lenny wanted nothing more than to go home, take a long, cold shower, and guzzle a couple of cold beers. He bid his partner Betty good night, walked down the stairs to the housekeeping office in the basement, and punched out at the time clock. He made his way to the parking lot, where his old Buick waited for him under a tree, like a faithful old dog. The car often made him think of his dad, who had left it to him when he died.

Lenny fired up the big V-8, enjoying the low rumble of the big block and the way the car rocked gently when the engine first turned over. He drove out of the parking lot onto Germantown Avenue. Looking left and right, he saw two older women standing in the shade of a kiosk waiting for a bus. Maurice, the messenger that everybody called "The Phantom," was standing out in the sunlight beside the bus stop as well. He had no hat on, apparently oblivious to the heat.

As Lenny turned onto Germantown Avenue, he saw the #23 bus pull up to the curb. The women queued, waiting patiently to enter, but The Phantom stepped away from them.

That guy really is strange, thought Lenny. *What's he waiting for if not the bus?*

Accelerating on a downhill gradient, Lenny turned the car radio to K-Y-W, the all-news radio station. The announcer said, "We'll have the weather report for you at the top of the hour. But you may not want to hear it, it's the same as yesterday's, the same as the day before that . . . You get the idea."

Lenny drove over the cobblestones past an old Ford Falcon with shiny chrome and a perfect paint job. He had thought about buying a classic car and fixing it up. He knew that Patience's kids would get a kick out of it. Maybe an old Impala, from the sixties. Or a Ford Fairlaine. In this heat, he would love to be driving a convertible. A '57 Lincoln. Or a Chevy Bel Air. Now *that* was a car. The kids could ride in the backseat, he'd ride with his arm around Patience in the old-fashioned bench seat.

The radio announced that the mayor was calling on people to cut back on their power usage or face rolling brownouts. He wanted all air-conditioning units set at seventy-five.

PECO was warning its customers that the Delaware Valley was in danger of the grid collapsing. They said everyone had to conserve energy, while they raised rates and shut people off when they couldn't pay their bills.

Lenny had argued the case of a few neighbors who were behind in their payments. He and the block club had prevented a few shut-offs. But it looked like the whole city was heading for a blackout if the weather didn't break.

He considered buying a huge block of ice and having it delivered to Patience's house. He would place a blanket over the ice and tell her kids they could sleep on it. Chuckling, he pictured Takia and Malcolm begging to try it and Patience giving him that last raw nerve look.

After parking the Buick, Lenny walked through the porch of his small row house, unlocked the front door, and stepped into his living room. Silence greeted him. For the first year after his wife's death he had felt the emptiness each time he came into the house. But lately the silence of his home had felt more like a sanctuary than a curse.

He welcomed the relief from his coworkers' endless pleas for help. He didn't know how much longer he could deal with the alcoholics who wanted a 32nd chance to dry out and who insisted with angelic innocence that they deserved it. The battered wives who stayed with the abuser. The pregnant teens and runaway children. The out-of-work spouses sitting in front of the television. It was a long line of needy people.

On the weekends he gladly gave up his solitude to see Patience and her children. They were always a treat. He savored his time with them, looking forward to Friday night as a reward for working hard. As much as he treasured his time alone during the week, he was beginning to consider living with his new family 24/7. He just wasn't sure that Patience wanted to make their relationship that complete.

In the living room he eyed the little blinking red light on his answering machine. He debated whether to have his beer before listening to bad news. Duty won out. He pressed the PLAY button.

"Yo, Lenny, it's Legrand. We're goin' out Friday to visit the shut-ins, make sure they're not suffering too much from the heat. I wanna see they have working fans and stuff. Meet me at my place at six, but don't wear shorts, you got hairy legs. Later, bro."

Lenny smiled at his neighbor's reference to his hairy legs. One Christmas, Legrand gave him a woman's electric shaver "for his legs." He tried it on his face. It didn't do too bad a job.

Although he was looking forward to having pizza with Patience and her kids on Friday, he wouldn't let Legrand down. The block captain was the best thing to happen to his neighborhood in years. One Saturday a month Legrand went around in the morning with a bullhorn getting everybody out to clean their yards and alleys. Some of the neighbors came out onto their porches and cursed him, but they got to work and cleaned up their places.

Good old Legrand. A little crazy, with all his books on survival and martial arts. But he had the local drug dealers off the corner, thanks to a sizable arsenal and a willingness to rumble.

Waldwick Street would never win a beautiful streets contest, but it was clean and free from gunplay—a big victory in Germantown.

Lenny recalled Legrand's "Spring Spruce Up" campaign, when he solicited donations of old cans of exterior paint from MAB, Sid's Hardware on Chew, and every other place that sold paint. He showed the store owners the official city letterhead recognizing him as Block Captain and sweet-talked them into giving him their old cans of paint.

A lot of the cans were rusted and bent and needed vigorous thinning with turpentine or water, but they had all gone to good use. Several of the men on the block painted the porch for old Alma and her daughter, as well as the seniors who had no grandchildren willing to help.

Lenny went to the fridge, grabbed a mug from the freezer, and poured beer into the frosted mug. A long pull was like liquid ice coating his throat. Sublime! When the cold reached his stomach it began to absorb the heat and the frustrations of the day.

Carrying the bottle and mug up the stairs, he stripped and stepped into the shower, turned on the cold water, and drank more beer while the cool water ran over his body, washing away a day's worth of hot, dirty work.

Kate drove her old Subaru out of the hospital parking lot. It was Wednesday, so her mom would be working late at the Oak Lane Diner. Sarah would be arriving home from her after-school program. Kate decided to make up a big tuna salad and cut up some fruit for dinner; it was too hot to cook.

The Subaru growled as it climbed a modest hill. If it would hold up one more year until she graduated, she could get a loan and buy a new car. Nothing extravagant, just a good sensible car. She liked the Honda pickup, though it screamed southern California. But it would be great with Sarah. Throw their bikes in the bed and roll on down the Schuylkill.

Shifting into third, she thought about how to help Cleopatra and M-SOC investigate Odom, even without Lenny's help. What Odom had done to Charyse Desir was a crime. A killer had to be punished for his crime, even if he was an attending physician at James Madison University Hospital.

Chapter Ten

Doctor Odom dialed the operator and told her to connect him with the Human Resources Department. He soon had the director, Warren Freely, on the line.

"You have a nurse on your staff who does not deserve her license," he said without benefit of salutation or introductory remarks.

"What seems to be the problem?" asked Freely. He had been listening to physician complaints about the nurses for years. Many of them were groundless, but on occasion they revealed a deficiency requiring strong measures.

Freely listened as Dr. Odom detailed a story that was alarming, if true. When the physician was finished, the director promised to look into the matter.

"You will give it your immediate and full attention?"

"Yes, Doctor Odom, I will."

The physician hung up without saying good-bye.

Freely was peeved at Odom's poor manners, but realized that the last thing he needed was to have a nurse on staff who didn't have a valid license. If the State ever heard about it, the hospital would be cited and fined big-time.

He hung up, buzzed his secretary, asked her to pull the employee file on a Mai Loo. Then he opened his Palm Pilot and checked the current time in Saudi Arabia, in case he needed to make a long distance phone call.

★ ★ ★ ★ ★

Lenny emerged from the cold shower refreshed and relaxed. As he toweled his body, he saw that the spot on his leg where the needle had stuck him was red. That didn't seem to go with HIV, from what he knew. Should he take the AIDS medicine anyway?

He thought of what his father used to say: *In life you will make many mistakes. There will be a price to pay for every mistake, but you still have to make them, it's the cost of taking action.*

Then he recalled Moose's more succinct version: *Shit happens.* Take the meds and maybe get sick. Don't take the meds and maybe risk coming down with AIDS. The damned needle seemed to be clean. It had no blood in it. There was no evidence a patient had been stuck. *Fuck it.* He put the matter out of his mind.

He turned on the air conditioner in the bedroom, slipped on a set of boxers, then went downstairs to make himself a sandwich and get another beer. He made a sandwich of sliced ham and cheese, thick tomato slices and pickles. He bit into a potato chip, found it soggy, tossed the bag in the trash. He went back to the bedroom, now cooled a bit by the air-conditioning.

He flicked on the TV and caught the early local news. A reporter had actually cracked an egg into a solar oven placed on the sidewalk. The egg was bubbling in the heat.

The coverage switched to a female reporter pointing at the Shuylkill Expressway. She was a slim blonde woman with Jackie Kennedy–sunglasses, cool and sophisticated beneath a large umbrella. Behind her, cars on the Schuylkill were bumper to bumper. One vehicle was on the narrow shoulder, steam rising from its engine compartment.

As the camera focused on the wilted driver seated in the

car, the announcer described other cars overheating and abandoned all over the city.

She ended her report with the tag line, "When will the heat wave break? Stay tuned, we'll have it for you later in the broadcast."

Lenny shook his head in disgust at the crass effort to manipulate the viewers. Everyone knew there was no end to the heat wave in sight. The chance of rain? Zero. A shift in the wind from the north? No chance. The mosquitoes and the rats were in seventh heaven.

He sat in bed and ate his sandwich. Crumbs fell on his hairy chest. He brushed them off. He did have a lot of hair. Patience called him her "wild man of Borneo." He liked the way she sometimes twisted his chest hair around her finger. The way she talked to her kids. And the way she let him be a kid when he was with them.

Pouring the last of the beer into the mug, he thought about where their relationship was heading. He had never told her, but the fact that she had given birth to two kids turned him on, he didn't know why. He had a suspicion that if she were ever pregnant with his own child, he would be jumping her bones every day and every night.

He called Legrand and told him he'd be there Friday to help with canvassing the block. He would tell Patience at work he'd be late coming over. Friday was her night to order pizza. In this heat, he'd be happy to eat it cold. He would offer to bring ice cream. And butterscotch syrup. The kids loved butterscotch.

Settling into bed, he pulled a book out from a pile on the bedside table that was forever threatening to fall over. A doctor at work had recommended *Guns, Germs and Steel*. He found his place and began reading about indigenous grains and livestock on the different continents.

As he read, the reading light dimmed and the air conditioner fan slowed. K-Y-W had been warning about brownouts all week. He considered turning the machine off.

Fuck it, he thought, it was an old machine. If it died, he would trade up to something more efficient. And quieter.

He recalled buying the air conditioner the year he had married Margaret. On hot, sticky nights they used to take their dinner into the bedroom, watch the news and talk. He slept every night with his arms around her. Until the cancer. And the surgery and chemotherapy.

When she lay dying in a hospital bed, Margaret's biggest regret had been her failure to bear Lenny a child. Now he had a ready-made family who embraced him without question. Life was funny.

For a long time the thought of a new romantic attachment had felt like a betrayal. But that feeling had waned, as had his memories of Margaret. He was comfortable with Patience and her children. The kids didn't think anything of his being white; he hardly gave a thought to their being black. They were kids, he was Lenny. When they were together, nothing else mattered.

He'd even gone on a couple of school trips with the kids. Once on a trip to a farm with Malcolm, he fell asleep on the ride back to school. As the last child was ushered off the bus, he opened his eyes to find the teacher looking down at him. The teacher said, "We didn't know if we should wake you. Do you work nights?"

All the kids laughed, but none as hard as he.

He put the book down, closed his eyes, and drifted off to sleep with a smile on his lips.

In his cool Center City penthouse apartment, Dr. Leslie Odom mixed a very dry martini. He drew back the curtains from the sliding-glass doors and looked down on the city sweltering in the heavy night air. No breeze stirred the trees in the street below. There was no hope of rain.

He sipped his drink and thought about the threads that were threatening to entangle him. It was always the same. For his courage and his principles he would receive accusations rather than praise. Fools and cowards always raised their tearful voices.

It was the same in America as it was in his home country. Weak minds struggled to pull down towers of intellect. The sheep dared question the shepherd's commands.

He knew that if he were to continue his mission he would have to employ bold action. It would all work out, of that he had no doubt. His hands were skillful, his mind was prescient, his purpose clear.

He would set the dogs on his enemies and watch as they ripped the flesh from their bones. The rule of the righteous would prevail, even in this godless country.

When he came in from his nightly walk, Maurice bathed, toweled dry, powdered his chest, armpits and groin, and put on silk pajamas. He placed three pillows at the head of his narrow bed; the one he'd slept on all through childhood.

On the bedside table was a grainy photo of Mai Loo, blown up from a hospital newsletter photograph of newly hired nurses. He liked the way the grainy quality made her look like an otherworldly angel.

Beside the photo was a paper bag. He reached into the bag and removed the Styrofoam cup he had retrieved from the trash at the Seven South nursing station. He held the cup up to the light and stared at the scarlet smear of lipstick on the rim.

Tracing the outline of her lips with his finger, he recalled the curl of her smile. The pink of her tongue when it poked out between her teeth. The musical chimes of her voice when she laughed.

Bringing the cup to his mouth, he began slowly licking the lipstick off the outer surface. He savored the taste of it. It was her taste. The taste of her lips. Of her mouth. As he ran his tongue over the surface, like a dog licking a bone, he became more and more aroused.

When the outer surface of the cup was white and clean, he turned the cup over and pressed his tongue along the inside. As his tongue followed the inner curve of the cup, he imagined that he was making love to her, and that his cock was a giant shaft of steel plunging inside her.

As he licked and tasted her lips, he imagined that his organ had passed through her vagina and had entered her womb. Her womb was contracting, as if in labor, and her eggs were floating toward the head of his cock as if drawn to an irresistible magnetic force. As he heard his beautiful Mai Loo moaning in ecstasy, he felt himself fill her womb with his seed, impregnating all of her eggs.

Later, as he nestled deeper into the bed to sleep, he imagined what his life would be like when she loved him. All of his old fears and doubts would be washed away. His whole life would be transformed by her love. As she began to show, their child growing in her womb, he would be reborn as well.

The other girls that he had sex with were losers. Wet blankets. He couldn't get excited when he was with them, or, if he did become aroused, he came at the first touch of their body.

The last girl he had touched had been especially cruel. When he couldn't perform, she asked him, "What's the matter, are you on drugs? Are you gay?" When he didn't answer, she put her clothes on and walked out. He had felt as ashamed as a child caught in a lie by his mother.

But with Mai Loo everything would be different. He would be a raging bull one moment, a gentle, patient lover the next. He would last for hours inside her, and he would always be ready to give her more.

He would go back to school, earn his degree, get a good job, be respected. He would earn piles of money and buy her whatever she wanted.

His life would be transformed. He would run and jump and do cartwheels, laughing and singing. Every day would be sunny when he had her love.

Wrapped in a milky plastic sheet and crudely tied with flat cotton string like a Christmas package wrapped by a child, the body of Charyse Desir lay on a steel stretcher in the hospital morgue's walk-in refrigerator. It was a small body, weighing no more than one hundred and ten pounds, and lightened considerably by the removal of the uterus and other internal organs from the chest and abdomen. Large black cotton sutures bound her skin together from her throat to her groin. The skull had been closed, the skin sewn together at the back of the head. The tangled hair awaited the loving hand of the undertaker. There was no outward sign that the body had been pregnant, or that the pregnancy had been recently terminated.

The face was set in a look of anticipation, the mouth slightly open. The tip of a purple tongue protruded from between the front teeth. The eyelids, open just a slit, would appear to be peeking timidly at the world, were it not for the total blackness of the thick-walled chamber.

There was no sound in the refrigerator for the small, round ears to hear, had they been able to listen. The cold, damp air was laden with the odors of decay, formaldehyde and bleach. Bacteria in the bowel slowed their activity, awaiting a warmer environment. The head, back, buttocks, legs and heels pressed against the icy metal surface, but there was no shiver of cold, no search for warmth. Only the silent acceptance of eternity. The grim victory of death.

Chapter Eleven

On Thursday morning Lenny emerged from the stairwell onto Seven South to begin his shift. Suddenly a voice called out, "*Freeze,* motherfucker!"

The first shot struck his open mouth. He stumbled back, took two more direct hits to the face.

Standing in the middle of the hall, the weapon in his big hand, Moose grinned wickedly as he tucked the water pistol into his back pocket.

Lenny took off his glasses to wipe them on his shirttails. "God damn it! You scared the piss out of me. I thought it was Joe West gunning for me."

"Heh, heh. Got you good, didn't I? A bunch of the guys brought in water guns. It's one way to cool off, heat wave as bad as this one."

Lenny walked toward the housekeeping closet, his friend beside him. "I have to take more readings down the laundry."

"You're gonna come to the kitchen, too, aren't you?"

"Of course. I'll see you later."

"Count on it," said Moose. "But when you come you better be armed." He grinned wickedly as he went off to pick up the menus for the late admissions.

Maurice stood in the window of the hospital lobby and watched Mai Loo walk up the broad marble steps. He noticed that her white nurse's shoes were bright and shiny in the morning sun, and that she was wearing the lab coat with the colorful animals on it—one of his favorites.

Here comes my angel divine, he thought, smiling inside himself. He saw that she was already sweating. The air was so unhealthy for her. He liked it when the breeze stirred her long hair. As she approached the revolving door, he hurried out of the lobby.

Gary greeted Mr. Darling with a smile and a warm hello, then got to work. He performed the neurological exam first, not wanting to repeat his mistake of the day before. Breaking a Q-tip in half, he ran the soft and sharp ends along Mr. Darling's hips and legs, noting the point at which the man lost the sense of sharp and dull.

"Those legs of mine used to buck some beautiful women," said Darling, his eyes following the nurse's examination. "I used to really make them moan. In my day I've visited the best brothels in the world."

"I hope you took precautions," said Gary, entering his results on a flow sheet.

"Back then the worst you could get was the clap. Two shots of penicillin, one in each cheek, and you were good to go. Those were great days, my friend. Great days."

The patient's happy memories faded as his thoughts returned to his present condition.

"Don't bullshit me, Gary. The paralysis is worse, isn't it?"

"It's progressed a little, but that doesn't mean it will continue to your lungs. It may stop at this point."

"I've seen black thunderheads on the horizon, son. I know when trouble's coming. The doctor said nine out of ten folks with this disease make a full recovery."

"That's right. Guillain-Barre is *usually* a self-limiting paralysis."

76

"I still got a one in ten chance of *not* getting better. Would you stake your life on those odds?"

Gary sat on the edge of the bed. "I can hear that you're afraid of dying. That's a normal response to an illness like this."

"*Normal?* There's nothing normal about having your legs go numb and waiting for your breathing to quit. I don't want to talk about how I *feel*. I want somebody to tell me I'm not gonna be carried out of here in a body bag!"

After giving the corridor on Seven South a quick mop and emptying the trash in the patient rooms, Lenny took out his digital thermometer. He stood in the middle of the hall, holding the instrument chest high. The numbers on the instrument rose until they reached ninety-three degrees.

"Look at this, Boop," he said, extending the thermometer.

"Lord have mercy. We're gonna need to put a fan in every one of the patient's rooms."

"It's outrageous. I'm going to Engineering. Cover for me, okay?"

"Like I always do," she said. "You give them hell down there."

He crossed over to Seven North, found the temperature two degrees cooler, probably due to less sun on the windows facing north. He went down the stairs to the sixth floor and took more readings, which were no better than on his floor. Then he went down to the kitchen. It was ninety-eight degrees, and they still had the heavier meals of the day to prepare.

Going on to the laundry, he felt a wave of humid air envelope him. The women were already feeling the heat, their scrub suits dark with sweat.

"You don't need no thermometer," said Big Mary, a tall,

big-boned, Italian-American woman with thick gray hair gathered in a net.

"They about to kill me with this heat!" said Little Mary, a short, compactly built black woman, her bare arms glistening with sweat. "I might as well be picking cotton in Mississippi!"

"I'm going to take a few readings and bring them to the engineer," said Lenny. He found the washing room was one hundred and one degrees. The drying room was one-ten, and they hadn't turned on the driers yet. Once they did, the temperature would climb even higher.

"Engineering has got to get some cool air down here," said Lenny. The women grumbled, not expecting any relief.

Lenny made his way to the chief engineer's office, a thickly carpeted room with handsome leather furniture. He approached a curvaceous secretary dressed in a miniskirt and a tank top that revealed a belly button with a gold earring.

"My name is Lenny Moss. I have an eight o'clock appointment," he said.

He followed her swiveling buttocks into the office of the Chief Engineer. Lenny shivered as he felt a blast of cold arctic air from the huge air-conditioning unit in the window.

Frank Fennerty rose from his chair and extended his hand. "Mr. Moss, what can I do for you today?" He was a hearty, blustery man with a ruddy complexion and watery brown eyes. Rumor had it he enjoyed his scotch neat and his secretary on her knees.

"It's the air-conditioning," said Lenny. "Or the lack of it. I've taken readings in several areas of the hospital the past several days. Take a look."

He handed Fennerty a paper that contained tables showing hospital departments, dates and readings. Fennerty put on half-shell glasses, wrinkled his brow, and studied the paper.

"I see that you have included the relative humidity. Very

thorough of you." He studied the document further. "Our numbers are a tad lower than yours. What sort of instrument did you use?"

"It's digital," said Lenny. "From Brookstone."

"Hmm. Not *bad* instruments, but . . ." Before Lenny could object he added, "I admit it does give a good ballpark reading." Handing the paper back, he added, "What level did you hold the thermometer?"

"Chest high."

"Not up at the ceiling?"

"Not at the ceiling."

"Hh-hmmm." Fennerty cleared his throat. "I want you to be assured that this department and the hospital administration are deeply concerned about the level of comfort throughout the facility. We're doing everything humanly possible to upgrade our systems."

Lenny felt a powerful urge to leap across the man's desk, grab him by the throat, and choke him to death. "You don't seem to understand, the women in the laundry are *dying* from the heat. Literally passing out. This hospital doesn't give a rat's ass about the health and safety of the workers."

"I appreciate the discomfort that some of them feel, but—"

"*Do* you? Four people have gone to Employee Health this week already. One kitchen worker ended up in the ER and had to have intravenous hydration for heat stroke. C*hrist!* You treat the meat in the kitchen better than you do the human beings who cook it!"

Gary was about to get up from Darling's bed and mix his medications when the patient grabbed his arm.

"Hold on a second."

"Yes, Mr. Darling?"

"I haven't taken a dump in a week."

"I can give you a suppository. If that doesn't work, you can get an enema."

"Crap in a bedpan? No way! I'll wait 'til I can get up and walk to the toilet. On my own steam!" The patient tilted his head and eyed Gary as if studying an unusual specimen. "You a betting man?" he asked.

"No, I don't gamble very much," said Gary.

"I bet I've played cards in every major port city in the world. I won more than I lost, too, you better believe it."

"You're anxious about being intubated, aren't you?"

"Damn right I'm anxious. Once you get the tube stuck down your throat, the next stop is the morgue. Don't give me any sweet, sugary crap, I know what I'm talking about."

"Mister Darling, if you *are* intubated, you *will* survive it. You don't have lung disease."

"What do you mean I don't have lung disease? I smoked for thirty years!"

"I mean, you don't have lung cancer or pneumonia. Your lung capacity is good. You should tolerate intubation with minimal complications."

Darling looked at the nurse with a jaundiced eye. "You wouldn't call dying a 'minimal complication,' would you?"

Gary rose from the bed, pulled the top sheet to make it trim. "No, Mr. Darling. Expiration is definitely considered a major complication."

The hospital engineer looked Lenny in the eye. "Mr. Moss, you know from our previous discussions that the hospital has two new condenser units being installed even as we speak. Our people have been working 24/7 to get the new equipment up and running. We expect to have the system fully operational over the weekend, or by Monday at the latest."

Lenny had taken out a yellow legal pad. He thumbed back through his notes.

"Is that right? Two weeks ago you said that the new system was about to go on line."

"I don't recall saying—"

"And *last* week you told me the same thing."

"You have to expect a few glitches when you're upgrading an H-VAC system as old as this one. The latest OSHA and state regulations are mind-boggling. We have to answer to a lot of chiefs, and we're inspected at every step of the way. It's not like we're adding a deck to your backyard."

"How do I know you'll get the AC fixed before this heat wave breaks? The weatherman says it could last for weeks."

"You must have some faith in us, Mr. Moss. We're all on the same side here."

"Really? Two days ago I found that the temperature is fourteen degrees lower in the medical school than on the patient wards or the basement work areas. Why can't you shift some of the cool air to the laundry and Central Sterile?"

"The medical school is a newer building; it has a more up to date cooling system. There are also significant differences related to sun exposure and the insulating properties of the windows."

"The students aren't doing physical labor!"

"We are acutely aware of how the hospital environment impacts on the employees. And on the patients, of course. Believe me when I tell you, the upgrade is nearly complete."

Lenny rose. He looked at his shirt, realized the sweat stains had disappeared in the cool, dry office air. A pang of anger stabbed at him, knowing that as soon as he got back to Seven South the heat would begin sapping his strength and souring his mood.

"I'll give you until Monday morning, first shift. If you

don't have the temperature down by then in the laundry and Central Sterile, I'll expand the grievance to a class action suit against the hospital, and I'll call the Department of Health and file a formal complaint."

"You can't threaten me like that, I—"

"*And* I'll tell them in the laundry that if the temperature rises above a hundred degrees again, they should all report to Employee Health. It will shut down the laundry."

"That's nothing but a surreptitious walkout. If your people leave their post, the hospital will out-source the linen and close the department permanently. There will be layoffs, and the employees thrown out of work will blame *you* for their plight."

"We'll see who takes the heat," said Lenny. He turned and walked out without saying good-bye or apologizing for the bad pun.

After Lenny was gone, Fennerty picked up the phone. *Time to call in the exterminator,* he mused. He punched in the operator. When she answered after the tenth ring, he barked, "Page Security Chief Joe West to Engineering!" and hung up. Then he opened a cabinet, dropped some ice in a crystal glass, poured himself a shot of scotch, and settled into his deep leather chair.

The first taste of the day was always the best.

Doctor Leslie Odom was conducting rounds on the Postpartum Unit. One of the residents summarized the case of an emergency C-section.

"She is para four, gravida four," said the resident. "This was her first C-section. She is afebrile. Her WBC is nine point five." Riffling through a raft of notes and lab printouts, he said, "Her hemoglobin and hematocrit is . . . ."

Odom brushed by the young doctor without waiting to

learn the woman's blood count. Entering the room, he cast a stony glance at the patient, a very dark-complected woman from St. Lucia.

As soon as the woman saw Odom, she grabbed her abdomen and began moaning. "Oooh, doctor. I have so much of the pain. I am suffering terrible from the pain."

Odom pulled up the woman's gown without a word and pressed on the abdomen. His probing fingers elicited a shriek from the woman.

"I am sorry to complain to you, doctor," she said. "The nurse will not give me stronger medicine. She says she must have the okay from you. Oooh!"

"I will not order anything stronger than Tylenol," he said, staring at her with a lizard's hooded eyes. "Narcotics are addictive substances. I will not send you out of the hospital a junkie."

Tears welled up in the woman's eyes. "Please, doctor, just a little bit more medicine. *Please!*"

With a look of cold indifference, Odom led his team out of the room. In the hallway he stopped to say, "Always remember, opiates produce euphoria as well as analgesia. That is why they want so much of it. Do not give these women a taste or they will take the opiates forever."

As he started to continue the rounds, one of the interns said, "Excuse me, sir, I have a little problem with one of the clinic patients."

"What is it?" said Odom, a hint of irritation in his voice.

"Uh, it's a bit sensitive," the intern said, eyeing the other members of the team.

Odom told the Fellow to take the team to see the next patient. Once he was alone with the intern, he looked at the young man with impatient eyes.

The intern felt a lump collect in his throat. "It's about

Debbie Hawley. She's the fifth abortion on the schedule for Saturday."

"What's the problem—didn't she qualify for Medicaid?"

"No, sir, the insurance is fine. It's just that, according to the chart, she has a fetal gestation of fifteen weeks, based on the last menstrual period as reported in your note."

"So?" Odom glanced at his watch.

"On physical exam she appears to me closer to twenty weeks. I wanted to send her for an ultrasound to get an accurate estimate of the fetal age, but the Fellow told me not to bother. I just thought—"

"You're not paid to think, you're paid to listen and learn. Medicaid will not reimburse for an outpatient ultrasound without a bona fide medical reason. The hospital won't be paid."

"I understand that, sir. I simply wanted to be sure—"

"Do what you're told and let the Fellow do the thinking."

"But—"

"Do you want to be dropped from the program?"

"No, sir," said the intern, his face coloring in fear.

"Then forget the ultrasound and get back to work."

Odom turned and walked toward his team, leaving the intern standing openmouthed in the hallway.

Chapter Twelve

When Mai Loo saw Maurice approach the nursing station with the morning mail, she felt a chill run down her back, despite the oppressive heat. *He was watching me from the window,* she thought, recalling her walk up the marble steps to the main entrance that morning. *What does he want from me?*

She bent her head to concentrate on the doctor's orders, checking for errors in the medication Kardex. She felt his eyes on her as she looked from chart to medication.

Maurice dropped off the mail and picked up the outgoing material.

"Got any specimens?" he asked.

"There are some in the fridge," she said, not daring to look at him.

Maurice went to the small refrigerator labeled SPECIMENS ONLY—NO FOOD OR MEDICATIONS. He found a few urine samples and placed them on his cart. As always, his face was a stony mask. When he wheeled his cart away he leaned slightly forward, walking stiffly down the corridor.

Even though the ward was already warm and humid, Mai Loo felt cold. Entering the medication room to draw up the morning meds, she couldn't get the image of the messenger's face in the window that morning out of her mind. She was afraid to think how often he had been watching her. For how long? To what purpose?

What did that strange man who never seemed to smile want?

As Gary entered his vital signs in the flow sheet, Crystal, the charge nurse, came to the bedside and handed him a stack of papers.

"Here's an article on ascending paralysis and another on mechanical ventilation," she said. "Oh, and I added one on electrophoresis. Dr. Singh put in a consult to oncology for the treatment."

"Thank you," said Gary, scanning the titles of the articles.

"How's your patient doing?" asked Crystal, settling into a chair beside him. She was wearing lavender lipstick that matched the lavender of her stethoscope, which was draped casually around her neck. Gary realized that Crystal had several different colored scopes, each one matching a different shade of lipstick.

"His level of sensory loss is higher." He described the landmark where he had found the sensory deficit. "He's expressed some anxiety about intubation."

"He saw the young woman code and die yesterday. It's an appropriate fear response," said Crystal.

Gary crossed his arms across his chest, chewed on his lip.

"Yes?" said Crystal. "Is something wrong?"

"I was wondering. I know she wasn't my patient and all, but I heard Dr. Singh telling Dr. Odom that Charyse Desir should have gone right to the OR for a D&C. Is it true she coded because she was infected from an abortion?"

Crystal shook her head sadly. "Dr. Singh told me the autopsy showed exactly what we knew it would. She had necrotic fetal remnants adhering to the uterine wall. The infection invaded the muscle and she perforated."

"Didn't her doctor put her on antibiotics?" he asked. "If you have signs of an infection . . ."

"Gary, if you work here long enough you tend to become cynical. I hate to suggest something totally mean-spirited."

"Like what?"

"If a patient dies in surgery, the statistic goes on the surgeon's mortality record. If she dies in the ICU without going to the OR . . ."

"But the infection happened so soon after the procedure," said Gary. "Won't the death be attributed to the procedure?"

"Don't be so sure," said Crystal. "Some of these doctors have all kinds of tricks to keep their numbers low. So many hopeless cases come here and die, sometimes I think the other services dump their disasters on us so we can take the hit for the death."

Gary hoped that Charyse Desir's death would be assigned to the physician who deserved it. Leslie Odom.

Mai Loo was mixing the last of the intravenous antibiotics for the morning, trying not to think about Maurice. *The Phantom.* Trying not to think abut what she had said to Dr. Odom the day before. She wanted to kick herself for being so stupid and opening her mouth that way.

She held the IV bag upside down and stabbed the rubber stopper with the needle.

" 'Mornin', sweetheart," came a voice in the doorway. "Isn't it a blessed—"

"Ooh!" cried Mai Loo, dropping the syringe and bag on the floor at the sound of Betty's voice. "I stuck myself!" She bent down to pick up the syringe and discard it in the sharps container. Then she opened a gauze dressing and pressed it against her finger.

"I'm sorry, dear heart, did I surprise you?" Betty stepped into the room. "Or is something troubling your soul?"

Hunting for a Band-Aid in the cabinet, Mai Loo said, "My mind was a million miles away. I'm sorry."

"No need to apologize. There's nothing wrong with having a young man in your thoughts."

When Mai Loo gave her a questioning look, Betty told her how she had seen Maurice mooning over her.

"He isn't somebody I want to think about." Mai Loo explained how she thought she'd seen The Phantom leaving the hospital lobby just as she came in. "It's not the first time, either. One time at night I saw a man in the street looking up at my bedroom window. I think it was him!"

"This is the Devil's work," said Betty. "Have you thought about going to the police?"

"I couldn't do that!"

"Well, if you aren't willing to file a complaint, there's not a whole lot you can do, but there's sure something *I* can do about it."

"What?"

"I'm going to tell Lenny. He has a way of talking to people. I bet he can fix this."

"Oh, no, he's not going to talk to the messenger, is he?"

"Don't fret, child, Lenny knows what he's doing. You leave everything to him."

Betty went on with her housekeeping duties, after deciding to tell Lenny about Mai Loo's troubles as soon as he got back from his meeting.

Kate hurried from morning lecture as soon as the speaker opened the presentation to questions. Going to the medical school library, she sat down at a computer terminal and logged on to the laboratory. Calling up Charyse Desir's lab work, she quickly ran her eyes over the results. The numbers sent a chill through her.

The white count was terribly high: 39. The patient had an overwhelming infection in the blood. The B-U-N and creatinine were off the scale as well. She knew that several kinds of infections could injure the kidneys, causing the build up of waste products like urea. But what organism would hit them this hard this fast?

It was too soon to get back a result of the blood culture, but she clicked on the microbiology tab anyway, hoping for initial findings. The blood culture read: *Gram negative rods–species to be identified.* The vaginal culture had the same entry.

Kate knew there was a long list of gram negative pathogens that excreted toxins. She felt a need to speed up time and deliver her the results, but knew the species identification would take at least another day, assuming it was a fast-growing bacteria. The bug might not be identified until Saturday.

She thought about the other women who had developed infections after Odom aborted their babies, and wished she could look at their lab results, but didn't have the names or medical numbers. M-SOC had a list, she was sure. No way would Cleopatra share them with her, a white student.

Kate didn't see how she could get the information that she needed without Lenny. He had so many friends all over the hospital who trusted him and would bend the rules. She decided that if she was going to really dig out the information she needed, she would just have to convince him to get on the bus.

Chapter Thirteen

Betty greeted Lenny on his return from engineering. "Dear heart, I'm so glad you've come back. What did the man say about the air-conditioning—the patients are suffering something terrible."

"We're supposed to have the new cooling system up and running this weekend. I'll believe it when I see it."

She walked along beside him with a little duck walk because of her bow legs. "I think you should talk to that weird messenger guy."

"The Phantom?"

"Uh-huh. Is it true what they say, he went crazy in the Gulf War?"

"I don't pay attention to rumors. People love to make that kind of shit up." They arrived at the dirty utility room, where he poured some bactericidal soap into a bucket and threw in a rag, preparing to wash down an empty bed.

"I never see him smile," said Betty. "That's not natural. And he don't hardly say nothin' when he comes through."

"Okay, he's unhappy and he's quiet." Lenny carried the bucket to the room that needed cleaning. "Maybe he had a tragic childhood and he doesn't see much humor in things."

She told him how the messenger had taken one of the trash liners stuffed with garbage.

"That *is* weird," said Lenny. "I can understand somebody

searching the beach with a metal detector for rings and coins, but taking our trash . . ."

"Will you talk to him?"

"Why come to me? Why not talk to the chaplain?"

"I *do* talk to the chaplain, and I pray hard every day. But some things need the hand of man, and that's *you*."

Lenny lifted the mattress and began washing the metal frame. "Yeah, okay, I'll talk to him. After my break. Which I'm taking as soon as I finish this discharge bed."

He completed his cleaning, gave the floor a good mop, then entered the stairs and headed for the cafeteria.

Mr. Darling grimaced when he saw Gary coming toward him with a bedpan.

"I'm not using that thing, I'm getting up on the crapper." He grasped the side rail and pulled himself to a sitting position.

"I'm sorry, Mr. Darling, you're too weak. You don't have the muscle strength to sit up on the commode."

"Then I'll wait till my strength comes back."

"That may not be for several days. Or weeks."

"Let it go."

"I can't; this is a medical problem," said Gary. "If you become impacted you could damage your colon."

Darling scowled and crossed his arms across his chest.

"You'll feel a lot better after you move your bowels," said Gary. "You really will."

The patient felt his resolve weakening under the nurse's gentle insistence. The feeling of constipation was driving him almost as mad as the loss of sensation in his legs.

"All right, pull the curtains," he said, falling back in bed.

Gary pulled the curtains around the bed. Then he helped

the patient turn on his side. He inserted a suppository in the rectal vault. After that he pressed the bedpan against the man's buttocks and rolled him onto his back.

"Check and make sure I'm on it right!" said Darling.

"It's fine, Mr. Darling, it's—"

"Check it!"

Gary looked at Darling, surprised to see fear in his eyes. He pried Darling's flaccid legs apart, saw that the bedpan was a tad off center and adjusted the man's hips.

"You're right on target. Here's a urinal for number one." Gary pulled the covers over Darling and raised the head of the bed to make him more comfortable.

"This is worse than the toilet in a Turkish whorehouse," said Darling. "You have to squat down and drop your load in a hole in the floor."

"Wait," said Gary, "you need one more thing."

Slipping out between the curtains, he hurried to the nursing station, picked up a copy of the *Daily News*, and came back through the curtains. He handed the paper to Darling. "Here you go. Now you'll feel right at home."

Darling allowed half a smile to curl his lips. He reached for his eyeglasses, flipped to the sports section, and began looking at the pictures.

On the way out Gary told the patient to be sure and yell when he was finished.

"Don't worry, you'll know," said Darling. A loud burst of flatus erupted from the bed. "See what I mean?"

As Lincoln came out of the lecture hall, he said to Cleopatra, "I still don't see why it would be so terrible to allow Kate Palmer to help M-SOC."

"Lincoln! I've told you a thousand times, we have to stop relying on white people to do our thinking for us. People of color have to become self-sufficient. Self-sufficiency builds self-confidence."

"I'm not asking her to think for me. We have a dozen minority students examining the medical records. What difference does it make if we add one more?"

Cleopatra glanced at her watch, saw she was due for her clinical rotation.

"If you don't know by now what M-SOC and I are all about, you better get your head screwed on right. Martin's dream of reconciliation died with him. Suck it in and get used to it. They don't want *us*, and we don't need *them*."

She strode rapidly away, leaving Lincoln feeling as if he had been put in the corner by a stern teacher and might never be allowed out again.

As Joe West slipped into the office of the Vice President for Patient Services, formerly known as the Director of Nursing, he seemed to materialize out of thin air in front of the secretary. His blue blazer was crisply starched, his trousers pressed knife-edge sharp. A large, stainless steel watch on his wrist and a pair of handcuffs dangling from his belt were his only jewelry.

The secretary gasped upon seeing him. She had never had to deal with West or anyone in security on a personal level. From the stories she had heard about West, she fervently hoped that misfortune would never befall her.

"Miss Burgess is ready for you," she said, indicating an office door.

West passed through the door, as silent as a shadow.

In the office, he found Miss Burgess seated at a large desk cluttered with files, memos, computer printouts and knick-knacks of all sorts. Several small clown dolls sat on a shelf on the wall. A photo of President George W. Bush hung on the wall behind her chair.

In another chair to the side of the desk sat Warren Freely, Director of Human Resources. Freely was a tall, slender man with delicate features. He wore a double-breasted suit, a pale lavender shirt, and a plum-colored bow tie. He gave West a curt nod.

Miss Burgess, with frosted hair and frosty eyes, gestured to a chair.

"I prefer to stand," said West.

"Suit yourself." She opened a file on her desk. "Since Dr. Odom spoke with Mister Freely yesterday, he and I have made several inquiries." She handed the file to West.

Freely took up the narrative: "His statement that the nurse in question falsified her application for employment is correct. The young woman *was* terminated for stealing narcotics from a hospital in . . ."

"Saudi Arabia," said Burgess.

"She stated that she worked there for three years and that she left that facility voluntarily. The hospital faxed me a report that she was terminated after six months on the job. That leaves two and a half years on her résumé unaccounted for."

"She probably turned to prostitution," said West.

"Whatever she did, the important fact is that her application contains false statements," said Burgess.

"There are other false entries on her application," Freely continued. "Failing to admit that she has been terminated is by itself grounds for immediate dismissal."

"My one concern," said Burgess, "is that we have another nursing shortage on our hands, and we employ a lot of registered nurses from the Philippines."

"She stole drugs, she'll do it again," said West. "We don't want a junkie holding the keys to the narcotic cabinet."

"I asked in pharmacy if there have been any discrepancies

on the narcotic log for Seven South. They haven't noted any since she began working there."

"That just means she's clever," said West. "She gives the patients sterile water and keeps the morphine. The record is clean."

Freely looked at Burgess. "It's your call."

Miss Burgess turned humorless eyes on Joe West. "Show her the door."

Almost letting a smile creep onto his face, West growled, "With homeland defense, we can have her out of the country in three days."

"Do we need to be quite so draconian?" asked Freely.

"Once she's terminated, her immigration status is not our concern," said Burgess. "Just send her away as quietly as possible."

West said, "Do you want me to wait for the end of her shift?"

"No, do it now. I'll pull a nurse from Seven North to cover."

"Give me fifteen minutes to prepare my people," said West. "By the way, that pesky janitor, Moss, is stirring up the people in the laundry. There's talk of a walkout."

"Wouldn't that allow us to outsource the linen without fear of a grievance?" asked Burgess, turning to Freely.

"There are always grievances. But if they walk out it strengthens our hand considerably."

Burgess said, "As far as I'm concerned, if they walk, they're history." She nodded to West, who turned and left the room.

As Freely collected his papers, Miss Burgess said to him, "You know, Warren, we may have problems with Doctor Odom's employment as well. There have been complaints made about Odom's medical practice."

"Really? From whom?"

"A doctor wrote a letter to the Medical Board." She picked up the phone. "He brings in a million plus with his fertility clinic, so the Board is inclined to be tolerant. But I don't entirely trust our Doctor Odom."

As Lenny entered the laundry room, a bag of linen came flying out of the chute and fell with a loud *WHUMP* into a big cart. A tall Italian-American woman with a ruddy complexion and gray hair lifted two bags from the cart and carried them to the laundry room.

"Hey, Big Mary, how's it going?" said Lenny.

Big Mary tossed the bags onto the floor in front of a washing machine and wiped her face on the sleeve of her scrub suit. Her eyes had dark circles around them and her feet were swollen from retained water. Lenny knew she hungered to retire, but her retirement was far away, thanks to her own folly.

Years ago, when she applied to work at James Madison, she wrote that she was forty when she was really fifty, knowing that a fifty-year-old woman had little chance of being hired. Now she was turning sixty—fifty on her record. Although the laundry work was beating the life out of her, she didn't dare tell the truth for fear she would lose her retirement benefits. At the same time she knew she could not possibly survive another fifteen years in the laundry.

Lenny had tried to find her work as a unit clerk, but Big Mary had flunked the test for computer entry. So far he had found no way out of the dilemma.

"I'm as damp as a wet nurse who can't find her baby." She took a plaid handkerchief from around her neck and dabbed her face with thick fingers. "When are they gonna fix the bleeping air-conditioning?"

A short, dark woman with wide hips and thick legs came

storming up to Lenny. Little Mary could hoist the heaviest bags of laundry over her shoulder like a sailor. She, too, was dripping sweat. "It ain't fixed!" she cried. "The lying mothers promised to fix the air-conditioning!"

"I can't work more than an hour at a time," said Big Mary. "I have to go to the lounge and put my head under the faucet. And then my supervisor yells at me for takin' so many breaks. They about trying to kill us is what they're doing!"

"I know," said Lenny. "I showed the engineer the temperature readings I took down here. I was in a step-two meeting with him this morning. He says Saturday night, Sunday at the latest, they'll have the new condensers on line and you'll get some relief."

"He's a lyin' sack o' shit," said Little Mary. "He's been feeding us that crap for weeks."

"I'm sorry. I'm doing everything I can."

"Why don't we all walk out?" said Big Mary. "That'd show the boss we mean business."

"That we're not pussies!" said her smaller coworker. She put her face up close to Lenny's. "Are *you* a pussy? Are you scared of them bastards?"

"Of course not. The only reason I haven't called for a walkout is that the hospital will hire an outside contractor and privatize the laundry and you'll all be out of a job."

"We'll all be out of a *life* if this place don't get a whole lot cooler," said Big Mary.

Both women crossed their arms across their chests and waited to hear what Lenny had to say. As he looked at the two tired, angry women in the laundry, the sweat running in little streams down his chest, he realized that, as hot as it was on his ward, it was arctic compared to the conditions in the laundry.

"If you feel weak from the heat, you should go to Employee Health. Dr. Primeaux will let you rest there as long as you need to, and if you're really dehydrated, he'll send you to the ER for an infusion of water."

"Let them stick a needle in my arm?" said Big Mary. "They can't hardly find a vein in all this fat come time for the annual blood drive. No, thank you, I'll go out on Germantown Ave. and get me something good and cold to drink."

"Well, don't let one of Joe West's snitches see you coming out of the Cave. He's already threatening to do drunk tests on anybody coming out of the bar."

"He can kiss my sweet black ass if he thinks he's gonna test *me*," said Little Mary. "K-Y-W says there ain't no relief in sight. No rain no way."

"If the supervisor tells you you can't go to Employee Health, page me and I'll get in her face. If you don't want intravenous fluids, let them give you Gatorade to drink."

"I need something a whole lot stronger than that!" said Little Mary.

"And give me until the weekend. If the system upgrade isn't in place by then, we'll all meet together, both shifts, and we'll talk about a job action. Okay?"

He looked into their sweaty faces, heat radiating from their bodies as if from an oven, and he cursed the system that put the women into this dungeon. Maybe they really would be better off out of work rather than burning up in the laundry.

With the bedpan nearly overflowing with foul-smelling stool, Gary turned his patient on his side, dipped a washrag in a basin of warm, soapy water and was about to clean Mr. Darling's buttocks when the patient snapped, "I can clean myself up, I'm not a little baby!"

Handing the rag to Darling, Gary spread a blue pad over the bed to keep the sheets dry. He went to empty the bedpan in the hopper while Darling cleaned himself thoroughly. Returning to the bedside, Gary picked up the washbasin and dirty towel.

Darling said, "You're sure there's no shit in the bed?"

Gary reassured him.

"Not even a spot?"

"I had the bed padded with chux."

"Taking a shit in the bed is as bad as being keelhauled," Darling said.

When Gary confessed he didn't know what "keelhauled" meant, Darling explained the maritime punishment of tying a rope around a sailor and dragging him under the boat.

"The barnacles raked your skin so you were filleted like a fish, but if you survived your wounds you were okay."

Back at the nursing station, Gary reflected on the odd things people feared. He found it fascinating that a man who could challenge the sea and ride out a furious storm was deathly afraid of soiling his bed. His mother's voice still blew like a gale in the winds of memory.

Mai Loo closed the drawers of her medication cart and locked it. She poured a dollop of rubbing alcohol on the top of the cart and began wiping the surface with a gauze pad. As she scrubbed a stubborn medication stain, she felt the presence of someone behind her. Thinking it was the messenger stalking her, she continued rubbing with the pad, determined to not look him in the eye.

Suddenly a steely hand squeezed her shoulder. She turned around, gasped, saw the cold, dead eyes of Joe West.

"Yes?" she said in a quivering voice. "Can I help you?"

"Come with me to the Nursing Office," he said.

"But I have work to do. I have to write my notes and check my orders."

"Miss Salvecchio will take charge of your patients."

When Mai Loo saw a nurse from Seven North standing a few feet behind Joe West, fear began spreading over her. The other nurse was taking over her assignment in the middle of the shift. She knew what that meant; it had happened to her once before. A terrible blow at the time, it was even more terrible now.

She walked numb behind the silent, implacable security chief. The corridor seemed to stretch out for miles ahead of her. She wished that she could melt into a puddle on the floor and evaporate away.

West opened the door to the Nursing Office and allowed Mai Loo to go in before him. Miss Burgess was seated at a conference table beside Mr. Freely. An administrative assistant sat across from them with a legal pad, ready to take notes. Mrs. D'Arcy, Mai Loo's Head Nurse, sat off to the side and did not look at the young nurse.

West pulled out a chair and indicated that Mai Loo be seated. She sat on the edge of the chair, her back straight, looking at her lap.

Miss Burgess began. "Miss Mai Loo. It has come to our attention that your application to practice nursing at James Madison University Hospital was not entirely honest. Isn't that right?"

The young nurse kept her head bowed. "I . . . I don't know what you mean."

The administrative assistant placed a copy of Mai Loo's employment application in front of her. Several sections were highlighted with a yellow highlighter.

"First of all," said Burgess, "the dates are not right. It says here that you worked at the King Faisal Royal Hospital in Jeddah from nineteen ninety-six to nineteen ninety-nine. Do you see where it says that?"

Mai Loo wordlessly nodded her head, knowing what was coming.

"But you didn't work at that facility up to ninety-nine. You left there in nineteen ninety-seven. Where did you work the following two years?"

Mai Loo feverishly debated in her mind whether she should tell the truth or make up a story. She wished her Head Nurse would come to her defense, argue her case, plead on her behalf. But the supervisor sat in stony silence, making no eye contact with Mai Loo.

"I left a little early from that job. It's true. I'm sorry."

"You left because you were terminated," said Mr. Freely. "Isn't that so?"

"Yes," said Mai Loo in a weak voice.

"Where did you work, my dear?" asked Freely, taking a conciliatory air.

"I worked for my Uncle in Manila. He has a store. I helped him with the bookkeeping and ordering the stock."

"A letter from your family is not a credible work history," said Burgess.

"You haven't explained *why* you left early," said Freely. "Tell me the truth. It is always better to tell the truth."

Mai Loo felt her throat constrict with fear. She was not sure she could even get the words out.

"I . . . had some difficulty."

"You were terminated for stealing narcotics, weren't you?"

"I didn't take anything! Not even an aspirin! I swear it!"

"Narcotics were found in your locker. I have the fax from the hospital in Saudi Arabia."

"It's not true," said Mai Loo, her voice weakening.

"And on your application to work at James Madison you wrote that you were never terminated from a place of employment. Do you see where you wrote that?"

"Yes," she said in a whisper.

"But that is a lie, isn't it, young lady?" said Burgess. "You lied several times on your application. Isn't that so?"

Mai Loo kept her head bowed and her eyes fixed on her lap. The fear squeezed her so hard, she thought her heart would burst and she would die right there in Miss Burgess's office.

"Isn't that so?" repeated Burgess with contempt in her voice.

Mai Loo looked up from her lap and stared at Miss Burgess.

"I did not take any drugs. Never would I do that. I was accused because Dr. Odom did not want me in the hospital with him."

"It will do you no good to blame a highly respected physician for your misconduct," said Freely.

"But it's true! He didn't want me there because I saw how he killed the babies."

"Young lady!" snapped Miss Burgess. "You would do well to watch your tongue. Accusing a physician of misconduct is slander. You could find yourself in worse trouble than you are already in."

Mai Loo fought against the impulse to cry out loud, not wanting the bosses to see how great was her shock. And her fear.

Freely said, "Whatever happened in Saudi Arabia, the fact remains you made false statements on your application. You denied being fired from your former employer. You lied about how long you worked at that facility."

Sliding a piece of paper toward her, the Director of Human Resources continued, "I am terminating you, effective immediately. Mr. West will accompany you to your locker and observe you emptying it out. He will then escort you out of the hospital. You are not to return except to report to the Security Department on the next payday, when you may pick up your terminal pay."

"What about my Green card? I can't stay in this country if I do not have a job."

"That is not our problem," said Burgess.

Joe West opened the door, gestured for Mai Loo to accompany him. She walked behind him, her head bowed, her feet shuffling along the corridor. A terminal patient stumbling to a freshly dug grave.

When they reached Seven South they went into the lounge. Mai Loo opened her locker, with Joe West standing behind. When she hesitated, not knowing how she would bundle all of her things together, West opened a large heavy-duty trash bag and haphazardly shoveled everything into the bag.

He looked over the open locker once more. Satisfied that there was nothing left, he knotted the plastic bag and handed it to her.

"Don't say anything to anybody," he instructed her.

He opened the door of the lounge and led her back out to the hall. Like a condemned prisoner, she followed silently, the bag dragging along the floor.

Betty saw Mai Loo with the trash bag and Joe West coming out of the lounge.

"What is it, child?" she said, stepping closer. "You in trouble?"

"Don't talk to her," West growled at Betty.

"They are making me go," said Mai Loo, fearful of West's wrath.

"I ain't scared of you, I'll talk to whoever I want." Betty walked a few steps beside Mai Loo. "Are you all right? Do you want me to call somebody?"

"No . . . well, could you please tell Dillie in the ICU. Would you do that for me?"

"Of course I will. And I'll tell Lenny, too." Betty stood and watched the young nurse being led away, feeling powerless and sad. And angry.

West punched the button for the down elevator and stood, arms folded across his broad chest. He looked like he wanted nothing better than to use the handcuffs dangling from his belt on anyone who tried to interfere with his mission.

Mai Loo saw Maurice, the scary messenger, down the hall. Her gaze locked onto his as he stood frozen in the hallway. She felt naked and vulnerable.

As she stepped into the elevator, her legs became weak. She feared she would collapse in front of the wooden security chief. Her mind was numb, as though she'd suffered a stroke. It was difficult for her to hold a coherent thought for more than a few seconds.

With the elevator doors closing, she reached for the grab rail and held on as if riding a roller coaster into hell.

Chapter Fourteen

Dr. Singh tapped lightly on the chief pathologist's door and stepped into the office. He saw piles of journals stacked higgledy-piggledy, jars with organs floating lazily in formaldehyde, and a skeleton standing in the corner, its bones yellowing with age, a pair of sunglasses covering its empty eye sockets.

"Good morning, Nelson," said Singh.

Dr. Fingers looked up from the report he had been reading, smiled, stood for his guest. Wiping his hand on his lab coat, which badly needed laundering, he shook his colleague's hand warmly.

"Good to see you, Samir. How are things in the unit?"

"Busy, as always." Accepting Fingers's offer of a chair, Singh sat lightly, his body loose and relaxed.

"What's on your mind?" the pathologist asked.

Singh's face turned serious. "I read the copy of Charyse Desir's preliminary autopsy report. Thank you for sending it to me."

"It was the least I could do," said Fingers.

"I understand the infection invaded the uterine wall. It must have had a high degree of virulence."

"There was evidence of widespread septic inflammation. Not just around the endometrial lesions, but in the kidneys and liver as well. Has the Microbiology Lab identified the bacteria?"

"Not as yet, but I am checking the computer frequently." Singh let a moment of silence pass between them. His colleague saw the indecision, so uncharacteristic of the intensive care physician, and waited. Finally Singh said, "I have such a bad feeling about this case. The patient was young and otherwise healthy. The infection could have been treated, but there was no evidence that she was prescribed an oral antibiotic."

"You believe that her case was mismanaged?"

"I fear so. Her endometritis would most definitely have caused her to feel severe pain. She would have experienced fever and chills. Why she was not receiving antibiotics is a mystery to me."

"I agree," said Fingers. "She would have been symptomatic for days prior to the admission."

Now it was the pathologist's turn to look perplexed.

"I, too, had a bad feeling when I performed the autopsy." Fingers described the slide of the premature infant's hand imbedded in the uterine tissue.

"That is a ghastly image," said Singh.

"It shook me up, and I've seen some grotesque pathology in my day. I felt as if I were examining the fruit of something evil."

"This practice of Odom's, his performing vacuum abortions in the second trimester, it cannot continue," said Singh. "My friend in the Emergency Room tells me Odom's abortion patients frequently come in with pelvic infections."

"I agree, it's monstrous, but I'm not sure what we can do about it."

"I'm going to speak with Dr. Slocum."

Fingers liked the Chief of Staff, although he felt Slocum was more a politician who hated to make waves than an insightful clinician. Still, if anybody was going to stand up to Odom, it would have to be Slocum.

"When you talk to the Chief, tell him I am in complete agreement with you," said Fingers. As he stood and shook Singh's hand in parting, he added, "Tell Slocum that if he ever came down here and viewed the slides from the autopsy, he would fire Odom in a heartbeat."

Gary went to the bedside to tell Mr. Darling that the oncology doctors were on their way to give him his treatment. "Did the doctors explain everything to you?" he asked.

"Yeah," said Darling. "They suck out all my blood, they pull off the clear part and give me back my blood cells."

"It's called serum plasmapheresis," said Gary.

"I know they're experimenting on me. It won't do you no good to tell me different."

"Just because the treatment is new doesn't mean it's experimental. It definitely removes antibodies from your bloodstream that contribute to the paralysis."

"Hmmph. You just be sure after they kill me they leave my body alone. I don't want my organs given to somebody else. I want to go out of this world the same way I came in. In one piece." Darling picked up the *Daily News* and tossed it toward the foot of the bed. "Can't you get me something hot to read?"

"Like what?"

"Give me some pictures of girls with bare asses and tits." Darling cast a doubtful look at Gary. "I don't suppose you go for that kind of thing."

"No, I don't," said Gary.

"You never been to a brothel?"

Gary shook his head, no.

"I've been to whorehouses all over the world. The Jap houses and the Korean and the Vietnamese. South America and Africa, too. I been to them all."

107

Gary listened without comment.

"You know who's got the best prostitutes in the world?"

Gary shook his head.

"The French girls. They're incredible. They have a way that makes you wait and wait and then, *bam!* You feel like you're leaping off a mountaintop and sailing through space." Darling's eyes twinkled. "Their skin is as soft as a baby's bottom. And their hair is perfumed." He winked at Gary. "*All* their hair."

Gary listened, not wanting to criticize his patient.

"And they have this bed with a thick comforter you could bury yourself in." A smile came over his lips. "The French whores are the best. Take my word for it."

Gary left to mix his afternoon medications. As he worked he couldn't help note that Mr. Darling's fear of dying seemed to have been eased by his memories.

When Lenny returned to Seven South after his meeting with the laundry workers, he found his housekeeping partner sitting in the little pantry across from the nursing station, her head buried in a small, well-worn bible.

"Oh, dear heart," she said, looking up at him. "I'm so glad you're back."

"What is it, Boop? Are you okay?"

"Me? This old body and soul are fine. It's Mai Loo. That devil Joe West came and made the poor girl empty out her locker. She's gone."

"Jesus Christ, they fired her? Why? What happened?"

"I don't know what it's about. West was on top of her like shit on your shoe so I couldn't get a word out of her. He took her away about a half hour ago."

"She's out of the building then, I won't be able to talk to her. Shit!" He poured himself a glass of water and gulped it down. "That laundry is an oven." He tossed the cup in the trash. "Did she say anything?"

"All she did was ask me to tell her friend Dillie. I was gonna go down and tell her, but I wanted to let you know first."

"I'll go. Dillie might know what the hospital has against her. I don't know what I can do, she's not in the union. Maybe I can hook her up with a labor lawyer. She's such a sweet kid."

"There's the devil behind it, you can believe me."

"Cover for me. I'll go down to the ICU and talk to Dillie."

"I will, dear heart. I surely will."

Lenny hurried off the ward, taking the stairs to the Intensive Care Unit on the third floor. As he descended the empty stairwell, he had a familiar feeling, like he was beating his head against the wall over and over, and all he would get for it was another headache.

Chapter Fifteen

The technician set ten bottles of plasma on the top of her electrophoresis cart along with drapes and a disposable razor. Drawing the curtain around Mr. Darling's bed, she told the patient she was going to shave his groin.

Mr. Darling placed his hands behind his head. "You go ahead, sweetheart. Just be careful with the family jewels."

Wetting a pre-soaped sponge, the technician pulled back his top sheet, draped a towel over his penis, and said, "Sir, I haven't cut anybody's organ off for over a year. You've got nothing to worry about."

"I'm gonna itch like a dog with fleas when the hair starts to comes in."

"Uh-hmmm," said the tech, deftly running the razor over his skin.

"What's the chance you could help me with my itch once I get back on my feet?"

The tech finished the shave. She wiped away the excess soap and pulled the sheet back over him.

"You wouldn't want that, Mr. Darling. My husband's a cop. He has several guns."

She drew back the curtain, washed her hands, and then began priming the machine with plasma. She hung ten bottles above the machine, each one linked by intravenous tubing to a single line. While she prepared the plasma, the oncology Fellow came to the bedside.

"Do we have the consent?" he asked her.

"It's in the chart."

"Good." Without addressing the patient, he put on a sterile gown, a mask, and gloves. Once he was ready, the technician exposed the cleanly shaven groin. The fellow cleaned the region thoroughly with iodine. After numbing the area with xylocaine, he deftly inserted a large double-lumen catheter into the femoral vein. As soon as he had it secured, the technician handed him the tubing, which he connected to the catheter.

"Ready?" he asked the tech, not looking at Darling.

"What if *I'm* not ready?" said Darling.

"Sir, you have a paralyzing autoimmune disease that can cause your death. You don't want to refuse a treatment that will in all probability save your life."

"I'd spit in the Devil's eye if I thought he wasn't playing straight with me. I don't trust you people for a minute."

"That is most unfortunate," said the Fellow, pulling off his gloves and ripping off the sterile gown. "Without our treatment you will not survive."

The tech unclamped one of the intravenous tubes. Bright red blood ran merrily down the tubing. In a few seconds the blood was passing through the machine, which separated the red cells from the clear fluid.

"That's a shit load of blood you're taking out," said Darling, raising himself up into a sitting position.

"Everything is fine, sir; lie back and relax. We're going to give you back all of your cells, we're just keeping the water and the protein."

Darling fell back into bed. He turned his face to watch the tubing as the machine hummed and his bright crimson blood ran out of his body. He felt like a fish on a line that would soon be gasping for breath.

A few moments later Gary was surprised to see Lenny come through the ICU doors. Greeting his friend, he learned that Mai Loo, with whom he had worked on Seven South until transferring to the ICU, had been fired.

"That is a tragic thing," said Gary. "What did she do?"

"Probably something good! Haven't you learned anything in all the years we worked together?"

"I know, it's a corrupt system," said Gary. "She must be devastated."

"I didn't see it go down," said Lenny. "I was in the laundry dealing with the heat, but Betty told me she looked like she was shaken up pretty bad. I came to see if her girl-friend knows anything about it."

"Dillie is at the station," said Gary.

Lenny went to the desk and told Dillie what had happened. The nurse shook her head slowly. "Mai Loo is a good girl. She does not deserve this."

"I'd like to help her if I can. I could hook her up with a lawyer if she needs one."

"That is very kind of you," said Dillie.

"It would help me help her if I had some idea what it was about."

Dillie looked past Lenny, as if peering into a distant past. "We were in school together in the Philippines," she said. "After we graduated, we worked for two years in the Island Provinces. The people are very poor. It was hard, but we helped many people."

Folding her arms across her chest, she looked into Lenny's eyes. "Mai Loo accepted a work contract in Saudi Arabia. A lot of the girls take jobs there. The money is very good. But the men are very bad. I came to Philadelphia to work."

"I've heard the stories," said Lenny.

"Some of the doctors were very mean. The worst was Dr. Odom. He is from South Africa. He acts like he is a king and we are all his servants."

"What happened with Odom?"

"Dr. Odom was involved with her losing her job, but I don't know how. She went back to the Philippines before her contract was completed. After a few years I asked her to come here, and she did."

"Do you think Odom had a hand in her termination at James Madison?"

"He must have. He is the only one who knew about what happened in Saudi Arabia."

Lenny had a sense that Dillie was holding out, as people often did, even when he was on their side. But he also recognized that she was a very private person and decided not to push her.

Dillie wrote down Mai Loo's phone number and address on a pink three-by-five card and handed it to Lenny. "Here is her address. You will have to visit her. She will not answer the phone."

"Okay," said Lenny. "I'll need some time to line up a lawyer."

"I will visit her tonight," said Dillie. "Tomorrow I will tell you how she is doing."

As Lenny turned to go, she grasped his arm with a hand as strong as a man's. "You must understand about Mai Loo. She is not a strong person. I am afraid for her."

"What do you mean?" asked Lenny.

"Some people are like a rock. They can be stepped on and be okay. Mai Loo is like a flower. She needs someone strong like you to fight for her."

"Well, I'm kind of limited in what I can do, other than recommend a good lawyer. She's not in the union."

"I know you can help her," Dillie said, releasing his arm. "And I will do what I can."

As he made his way back to Seven South, Lenny thought about other terminations he had handled. He had seen the job loss drive one worker into alcoholism, another into crime and prison. One had committed suicide.

He silently cursed himself for not having paid more attention to Mai Loo. But he hadn't wanted her to think that he was hitting on her. And he had enough on his plate already. He decided the most he could do was to try and dig up information about her work infraction and feed it to her lawyer, once she hired one. He hoped it would be enough.

While his patient received the plasmapheresis treatment, Gary caught up on his nursing notes. When he began to write about Darling's psychosocial needs, he wondered why Mr. Darling hadn't had any relatives visiting him. Perhaps he had none in the Delaware Valley area?

Turning to the front of the chart, he read the face sheet, with its list of personal information. He was surprised to find listed under nearest relative a brother, Ray Darling. He lived in Quakertown, just outside Philly.

Gary went to the bedside. "Mr. Darling, do you have a brother living in Quakertown?"

"Yeah, I suppose I do."

"Do you want me to notify him that you're in the hospital?"

"Don't bother," said Darling.

"Wouldn't he want to know about your condition?"

Darling looked at the bottles of amber fluid hanging on the plasmapheresis machine. "You sure they're not filling me up with scotch? I feel a little drunk."

Gary waited, not responding to the joke.

"Look," said Darling, "Ray and I haven't talked in a long time. We kind of drifted apart. I'll call him up when I'm feeling better. Okay?"

"But given your present condition—"

"If I croak you can call him! Otherwise, let sleeping dogs lie."

"All right," said Gary with deep reluctance. "If that is your wish."

"It is," said Darling, placing his hands behind his head, his bony elbows sticking out. "Are you sure you can't get me that scotch?"

Lenny put away his supplies, emptied his bucket and rinsed out his mop. Before leaving the ward he decided he had one more chore that had to get done. He had a feeling he would regret it, but he didn't care. The heat and the faulty air-conditioning had been bad enough, but Mai Loo's termination was too much. It was time to take action.

He paged Kate Palmer from a phone at the nursing station, stood and waited for the answer. He picked up the receiver before the first ring had finished.

"Kate? Lenny. I'm going to help you nail Odom."

"Really?" said Kate, her voice rising with excitement. "This is great! Can we talk about it tomorrow morning?"

"Yeah, I guess so. I don't have any information myself . . ."

"That's okay, I'll fill you in on everything I have. I should have more of her lab results back by then."

"Okay," said Lenny. "Talk to you tomorrow."

"Thanks, Lenny," said Kate.

He hung up without replying. He knew they were treading a dangerous path. There were multiple ways that he could get in trouble with Joe West. *Fuck it,* he thought, thinking of Mai Loo, sweet and decent, out of a job. Maybe even out of a work visa. *If they want to play rough, I'll show them what rough is all about.*

In the M-SOC office, Cleopatra called the *Voice of Africa* and asked for the editor.

"I have an update for you. Is it too late to add it to your article?"

"Girl, if the story's hot, I'll hold the press for you. Give it to me."

"Yesterday a victim of Odom's racist abortion died. Her death was a direct result of his butchery."

"This is great," said the editor. "What's her name."

Cleopatra spelled the name out slowly. "She developed an infection due to his callous methods and complete disregard for sterile procedures."

The editor promised to lead off the story with the dead woman. "You understand," he said, "I have to call the hospital and try to get a statement."

"They will refuse to talk about it, as they always do."

"No problem. I can print their refusal. It will make our case against them stronger."

As Cleopatra hung up the phone, Lincoln turned around from his desk. "Baby, are you sure you want to feed them so much detail? The confidentiality laws are awfully damn strict."

"Screw confidentiality. There's a bigger law to consider. The law of justice. When you murder someone you can't expect to keep your name out of the press."

"I know that. I just worry the Dean will come down on you and kick you out of the program."

"Let him try. It will just add to their guilt. If I have to finish my last year somewhere else, it will be worth it to see them brought to their knees."

Lincoln turned back to his desk. He was finishing an article for the M-SOC newsletter about residency opportunities for minority students in other countries. He worried about his fiancé. She was too headstrong. Lincoln was afraid that this time she was running smack into a brick wall. Or a barbed-wire fence.

Dillie followed an elderly gentleman into the apartment building and rode the elevator up to Mai Loo's floor. Reaching the apartment, she knocked gently on the door.

"Mai Loo? It's Dillie. Come open the door for me. I know you are home. Let me in."

She heard a rustle inside, then the sound of the chain being slid out of the metal slot and the lock being turned. The door opened slightly. She slipped through and stood looking at her friend.

Mai Loo was in her nursing uniform. Her hair was tangled and matted. Her eyes were red and swollen.

"Why haven't you changed your clothes?" said Dillie. "It's so late!"

"I don't want to sleep; I'm afraid I will have nightmares."

"I will make you tea. Come, let's sit in the kitchen."

While she filled the kettle, Dillie looked at her friend, who slumped listlessly in her chair. She saw despair in her eyes and heard defeat in her voice.

"You must not give up," said Dillie, placing the kettle on the stove.

"What can I do? I will lose my visa. I will have to go back home and work for pennies."

"No. You will stay. You have rights."

"I have nothing."

"You have rights and you have friends. I already spoke to somebody."

"Who?"

"Lenny Moss."

"But I am not in the union!"

"No matter. Lenny is going to find a good lawyer for you."

"Lawyers are expensive!"

"We will find the money." Dillie looked around the kitchen. She saw dirty dishes in the sink. Setting out two tea cups on the dining-room table, she saw that the window was open and the air-conditioning turned off.

"No wonder it is so hot in here, you have the window open!"

"I don't care; I feel cold."

Dillie crossed to the living room and closed the window. She turned on the air-conditioning and lowered the curtains. Standing in the middle of the room with her hands on her hips, she said, "You will feel better when the apartment is clean. I will clean up, you will drink your tea, then we will cry and make our plans. I have a friend at a nursing agency. She will give you work, I am sure of it."

"No one will want me!"

"Of course they will want you, you are a good girl. You will work and you will feel better."

"I will never feel better."

"You must not let Doctor Odom win. If you sink into despair, he has beat you. You must not let him do that."

"He has already won," said Mai Loo, her head tilted down.

As the kettle whistled, Dillie ran water over the dirty dishes in the sink. She made a pot of tea and cleaned the dishes while the tea steeped, all the while casting glances at her friend and looking for a sign of hope in her eyes.

Chapter Sixteen

This time Lenny was *really* pissed off. It wasn't just the heat making him sweat like somebody in a sauna, though he'd barely started his shift. It wasn't the pieces of dried crud he was loosening from the marble floor with his paint scraper as he mopped the floor, either. He was angry that that monster Odom was getting away with murder.

Bad enough him doing those botched abortions and refusing to help when the patient went critical, but getting Mai Loo terminated was above and beyond.

Kate had told him Odom's victims routinely came back to the ER with infections in their womb. Lenny decided to call a few friends and get some help.

Inside a room were two female patients, one suffering from Alzheimer's, the other deaf. Waving to the women, who smiled and waved back, Lenny picked up the phone and called down to the morgue. When Regis answered, Lenny asked if the young man would do him a favor.

"Sure, man. Name it."

"Did your department do an autopsy on a young woman named Charyse Desir?"

There was an interval of silence long enough to make Lenny wonder if they had been disconnected.

"We autopsied her," said Regis. "What's up?"

"Well, between you and me, I'm helping some people investigate this doctor named Odom."

"We know the bastard down here," said Regis.

"You do?"

"Yeah. When Dr. Fingers did the autopsy he found the uterus had pieces of the baby sticking to it, all infected."

"I hear the infection killed her," said Lenny.

"That's what Doctor Fingers said."

"You think you can get me a copy of the autopsy?"

"Sure I can, if you promise me one thing."

"What's that?"

"Get it to the papers. Get it on the six o'clock news. I want the whole world to know what kind of a sicko we have working in this place."

"You got it," said Lenny, encouraged that others recognized that Odom was a monster. Hanging up, he reflected on a sad, historic fact. Practices as horrendous as Nazi medicine can go on and on, unless somebody stands up and yells "Stop!"

Kate Palmer fidgeted in her seat as the lecturer talked on about autoimmune systemic processes. She simply couldn't pay attention. The pending lab work for Charyse Desir was on her mind. Especially the microbiology report.

"I can't sit another minute," she whispered to her friend, Jennifer. "I've got to check some lab results."

She stood up and made her way down the aisle, trying not to step on any toes or to draw attention to herself. As she reached the end of the row, the lecturer said, "I seem to be losing somebody. Are you ill, my dear?"

"Uh, no sir, I got a page from my daughter's school. I have to check on her."

"Ah. I hope all is well with her. Those schools are a teeming reservoir of communicable diseases. Now, where was I?"

Kate hurried out of the lecture hall as the instructor resumed his lecture.

A Race Against Death

★ ★ ★ ★ ★

After taking the report on Mr. Darling from the night nurse, Gary stepped to the bedside. He was worried. During the night the level of paralysis had risen to the lower thoracic region. In spite of the one hundred percent oxygen delivered by mask, the patient's oxygen level was barely ninety and his heart was racing at a hundred twenty.

Dr. Singh came to the bedside with his team. The resident who had been on call the night before read out loud the latest blood gas results.

"Hypo-ventilation is evident," said Singh. "You see the high carbon dioxide? He is not moving enough volume to expel it. Very little oxygen is reaching the alveoli."

"Then we intubate?" asked the resident.

"Yes. It is time." Singh turned to the anesthesia resident, a Korean man with small, nervous hands. "Koo will do the intubation."

"Yes. I will do," said the resident, smiling at the opportunity to practice his craft. He went for the intubation kit while another resident replaced the oxygen mask with an ambu bag and began forcing oxygen into the patient's lungs.

Only semiconscious due to the high level of carbon dioxide in his blood, Darling made a feeble effort to push the ambu off his face, but soon gave up and let his arms fall to his side. He closed his eyes as if to shut out the whole affair, certain that his ship was sinking and he was going down with it.

The anesthesia resident forced open Darling's mouth and inserted the rounded blade of the laryngoscope. The little light bulb in the smooth blade illuminated the throat. He peered into the shadows looking for the trachea. Just as he got a clear view of the vocal cords—the landmarks that told him he was in the right opening—Darling gagged violently. Brown vomitus spewed out of his mouth and ran down his chin, making it impossible for the resident to see the opening of the trachea.

"Suction, please," said Dr. Singh, his voice calm and direct. Gary hurriedly handed him the suction tube. The physician deftly inserted it deep in the patient's throat.

Dr. Singh told the young resident, "If the patient aspirates his gastric contents, he will develop a florid pneumonia. That would be disastrous."

Once the airway was cleared of vomitus, the resident was able to insert the breathing tube.

"Do you wish x-ray?" he said, looking at Dr. Singh.

"Always," said Singh. "And be sure to lavage the trachea until it is clear."

Moose was working the line, dishing out breakfast. He scooped oatmeal into a bowl and covered it with plastic wrap. Another tray got cold cereal and a container of milk. The pats of butter were rapidly melting into puddles in their wax paper wraps. All the patients who had requested eggs received the same order: cold hard-boiled eggs, which the chef had boiled at five in the morning, saying he would not fry a single egg or slice of bacon until the air-conditioning was fixed.

The kitchen supervisor argued and yelled and threatened the chef with discipline, but the chef held his ground. The room thermometer read a hundred degrees, and it was only seven-fifteen in the morning.

As he dished out the food, Moose thought about the young woman Lenny had told him about at the time clock that morning. It seemed everybody was talking about her. They all wanted Odom to get what was coming, preferably up the ass. Moose decided to visit a friend in Medical Records the first chance he got. He had a feeling someone in that department could help him nail Odom to a tree.

A Race Against Death

★ ★ ★ ★ ★

Once the breathing tube was in place, Mr. Darling's color rapidly improved. His lips became a healthy pink and his oxygen level returned to the normal range. But the tube in the airway was irritating, and the force of oxygen being rammed into his lungs even more uncomfortable.

When Gary saw the patient's hand reaching for the endotracheal tube, he grabbed hold of Darling's arm. "Don't pull on the tube, Mr. Darling, it has to stay in for a while." Gary asked Dr. Singh what type of sedation he wanted.

"Interesting question," said Singh. "I have a strong preference for dropidol."

Gary hurried to the medication room for the dropidol. Returning with the pre-mixed intravenous solution, he asked, "What dose would you like, doctor?"

"Let's begin with twenty-five mikes per minute."

Gary dialed in the dose on the intravenous pump, letting the machine calculate the drip rate.

Singh turned to his team. "I prefer dropidol. In addition to providing effective sedation and amnesia, it has an added side effect that can be beneficial."

"What is that?" asked Dr. Koo.

"Dropidol can produce vivid sexual dreams. I have believed for some time that if a patient must be asleep for long periods, why not let him enjoy himself?" Leading his team on to the next patient, Singh added, "In spite of what your mother told you, a wet dream never hurt anybody."

Chapter Seventeen

Mai Loo sat at her little dining-room table, her hands in her lap, her eyes staring into space. A half-filled cup of tea sat on the table. Despite the hot, muggy air coming in through the open window, she felt a chill. After Dillie had left the evening before, Mai Loo turned off the air-conditioning and opened the window.

She turned her head, looked at the open window. No breeze stirred the sheer curtains hanging there. She knew how many stories it was from her window to the ground. Knew that there was a cement sidewalk and steps directly below, and that the impact would kill her quickly if she let herself fall.

She felt a magnetic force pulling her toward the open window. The thought of the wind rushing up at her as she sailed downward was appealing. It would obliterate the terrible ache that she felt. An ache that was so deep and so intense, she couldn't even tell where it originated. She only knew that she wanted the unbearable pain to go away.

Beside her cup of tea was a paper with the name and address of the nursing agency that Dillie had left for her. Mai Loo had promised her friend to go to the agency and apply for work.

She doubted that she would ever work as a nurse again. But she had promised her friend. Dear Dillie: the rock. Always strong. Always optimistic. Mai Loo felt she could not betray her friend, even though the job interview would be useless.

With slow, reluctant steps, she walked to the bathroom to prepare her face for the interview.

Kate called up Charyse Desir's lab results on a computer terminal at one of the nursing stations. Scrolling down to the microbiology report, she saw that the technician had identified the bacteria. It was E. coli, a common bowel flora. Not a surprising result. She knew from her Infectious Disease rotation that E. coli often caused bladder infections, so it wasn't surprising to find it in the uterus.

But then she saw that the report was amended. The full report listed the bacteria as sorbitol positive. It said: *Presumptive identification is E. coli 0:157. Department of Health notified by E-mail.*

This was surprising. Kate knew that outbreaks of the 0:157 strain sometimes occurred in the community, usually in contaminated processed meat or a polluted water sources. But in a hospitalized patient? It didn't make sense.

Kate didn't know enough about E. coli to understand how Charyse Desir became infected with the deadly strain. But she knew someone who did. As she printed out the lab results and hurried to the Infectious Disease department, she hoped Dr. Auginello was in.

Lenny had emptied all the trash liners from the patient rooms and was about to take the big rolling trash barrel to the service elevator when he spied Napoleon, one of the Emergency Room nurses, who had just brought a new admission up to the ward.

"Hey, Nate, how's it goin'?"

"Hi, Lenny. Ah, you know, *bon gre, mal gre.*"

"How's that?"

"It's from a French jazz song. It's, like, good days, bad

days." He stripped the sheet off the stretcher and dropped it in a dirty laundry bag. "Hey, I'm goin' to see Cedar Walton at the Melodeon Saturday night. You want to come?"

"I can't. I'm going over to Moose's with Patience and the kids for dinner."

"You two make a nice couple. Earth and wind."

"I mainly break wind," said Lenny. He stepped closer to the nurse. "Listen, you got a minute?"

"Sure," said Napoleon. He parked the stretcher along the wall and followed his friend to the housekeeping closet.

Napoleon settled lightly on the bucket. Though not tall, he was a solidly built black man with a shaved head, sculpted arms, and thick, callused hands that he used to break cinder blocks. Lenny knew that Nate was a black belt in Japanese karate, and that the young man preferred to keep quiet about his art so as not to invite challenges from the hardheads.

"Are things cool with you down the ER?" asked Lenny.

"Smooth as silk. Thanks for going to Human Resources with me. I still can't believe that I lost my cool that one time. I've meditated a lot on it."

"It's the heat, it makes us all crazy," said Lenny. "Still, calling that drunken postal worker white trash could have got you fired."

"He said he and his KKK buddies were gonna come back and lynch me."

"That's the only thing that saved your ass," said Lenny. "Here's my problem. Somehow I let myself get talked into poking around this doctor Odom's abortions. You've probably heard about him."

"Sure I've heard. His post-abortion women come in every week with fever and chills and abdominal pain. We even have a word for the syndrome. Instead of 'endometritis,' we call it 'Odometritis.' "

"That's fucked up," said Lenny. "I hear it's because he uses a vacuum to abort the fetus."

"The bastard should be inducing labor, like a stillbirth. He uses the vacuum because it's fast. It tears their limbs off and leaves tissue behind."

"Which get infected," said Lenny.

"And brings them back to us in the ER."

"An abortion mill here in James Madison," said Lenny. "Do you fricking believe it?"

"You're surprised? The man satisfies a social need, he does it on budget, and he brings in big bucks from the Main Line with his fertility treatments."

Lenny nodded his head. "I know all about the bottom line."

Napoleon rose from his perch. As he retrieved his stretcher, he called back, "Hey, Lenny. If you get something going that'll stop the bastard, count me in. I'll write a letter or testify anytime you want. That man is pure evil."

Gary called telephone information and asked for the number of Raymond Darling. He gave the operator the address and spelling of the name, then waited until a computer-generated voice uttered the numbers.

Writing the phone number down on his report sheet, he wondered if calling the brother would be violating the patient's privacy. There were so many restrictions on health personnel. They couldn't even call another facility for information on a patient without proving they had a need to know.

Gary brought his concern to Crystal, the charge nurse. Crystal was wearing a deep lavender lipstick and eyeliner that matched her stethoscope and socks. She considered the issue for perhaps ten seconds.

"Call the brother," she said.

"You're sure?"

"I always go by the rule, if it were *my* mother or sibling in the hospital, what would I do? In this case, I'd want my brother to know, even if I hadn't spoken to him in years."

As Gary looked at the phone number, trying to make up his mind, Crystal added, "He's family. When you're really in trouble, there's no substitute."

Gary picked up the receiver and made the call.

Chapter Eighteen

Maurice mumbled to himself as he pushed his messenger cart down the hushed, carpeted corridor of the Executive Suite. The hallway was so cold, it gave him goose bumps. He repeated over and over to himself, "I'll get her back . . . I'll get her back," his lips clenched and hardly moving, his voice only a murmur to those who passed him in the hall.

Although he was not assigned to this area today, he had decided to make a special trip to Human Resources. Maurice knew that whenever an employee was terminated, a letter was sent to the victim the following day by certified mail. He had carried many such letters over the years. Mai Loo would be receiving one. He wanted to know why she had been terminated. And who was behind it.

He left his cart in the hall and entered the Human Resources office. The secretary, a prim woman who must have looked middle-aged when she was a teenager, glanced up at him from where she sat behind her desk, then put him out of her mind as she typed a letter.

Clenching his lips together so as not to mumble—he didn't want to draw attention to himself—Maurice went to the OUT box on the edge of the secretary's desk, picked up the stack of mail, and carried it out to his cart, his heart thumping so hard in his chest, he was afraid the secretary would hear it.

He made it out to the hallway, grabbed his cart, and hurried out of the suite. Once he was on safer ground, he riffled through the mail, looking for the telltale certified letter. His fingers were stiff as he fingered the letters. Finally he found it.

Looking up and down the corridor to be sure no one could see, he stuffed the letter inside his shirt. He continued with his rounds, anxious to unload his cart in the mailroom so he could hide in the tiny break room behind the messengers' dispatcher and read the letter.

Carrying a plate covered with plastic wrap and a towel, Moose stepped into the Medical Record room. Making his way through a maze of desks, computer terminals and bookshelves overflowing with charts, he spotted his friend on a step stool, running her finger along a line of charts on a high shelf. Her long legs drew his eye up along her shapely body.

"Hey, Tiffany. You got a nice cool place down here. Wish we had it this good in the kitchen."

She looked down, saw Moose, smiled. "We have extra air-conditioning units. If we get any dampness in the department, the charts will mildew."

Stepping down, she eyed the plate in Moose's hand.

"I hope that's for *me,* all the things I've done for you."

"Who else would I be bringing breakfast to?" He followed her to her desk, sat across from her, slid the plate smoothly onto the desk. Removing the towel and plastic wrap, he said, "I got you stuffed crab, spicy noodles with shrimp, and your favorite—ambrosia."

"Good god almighty, this didn't come from the hospital kitchen, did it?"

"Sure it did. You think just 'cause we serve roast beef and buttered noodles, we can't cook? The Medical Board is interviewing some hotshot cardiac surgeon from New York. Supposed to have some new tricks or something. We got the order to knock the socks off the guy."

"It'll take more than good food for somebody to leave that town for little old Philadelphia."

Tiffany took the fork nestled on the plate and dug out a generous helping of stuffed crab. She put it in her mouth and let it sit there a moment, savoring the flavor.

"Where did your cook get his training, Paris? This is *fabulous*."

"Montreal." He handed her a napkin, which she used to dab her lips in a dainty gesture of sophistication.

"Listen, Tif, I do have one little problem you could help me with."

She rolled her eyes while sucking the ends of some noodles into her mouth. "How come you only come see me when you *need* something?"

"That's not true! I helped your brother get a job in the kitchen, didn't I?"

"Yeah . . ."

"And Lenny helped him when he got in that jam with the police. The possession thing."

"He was a little high, but he's been straight ever since."

"I know he has, I been keeping an eye on him." Moose folded the towel and placed it neatly on the edge of the desk. "See, me and Lenny, we've been investigating Doctor Odom. The way he's been butchering women by doing bad abortions."

"I heard something about him, but I didn't get what it was exactly."

"It's been going on for years, but the shit hit the fan when one of his patients died up in the ICU. Charyse Desir."

Tiffany chewed her food slowly, listening intently.

"He got a whole bunch of women sick. Mostly black girls

from North Philly. I was hoping you could get me a copy of her chart. You think?"

The Medical Records clerk put down her fork and wiped her mouth. "It's funny you should come down just now. The Department of Health was in here this morning, and they had Harriet make a copy of that very chart. Plus, her record from the OR."

"That's great. So you could just—"

"Get my ass fired for helping you and get arrested to boot? No thank you." She took another bite of food, sat back in her chair.

"Come on, Tif. Odom is a butcher. Don't you think the world should know what he did to that young woman that died?"

Tiffany covered her plate of food, rose from her chair, and walked away without a word. Moose sat, not sure what he should do. She returned a minute later.

"The chart you want is still on Harriet's desk. She goes on her break in an hour. I got to go up to the wards and pick up discharge charts. Where are you gonna be at ten o'clock?"

"I'll be collecting late trays and picking up menus."

"I'll put the copy inside your food cart."

A huge grin lifted Moose's face. "Thanks, baby. I won't forget you for this." He got up from his chair and started out through the labyrinth.

"You better be bringing me something good every week, you hear?" she said, covering her food with the plastic wrap. "Every week!"

As Regis Devoe came walking toward him, Lenny couldn't help but note the change in the young man. When he worked in the laundry the fellow was always in trouble. Now he looked serious and professional, dressed in scrubs and a crisp white lab coat. His job in the morgue had really turned him around.

"What's the new cologne?" asked Lenny, picking up the scent of formaldehyde. "I like it!"

"It's the damned preservative. I have to scrub with lemon oil soap before I go home, or Salina gives me hell. She's afraid the baby will have a reaction to it, or some crap."

"Mothers always worry."

"And complain."

Regis reached into his lab coat and handed Lenny an envelope.

"The autopsy report for Charyse Desir," he said. "I also printed a photo that'll make you sick."

"Thanks," said Lenny. "I'll get it to the right people."

"Good," said Regis. He watched a pregnant nurse's aide walk by. "You don't have any kids, do you?"

"No."

"It's kind of weird. After my son was born, I kind of looked at things different. I'm not saying there shouldn't be any abortions. But anybody who butchers babies the way that prick Odom does should be tortured and buried alive. You'll see what I mean when you get a look at the picture."

Lenny took the report back to the housekeeping closet and read it. The pathologist's description confirmed everything he had heard about Odom.

He picked up the photo and studied it. Lenny was not familiar with dissection and tissue analysis. But there was an area in the photo circled with red ink. The five small smudges on a gray background perplexed him until he read a note Regis had made in the corner of the photo with an arrow pointing at the circle. *Digits of fetus stuck to uterus.*

First, he felt sick in his stomach. Then, a rising fury. As a union steward Lenny had fought to see that justice was done, usually a fair shake for a coworker, sometimes a compromise on punishment. Seeing the photo of the tiny hand, he vowed to not give up until Odom was punished for his crimes.

Chapter Nineteen

Mai Loo stood in front of the office door and read the company name: *STAT NURSE*. She felt a powerful urge to turn and flee. Only her promise to Dillie kept her from leaving. She wiped her sweaty hand on her skirt and opened the door, stepped timidly into the room, stood quietly waiting to be noticed. A middle-aged white woman in a loose housedress and sandals sat at a cluttered desk, speaking on the phone while reading a computer screen.

"Of course she's fully qualified," the woman was saying. "She passed my nursing examination with flying colors!" The woman scribbled a hasty note on the pad. "I saw her diploma and her license, it's all in my employee records . . . Well, at least let her come back on the night shift. It's quiet. There's less stress and fewer people around . . . You will? *Fantastic.* I'll make sure she understands the next time a situation like this comes up. Thanks. Bye."

The woman hung up the phone, glanced up, and saw Mai Loo.

"Be with you in a second, honey. You can fill out an application form and a W-2 there on the clipboard. You bring your license?"

"Yes," said Mai Loo in a frail voice. She picked up a clipboard with an application and a pen chained to it and sat on a futon sofa. She wondered if the nursing agency had a night supervisor who slept on it.

She felt a powerful urge to run out of the office and never come back, certain the tough-talking woman would reject her request for a job. She could hardly believe that anyone would hire her as a professional nurse after the hospital terminated her. *What should I say when she asks why I left James Madison?*

She remembered Dillie promising that the woman at the agency was understanding. Mai Loo could not face her best friend and admit that she had run away without even applying for a job.

Staring at the form on the clipboard, she agonized over what to do.

Kate reached her hand to the keypad on the door of the Infectious Disease Lab, punched in the three-number code, and pushed open the door to the lab. Inside, she found the familiar black marble tables and sinks, the microscopes and jars of staining fluid, the odor of mold and decay.

Bent over one microscope was the tall, gangly form of Dr. Salvatore Auginello, Infectious Disease Attending Physician.

"Hi, Auggie," she called, stepping up to the table.

Auginello looked up from his instrument. "Kate Palmer! What a pleasant surprise." He stepped to the sink and began washing his hands. "What brings you back to ID?"

"I have a patient with endometritis. She died from it, actually. I was hoping you could look over her lab work and give me your take on it."

"Sure. Let's have a look."

Drying his hands, he took the lab reports from Kate and examined them. His vivid blue eyes danced from side to side as he skimmed the lines of data.

"Hmm. Our old gut flora friend, E. coli. It's a common gram negative, as you'll recall from your rotation. Finding it in a uterine culture is not surprising, although it does not commonly produce a fatal infection."

"I know," said Kate. "But this strain produced endotoxins."

"Ah. I see they tested for sorbitol," said Auginello. "Hmm." He settled on a bar stool. "This is very strange. I haven't had any reports of an E. coli o-one-five-seven outbreak in the Delaware Valley since last May."

"That's one of the things that's troubling me," said Kate. "I don't think she picked up the E. coli in the community."

Auginello gave her a guarded look. "Where, then?"

"I think she became infected during an abortion here at James Madison."

"That would be highly unusual, as well as reportable to the state." He wrote down the number of the culture on a three-by-five card. "I'm going to have to do a literature search, but I've never heard of this pathogen linked to a hospital-acquired infection."

"I was hoping you would run a ribotype on it," said Kate. "If you're not too busy."

A twinkle lit up in the physician's eyes. "Are you sure you don't want to do a fellowship in Infectious Disease after your residency is over? You were my best student."

"I gave it a lot of thought, Auggie. I really did. But I'm committed to Family Practice. Which means that I'll see a lot of infections!"

"Not the same," said Auginello. "But close enough."

He escorted her to the door. "I'll run down to Microbiology and pick up the isolate," he said. "I should have it ribotyped this afternoon. I'll page you."

"Great. My beeper is—"

"I know your beeper."

"Thanks, Auggie. I've got to run. I have a friend who needs to know about this."

"Don't be in such a hurry. Have you forgotten what I told you on your ID rotation?" he called after her.

"I know!" she yelled back. "Don't forget to take the time to stop and smell the pseudomonas along the way!"

As Mai Loo sat in the Stat Nurse office and filled out the application form, the woman behind the desk dialed a number, told a nurse that she could go back to Blessed Mother Nursing Home, but only if she worked nights. "It's just until you get back in their good graces," she said. "I had to fight like hell to get them to take you back! I know they're a bunch of repressed old hens, but what can you do, you screwed up the meds." She made an entry in the computer. "I know it's a Saturday night, but it's work, isn't it? I'll put you down as confirmed."

She hung up the phone, punched a button on the keyboard, then looked over at Mai Loo.

"What's your name, dear?"

"Mai Loo."

"Oh, yes. You're Dillie's friend."

"Uh huh."

"I wish I had a dozen more like her. Great nurse. Always calm. Can I see your license?"

Mai Loo handed the woman her nursing license and her Green card.

"My name's Silkie," said the woman, stepping to the fax machine to copy Mai Loo's papers. "It's my last name, but it's what everybody calls me, even my ex." She handed the originals back to Mai Loo.

"Are you willing to work nights, dear? 'Cause that's where I have most of my shifts, at least until you get some seniority and the supervisors in the nursing homes get to know you."

"I can work any time," said Mai Loo. "Umm. About my last employer . . ."

"Don't worry about that. Dillie told me how you got a raw deal. That's a shame, the way some employers treat their staff. They don't realize what it does to a person's mind to lose a job."

"It was a terrible shock," said Mai Loo.

Silkie nodded her head in sympathy. "It had something to do with a doctor you worked with in, was it Kuwait?"

"It was in Saudi Arabia. He is a very mean person."

"I know the type, believe me." She scanned the application for five seconds. "I can see you're a nice girl. Can you start tomorrow night at eleven? I have an opening at Blessed Mother."

Startled, Mai Loo said, "Yes. I can. Don't you have to check my references?"

"Child, if Dillie said you're okay and you've got a current license, that's good enough for me. Show up at the Home a half hour early, the evening charge nurse will get you oriented. You have a white uniform?"

"I do."

"Good. The Sisters insist all the girls wear white. Like they're so pure, right? Here's the address and directions. You have a car?"

"Uh-huh."

"Great. Then you're all set."

Silkie printed out a name tag and gave it to Mai Loo. As she escorted the young nurse to the door, she placed a hand on her shoulder and said, "I've been fired from more jobs than I can remember. They're run by idiots. Don't let yourself get too down, dear."

Mai Loo was close to tears, this time with relief. In a voice choking with emotion, she said, "Thank you for giving me this opportunity, Miss Silkie. I will not disappoint you!"

"I'm sure you won't. Just remember, dear, the only one who can hurt you now is you."

Chapter Twenty

Joe West stood towering over the young woman dressed in tight jeans and a clinging top. He ignored a walkie-talkie that squawked in the background.

"You understand, you can encourage the employee to drink, but you can't be overt. You have to be subtle."

"I know how to get them boys tossing down cold ones," said Baby Love. "Heat like this, it don't take much for them to chug a cold eighty." She put her hands on her hips and pouted. "What about some money for me? I shouldn't have to pay for my own drinks."

West glared at the young woman. "Don't have more than one. You have to keep your head and keep count of how much they drink."

He took a ten-dollar-bill from his wallet and handed it to her. When she made a face, he said, "*One drink.* You have the number to call to report the employee. Be sure the description is clear so that the officer can make the correct arrest."

"Don't you worry yourself about me," said Baby Love, slipping the bill into her bra. "I'm a natural born cop. I'll tell you who to pick up. And this time I'm getting my promotion. Right?"

"If you do this correctly, I'll see that you get bumped up a pay grade."

"With a title! I want a title."

Holding the door for her, West shoved it closed just as she cleared the doorway. He was not about to make any promises to a snitch.

As Gary sat at the bedside and updated his notes, he saw the red trigger light winking on the ventilator as Mr. Darling's chest rose and fell. The patient was comfortably sedated, making no effort to fight the machine or pull out the tube. Gary returned to his notes, while the ventilator made its rhythmic *whoosh-whoosh,* as if humming a lullaby.

In his sleep, Rupert Darling thought he heard voices. The voices were indistinct. There seemed to be music. And laughter.

After a moment he realized he was in a darkly lit bar. There were several beautiful, voluptuous women wearing low-cut dresses standing about. A tall brunette with enormous breasts that threatened to fall out of her dress stood behind the bar. She slowly wiped the inside of a glass with a rag and leered at him.

There was a huge supply of whiskey behind the bar, food set out on tables, and a place to dance. Darling had only to pick a partner and sweep her onto the dance floor, or take her upstairs to one of the private rooms.

As his gaze roamed over the women, he recognized, to his surprise, an old friend seated at the end of the bar, nursing a beer.

Lenny told Betty he was going for his break. Retrieving the autopsy report Regis had given him, he filled a cup with ice from the ice machine, grabbed a carton of juice and a sandwich from the fridge, and headed down the steps. In the basement he made his way to the sewing room where he had agreed to meet Moose. He gave the door one knock and entered.

A Race Against Death

Birdie was at her sewing machine, making pillowcases out of torn sheets. She had long, strong, slender hands that deftly fed the fabric across the platform of the industrial machine. Slouched in a beat-up folding chair, Moose was eating a salad.

"That smells good," said Lenny. "What is it?"

"Crab salad. With real crab, not that fake fish stuff. The chef made up a big platter for the administration."

"Lucky for you," said Lenny, unwrapping his sandwich.

"What's ya eatin'?" said Moose.

"Tuna salad, with relish and red onion."

"Mister gourmet," said Moose.

"I got a copy of Charyse Desir's autopsy report," said Lenny. "You better not look at it until after you eat."

"Amen to that," said Birdie. "It must be awful to read about."

Moose reached into his back pocket, pulled out an envelope, and handed it to Lenny. "There ain't nothin' like havin' friends."

"What is it?" Lenny wiped his hands on his pants, opened the envelope, and scanned the first page. "Holy shit! It's a copy of Charyse Desir's hospital chart! I thought *I* was hot, getting the autopsy report. This is fantastic!"

"No big thing," said Moose.

Lenny leafed through the papers. "Hmm. It says she had organ failure . . . Shock, too, I think . . . there's a lot of medical lingo."

"Why don't you show it to Gary Tuttle?" said Birdie.

"Good idea," said Lenny. "I'll stop by the ICU after—"

The door opened slowly and Kate Palmer stuck her head inside. "Hi, Lenny. The clerk on your floor said I'd find you here." She entered the sewing room and greeted Moose and Birdie while Lenny unfolded a chair for her. "I've found out some things about Charyse Desir."

143

"Us, too," said Lenny. "You go first."

She told them about the E. coli 0:157 recovered from the dead girl's blood and uterus. She explained that the strain was not supposed to be acquired while in the hospital. "Doctor Auginello, my ID Attending, says it's very unusual for somebody to become infected with this pathogen in the Labor and Delivery OR. It's supposed to be a sterile environment."

"Unusual, but not impossible?" asked Lenny.

"Auginello is always saying, 'The bugs don't read textbooks.' But he made it clear this infection should not have come from a hospital procedure."

"I say Odom did it on purpose," said Moose.

"I know he's cold," said Kate. "And very prejudiced. But knowingly infecting his patient?"

"I have to agree with Kate," said Lenny. "It's hard to believe he would intentionally infect his patients; it could jeopardize his license. It sounds more like negligence."

Birdie said, "Odom wants to stop black women from having babies. I bet that E. coli whatever it is makes women sterile."

"Is that right?" Lenny asked Kate.

"This bacteria secretes a powerful toxin. I suppose it *could* leave the uterus scarred."

"And unable to carry a baby to term?" asked Birdie.

"It's possible," said Kate. "I'll talk to somebody in OB-GYN."

"While you're talking to them, you might let them know about these," said Lenny. He handed Kate the autopsy report with the photo and the copy of Charyse Desir's chart.

Kate looked at the image and read the autopsy report. Tears welled up in her eyes.

"He's a monster," said Kate. "A living monster."

Birdie stepped behind her and looked over her shoulder. "What is it?"

"It's a section of the uterine wall," said Kate. "See those little gray lines? Those are fingers. The baby's hand is imbedded in the tissue."

Birdie turned away, sick and shaken. Moose put his arm around her.

"He hates black women," said Moose. "End of story."

"That's what they're saying in M-SOC," said Kate. She explained the charges Cleopatra had made at the medical students meeting.

Kate opened the medical record and read the progress report out loud, explaining the medical terminology. "It doesn't tell us anything we don't already know. She developed the infection after undergoing the abortion and the infection killed her."

She studied the operating room report. "I don't see anything unusual here, either."

"Who helped out in the delivery room?" said Lenny. "We could ask them if they saw Odom doing anything unusual."

"Like a lapse in sterile technique. Or improperly reusing equipment without sterilizing it between cases. Good idea," said Kate. "Let's see. Here's Odom's name. Doctors Margolis and Dobkin would be residents. Johnson, an intern, probably. And there's the scrub nurse. Looks like a Miss Munios."

"Could you talk to the residents?" asked Lenny.

Kate agreed to track them down. "When can we meet again? I might have more information about the bacteria that killed her."

"Moose and I are going jogging in the morning, then I'm going to the zoo with my friend and her kids. We could talk then."

"Saturday Odom will be performing his abortions again," said Kate.

"We can't stop him by then," said Lenny. "The best we can do is collect as much information as we can and let M-SOC release it to the press."

As they all stood up to leave, Moose said, "We're gonna nail the bastard. When the facts come out, Odom will be taken out of here in handcuffs. Trust me."

Chapter Twenty-One

In his peaceful slumber, Rupert Darling inhaled the sweet perfume of a woman aroused. He ran his fingers lightly over her soft, swelling breasts. The music in the bar was a distant hum as he and his friend settled into huge circular beds, each with a willing partner.

A luscious redhead with sharp nails ran her fingers along his chest. She drove her tongue deep into his mouth. It danced and frolicked in his throat while her hands grasped his hair and pinned his head to the bed.

Thrilled by her aggressive love, he wondered if his friend and the other girl might all end up in the same bed together. He had a feeling that Gary Tuttle was a lot more uninhibited than he let on.

Baby Love left the hospital and crossed Germantown Avenue to the Cave. Entering, she stepped to the bar and ordered a wine cooler. "Gimmie the peach flavor," she said. "And a big old glass of ice on the side."

She looked around the room, saw it was almost empty and there were no James Madison employees present. At least, none she recognized.

That was okay, she thought. She had plenty of time. She'd just sip her wine, chill, and wait for a pigeon to fly into her trap.

Tyrell had his head up in the ceiling and was checking to

see that the baffle in the cooling duct was open when his beeper sounded. He cursed the thing, climbed down the ladder, and made his way to the nursing station. He soon had his supervisor on the line, who told him to take a look at a leaking pipe in the pharmacy.

"I'm checking the duct work," he complained. "I'll never get done if you send me down there."

"The duct work can wait. If they have a flood in the pharmacy, it will ruin a lot of drugs. Get your ass down there right now."

"All right," said Tyrell. "But don't blame me if some of the wards don't have cool air."

"I'll blame you for a pharmacist drowning if you don't hurry up," the supervisor growled.

Tyrell went to the pharmacy. A phone was ringing and left unanswered. One of the pharmacists, a petite Korean woman in shorts and a tank top, sat on a bar stool in bare feet, filling prescriptions, her sandals on the floor. She pointed her thumb at the storage room.

He followed a trail of wet blue pads on the floor to the storage room. In a corner he saw the water dripping steadily through a brown-stained ceiling tile into an overflowing wastebasket.

He unfolded his ladder, reached up and pulled down the ceiling tiles, now crumbling with moisture. Shining a flashlight into the space, he saw the problem right away. A juncture where a pipe made a right angle was leaking around the nut. The threads might be worn, or the pipe could have been stressed by some weight pulling it down. Or it could simply be a loose nut.

Tyrell believed in trying the easy fix first. He found a shut-off valve upstream of the leak and tightened it down. The leak slowed and finally stopped.

Once he had the water off, he loosened the leaking nut and eased it back off the threads. The threads looked good; no sign of wear. He wrapped silicone tape several times around the threads, added a little plumber's jelly, then he replaced the nut and tightened it up.

He opened the valve back up, and presto! The leak was fixed. Not a drop came from the junction. He estimated that his repair job would last a thousand years.

Stepping off the ladder, he called his supervisor.

"How bad is it?" asked the supervisor. "You gonna need any help on this one?"

Tyrell knew that his supervisor hated to leave his air-conditioned office, where he spent hours playing video games on the computer.

"I can get it done by myself. I turned off the water. It looks like I might have to cut the pipe and put in a patch."

"Christ," said the supervisor. "How much time will it take?"

"About four hours. Unless I run into problems."

"Really? Okay, if you're sure you can handle it. Call me if you run into trouble."

"I will," said Tyrell, thinking about the cold beer waiting for him at the Cave. "I promise."

Maurice was relieved to find the tiny messenger's lounge empty. He put the kettle on the electric hot plate, a device that violated hospital rules and the city fire code. But the hospital safety director rarely inspected their little hole in the wall, it was too far off the beaten track.

When the kettle began to steam, he locked the door, then held the envelope over the steam. He was always surprised at how easily a letter came unglued. "They use cheap envelopes," he mumbled to himself. "Cheap, cheap, cheap." In seconds he had the envelope open.

He read the letter slowly, his lips moving as his gaze traveled down the page. *In light of Dr. Odom's statements reporting your prior unprofessional behavior . . . due to your falsified application for employment . . . the report of narcotics stolen from your previous employer . . . we have no choice but to terminate your employment effective immediately. You will surrender your identification badge and parking lot card . . . a terminal check may be picked up at the Hospital Security Office by appointment only.*

Maurice's hands shook as he read the letter. It was always the same. They were arrogant and heartless. The other termination letters had always made him sad. This one made him shake with rage.

He unlocked the door and peeked out at the office. The dispatcher was reading a weekly tabloid. Quietly, Maurice walked to the fax machine and copied the letter. When he was done, he put the original back in its envelope and resealed it. Then he went to the mailroom to deposit it where it belonged, wishing that he could tear it up in a million pieces. But Mai Loo had to get her letter.

And he had to get his revenge.

Baby Love was on her second wine cooler when three men from the maintenance department came in the door. A wicked smile formed on her face when she saw one of them order a sixteen ounce bottle of beer.

She sashayed up to their table, bent down to give them a peek at her breasts, and put her wine cooler on the table.

"You boys need some female company," she said, sliding smoothly onto a chair. She glanced down at a glass of soda. "What's the matter with *you*—can't handle a real drink?" She lifted her wine cooler to her lips and licked the rim of the glass.

"I can drink all I want," said the young man. "When I'm hot and tired I need a Coke to wake me up."

"What about you?" she said, looking at the second guy.

"You meet me here at three-thirty, I'll match you shot for shot," he said, holding his cold soda at arm's length.

Baby Love put an arm around Tyrell, leaning her breast into his arm. "Only one of you here is man enough for me, I can see that!" She clinked his bottle of beer with her wine cooler. "You must get awful hot, keeping that big building running in all this heat."

The others agreed, saying they were all on mandatory overtime and the system was strained to its limits.

"They need a whole new cooling system," said Tyrell. "The unit they have was built in the fifties."

"Don't forget they added two more floors and another building," another man said. "The compressors weren't made to handle all that load."

As Tyrell sipped his beer, Baby Love said, "You almost killed that one. Think you can handle another?"

"That's all right," he said. "I might have to work a second shift."

"I'm buyin'," she said, leaning her body into him again. She wished she could reach down to his crotch and really work up his thirst.

"Yeah, all right," he said. "I'll take another. Then I got to get back to work."

After the new drinks were served, Baby Love excused herself and went to the bathroom. It was a dirty little room with a cracked toilet seat and cigarette burns on the enamel sink. She took a tiny cell phone from her pocket and dialed the hospital security office.

"Get Joe West on the phone," she said to the guard who answered the phone. When the guard wanted to know who it was, she said, "Tell him Baby Love's got a drunk on duty to report."

A moment later West's flat voice came on the phone. "Who?" he said.

"I seen a guy from maintenance drinking on duty at the Cave. His name's Tyrell Hardy. He'll be on his way back in a couple of minutes, and you can catch him comin' in if you hurry."

She started to give West a description of Tyrell when she heard a *click*. West had hung up the phone. Cursing into the dead phone, she went back to the bar to order another wine cooler.

Chapter Twenty-Two

Dr. Auginello was deeply worried about the culture report Kate Palmer had given him. His literature search on the Internet had not found a single case of E. coli 0:157 causing a hospital-acquired pathogen.

He walked down the hall to the Microbiology Lab, intending to thaw out the frozen specimen of the last E. coli 0:157 they had seen back in May. It had come from a young woman living on a commune outside the city in Bucks County. They raised their own meat, slaughtered it, and smoked it. One of their members ingested the bacteria with improperly handled sausage. She was visiting a relative in Philly when she became violently ill, with bloody diarrhea and kidney failure. After ten days in the ICU and fourteen more on the ward, she was discharged. It had been a good save.

He found the door to the Microbiology Lab unlocked, though there was nobody in the room.

I've told them a thousand times, they have to lock the door when they go out, he thought. The equipment is ungodly expensive.

He went to a wall cabinet, pulled out a log book marked GRAM NEGATIVE ISOLATES, found the specimen number for the E. coli 0:157 he wanted. He hunted in the freezer, which was also unlocked, pushing aside a hodgepodge of Tupperware containers stacked in no apparent rhyme or reason. Finally, he found the right box, pulled it out, rooted among the plastic vials.

Try as he might, he could not find the frozen isolate for the woman from the commune. He tried other Tupperware boxes, thinking the specimen had been misplaced, with no better luck. The specimen was not there.

A technician came in and asked if she could help him. Auginello explained his quest. The technician covered the same ground, achieving the same results.

"It was probably thrown out by mistake," said the tech.

"That is most unfortunate," said Auginello. "I wanted to do a ribotyping and compare it to a new culture of o-one-five-seven."

"I plated that culture myself. When I called the physician to give him the report, he told me the patient died. Very sad." She found the isolate from Charyse Desir and gave it to the physician.

Auginello thanked the tech for her help, then took the isolate back to his own department. He rooted through his own records, picking out a battered notebook labeled "Ribos." Leafing through it, he found a printout for the virulent E. coli he had seen in May. He congratulated himself for being a packrat who never threw anything out, even though it made his office a jumble of notebooks and boxes of files.

Setting aside the first computer report from May, he took the fresh isolate from Charyse Desir and warmed up the ribotyping machine. As he waited for the machine to fire up, he made a mental note to stop by the morgue and have a chat with his friend, Dr. Leslie Fingers.

Tyrell was coming through the main entrance on his way back from lunch when he saw a chilling figure standing inside the sliding-glass door. The door opened. Joe West remained frozen in place, blocking his way.

"I have information you've been drinking on your lunch break," said West.

"Where'd you hear that? Somebody been whispering in your walkie-talkie?"

"Come with me to the security office. You're taking a breathalyzer test."

"I'm taking a what?"

"You heard me."

West's android hand clamped on Tyrell's arm. Tyrell counter-grabbed the man's wrist and twisted, loosening the security chief's grip. West brought his other hand up and jabbed Tyrell hard on the inside of his elbow, breaking his grip.

"If you give me any trouble," West said, "I'll handcuff you and arrest you for refusing a direct order. Do you want to spend the night in a city jail?"

"This is a load of crap and you know it. I'm not drunk. No way, no how."

"You take the test or you're fired on the spot," said West.

Cursing just loud enough for West to hear, Tyrell walked past the clerk at the information desk, who had heard the entire exchange.

"Page Lenny!" called Tyrell, passing the clerk's desk. "This fool wants me to take a drunk test!"

"I'm on it," said the clerk, and picked up his phone. He knew his union steward's beeper by heart.

Kate Palmer stepped into the Labor and Delivery Suite. The chill in the air reminded her of her obstetric rotation. It seemed wrong for a baby to be born into a refrigerator, but the staff had warming blankets for the babies, and the bassinettes were heated as well.

She spotted Miss McSweeny, one of the midwives, a middle-aged black woman from Barbados, whose grandfather had been an Irishman. She and Kate had laughed about the wayward ways of men during Kate's rotation, becoming good friends.

Kate smiled as she approached McSweeny. Shaking her hand, Kate recalled the strength in the midwife's firm grip.

"Katie, dear, look at you, all growed up and ready to be a doctor."

"I've still got a year to go, but, yeah, graduation is on the horizon." Kate smiled at her friend. "You look great. How have you been?"

"Me? I'm busy, like always."

"How's Harry?"

"That old man? He's still falling asleep after dinner. But I let him have his nap, and then we go out. We had a great time last weekend down in Atlantic City. I won two hundred dollars!"

"That's great. What did you do with the money?"

"He wanted to gamble it away, but I'm too smart for that. I took it home and hid it in my Christmas fund. For the grandkids."

"Can we find someplace private to talk?"

McSweeny led Kate to an empty birthing room. Through the open bathroom door Kate could see the Jacuzzi big enough for two. The room was decorated like a four-star hotel.

As she settled into a comfortable rocking chair, she explained how she and Lenny were investigating Dr. Odom and his abortions. She described the death of Charyse Desir, and the unusual strain of E. coli that caused her death.

McSweeny listened without saying a word, her brow furrowed in deep concern. When Kate was finished, she said,

"It's about time somebody did something about that man. He does treat those poor women terribly. And he's almost as bad with his residents."

"How so?"

"One of the OB residents quit in the middle of his rotation. He and Odom had a big fight, right in one of the exam rooms."

"Do you know what they were arguing about?"

"I think he couldn't take the abuse anymore. I believe he got picked up at Women and Children's."

"Miss McSweeny, I can't believe the hospital continues to let him practice. His abortion method is barbaric."

"He should be using a hypertonic saline solution and induce labor. But then, Doctor Odom would have to admit those women, and they don't have insurance. So it's wham, bam, thank you, ma'am. Suck out the fetus and send mom on her way."

"It can't go on," said Kate.

"I agree," said McSweeny. "What can I do to help you?"

"I'd like to talk to the people who assisted with Charyse Desir's abortion last Saturday. There was a Doctor Margolis, Doctor Dobkin and Doctor Johnson. And a scrub nurse, Miss Munios."

"Munios is out. I think she took a personal. Doctor Dobkin is post call, so he's gone home, but I'll give you his beeper. Doctor Margolis is probably in the on-call room playing video games. I don't know any Doctor Johnson."

McSweeny led Kate to the on-call room. She knocked once and opened the door. The doctor, a reed-thin young white man with long hair tied back in a ponytail, was on the bed reading *Road & Track*.

"Hey, Margolis, you got a visitor. Treat her nice, she's a lady."

The young resident took one look at Kate, sat up, put down the magazine, and slipped his bare feet into his clogs. Obviously, he didn't want her to smell his bare feet.

"How can I help you?" he asked, as Kate sat on a battered chair across from the bed.

"Dr. Margolis—"

"Call me Lee."

"Lee. I helped care for a young woman named Charyse Desir in the Emergency Room on Wednesday. She'd had an abortion by Doctor Odom. We admitted her to the ICU with sepsis and hemorrhage. Her coags were way off. Do you remember her?"

"I think so. But we do so many AB's on a Saturday, and if I didn't do the pre-procedure work up in the clinic . . ."

"She was a petite, slim black woman. She had delicate features."

"Was she light-skinned?"

"Yes."

"I remember her! Yeah, I assisted on the case." He began to adopt a guarded look. "Why are you asking about her? It was a routine case."

"She died," said Kate.

"Oh." The resident's friendly face instantly became hostile. "You're thinking I screwed something up?"

"No, of course not. It's just that she cultured positive for E. coli o-one-five-seven. Dr. Auginello in Infectious Disease says it's very unusual for someone to acquire that pathogen in the hospital."

"Makes sense," said Margolis.

"Do you have any ideas how E. coli might find a reservoir in Labor and Delivery?"

"None whatsoever." The resident's voice was now cool and crisp. "And I resent your suggestion that our technique was the source of an infection. She went home, anything could have happened. E. coli. I mean, come on, she probably contaminated her vaginal canal."

"Dr. Auginello doesn't think so."

"Oh yeah?" Margolis was holding the door open for Kate. "Well, you tell Auginello to come down here and swab every surface in the delivery room. I guarantee you, he won't find any E. coli."

Looking into the angry face of the resident, Kate decided to let the argument go. For now.

Tyrell was led into a small, windowless room deep inside the security office. Like a police interrogation room, it had no windows. A metal table was bolted to the floor. Three plastic chairs were at odd angles around the table. From across the hall came the static-filled sounds of reports called in over walkie-talkies to a guard at a central station.

Joe West, standing ramrod stiff, cast a cold eye on a young security guard. "Test him."

The breathalyzer apparatus was set up on the table ready to use. Tyrell considered the two beers he'd guzzled down in the Cave. *Two stinking beers,* he thought. *How bad can it be for two stinking beers?*

"I want my union rep here before I take this thing," said Tyrell.

"You don't get to have Moss holding your hand," West said. "He can represent you after you're fired."

"I don't think—"

"You don't have a brain to think with. The contract language is black and white. If you're suspected of being drunk on the job, you get tested or you're terminated on the spot."

As the junior guard held out the mouthpiece, Tyrell considered letting West have it with a couple of hard punches to his smug face. He looked at the handcuffs dangling from West's belt and decided to cooperate.

"Is that thing clean?" he asked, pointing to the mouthpiece.

"It's disposable," the guard reassured him.

Tyrell took a deep breath, closed his lips around the instrument, and blew. As he did, his eyes drifted to the meter attached to the flexible tubing.

The meter rose to the red zone.

"Do it again, just to be sure," said West.

Tyrell frowned, took another breath and repeated the maneuver. The needle rose to the same number. The junior security guard wrote the number on a disciplinary form.

"That's it, you're drunk. Roger will escort you to your locker, you can clean out your things, then you're out the door."

"This is bullshit!" said Tyrell. "I only had one beer!" He saw that West paid him no attention. "I've downed a case of beer in a night and still stayed on my feet. There's no way that test is accurate!"

"Tell it to the judge," said West.

As the security chief opened the door, indicating it was time for his assistant to accompany Tyrell to his locker, Lenny came rushing into the office.

"What the fuck's the big idea?" said Lenny.

West picked up the notice of discipline and held it an inch from Lenny's nose. "Your boy's legally drunk. I'm terminating him."

"There's nothing in the union contract stipulating a legal limit of alcohol. Or about administering a breathalyzer testing. You have no legal basis for this proceeding."

"You can cry a river for the arbitration officer, I don't

want to hear it," said West. "Anybody found drinking while on duty gets tested. Anybody fails gets fired."

Tyrell looked to Lenny with pleading eyes.

"I'm going to Human Resources," Lenny told him. "Just do what they say. I'll meet you outside the main entrance."

With fury boiling up inside him, Lenny marched out of the office and hurried to his locker in the Housekeeping department. He retrieved his copies of the contract and the hospital bylaws. He was familiar with the drunk-on-the-job clause: too many workers had come up against that particular regulation. But he wanted to be absolutely sure that there was no mention of alcohol levels before he started yelling and threatening legal action.

He thought of Freddie, the old alcoholic morgue attendant, and the times the fellow had been drunk on the job. A score of employees testified for him at his arbitration hearing, which convinced the arbitrator to give Fred a last chance, and he never drank another drop of liquor.

Lenny hoped that Freely, the chairman of Human Resources, would cut Tyrell some slack. Freely was the kind of administrator who sometimes listened to reason. Especially when the hospital's reputation might be sullied.

Kate Palmer called the ID Lab and asked Dr. Auginello if he had finished ribotyping the E. coli. Auginello told her that the bacteria in Charyse Desir's blood had the same DNA pattern as a culture taken from a woman who presented in the Emergency Room with diarrhea and kidney failure last May.

"I wanted to see if the two strains were distantly related," Auginello told her. "I expected them to share a few traits, but I was flabbergasted when I found they were a perfect match."

"Auggie, I'm confused. How could an abortion patient share a pathogen with somebody from a rural community?"

"I don't see how they could come from the same reservoir. There's no physical connection between them."

Kate was about to ask how much natural variation there was in this strain of E. coli, when she heard Auginello's voice take on a dark tone. "There's another thing that bothers me. I had to dig up my records to find the ribotype pattern of the earlier case. The specimen from May was not in the Micro lab freezer where it's supposed to be."

Kate began to have a sick feeling in her gut.

"Auggie, if the first culture is missing from the lab, does that mean . . . ?"

"One hates to think ill of a colleague, even a bastard like Odom. But you know what I always say about recurring pathogens."

"There are no coincidences in the hospital. Only contaminated surfaces."

"And careless caregivers."

Chapter Twenty-Three

Lenny brushed past the secretary in the Human Resources office and pushed into Warren Freely's office, where he found the director seated at his huge desk, writing a memo. Freely sat back and listened with a poker face, until Lenny finished his complaint about the drunk testing.

"Joe West has witnesses that the man had been drinking," said Freely. "That's a clear violation of hospital regulations in and of itself."

"There's nothing in the contract that states an employee has to refrain from drinking alcoholic beverages while on a break," said Lenny.

"You are still 'on duty' when you're on a lunch break."

"I don't think so," said Lenny, pulling out a set of papers and sliding it over to Freely. "Two years ago an arbitration panel ruled on a hospital worker who was seen drinking from a bottle of wine while sitting in his car on his dinner break. The arbitrator ruled that he didn't violate any hospital regulation."

"At the time we failed to produce evidence that the man was inebriated," said Freely. "The security officer did not document his abnormal behavior. That's the only reason he won his case. Being on or off duty was not the salient question."

"Tyrell Hardy wasn't drunk, not by a long shot, I saw him myself."

"West smelled alcohol on his breath and noted an unsteady gait. And the young man flunked his breathalyzer test. You can't argue with science."

"There's nothing in the contract that grants the hospital permission to invade a worker's body by forcing him to exhale into a machine."

"Wrong again. The breathalyzer test is well established in Pennsylvania. As an officer of the law, our security people are well within their rights to administer the test."

"How did you decide what blood level constitutes being drunk?" asked Lenny.

"We use the same standards as the Commonwealth of Pennsylvania."

"You have no precedent for that."

"We have twenty-five years of state police practice. Not to mention countless court rulings accepting the standard."

"That's fine for the state police," said Lenny. "But you and I know that an arbitrator will rule that the hospital failed to inform the employees *in writing* that they are adopting the state criteria for drunkenness *before* they actually applied it. It's a basic due process right."

Freely stood up, indicating that the discussion was over. "We'll let an arbitrator sort that out. In the meantime, the termination stands."

Lenny turned and walked away without another word. As he left the Executive Suite, he realized that he was drenched in sweat, despite the arctic chill in the department. The anger inside him was boiling up again.

Passing through the front lobby, then out the main entrance, he found Tyrell sitting under a tree on the hospital's broad lawn.

"I'm sorry, Ty," Lenny said. "I gave it my best shot. I'll

file an appeal before I punch out. We might get an expedited hearing first thing next week."

"A black man can't get justice in a white man's world," said Tyrell. "You were nuts to think you could."

"I don't think it's about race this time," said Lenny.

"It's *always* about race."

"Maybe. But I have a feeling somebody's leaning on Freely to lay down the law. I don't know what's going on, but I'll try and find out, even if I have to hide in his closet and listen. Can you hold out until I get you an appeal?"

"Sure."

"I have to get back to work. I'll call you as soon as we have a date for the hearing."

"I'm going to the Cave and have a beer. And I don't give one hard shit who knows it."

Lenny watched Tyrell walk down the sidewalk and cross Germantown Avenue. He worried, as he did so often, that another young man had been pushed off a cliff and didn't have so much as a pillow to soften his fall.

Gary was at the nursing station when he saw a tall, lanky man of around fifty, with a graying ponytail, plaid shirt, jeans, and cowboy boots enter the ICU.

"Can I help you?" Gary asked.

"I'm Ray Darling. Somebody left a message that my brother was in the hospital?"

"That was me." Gary saw the resemblance in the bones of the man's face and in his eyes. He rose to greet him.

"How's he doing?"

"He has a paralysis that we believe will be reversed." Gary led Ray to the bedside. "Right now your brother needs a ventilator to support his breathing, because of the paralysis."

"Wow, on the breathing machine?"

Ray looked at his brother in the bed. Saw the breathing tube dragging down the corner of the mouth, the catheter in the neck delivering intravenous fluids. Rupert looked old and vulnerable, the opposite of the hearty seaman who had been in more fights and more brothels than he could count.

Ray touched his brother's shoulder. "Hey, Rupe. It's me, Ray. How ya doin', bro? You okay?"

Gary stood beside him, "I have him on a fairly high dose of sedation. The breathing tube is uncomfortable, so we usually give them something to help them tolerate the ventilator."

Ray nodded his head as he looked down at his brother. "Can he hear me, sleeping like that?"

"Oh yes. Patients often wake up from their sedation and report hearing whole conversations. We have to be careful what we say at the bedside."

"Especially around Rupert. If you say something against him, he'll let you know about it when he's able. Rupe never ran from a fight, even when we were kids."

Gary brought a chair to the bedside and told Ray it would be helpful if he talked to his brother.

As Gary returned to the station to write his notes, he stole an occasional glance at the brothers. Perhaps it was a coincidence, but Mr. Darling's heart rate had come down twenty points. The brother's voice seemed to have a calming effect.

Or, as Dr. Singh had said, perhaps the intravenous sedation was giving Mr. Darling sweet, restful dreams.

Mary McSweeny washed her hands in hot water, building up a good lather, enjoying the sting of the heat. Returning from lunch, she liked the feeling of really clean hands. She patted the pink palms, then she squirted a dab of lotion onto her hand and rubbed it in.

She went to the medication cabinet and looked over her

supplies, to be ready for the morning. As she checked off the pharmacy requisition, she noted that no one had written in any unusual drug requests. *Good.* She wasn't in the mood for the pharmacist telling her not to order any more drugs they didn't need.

And hadn't it been an odd drug? Doxycycline was an antibiotic *and* a sclerosing agent. Just the thought of it made her shudder. Nobody used a sclerosing agent in OB. There was no medical need. But the pharmacist showed her the requisition with the drug clearly written in at the bottom. No initial by the order, but that was not unusual; most of the girls didn't initial their requests.

But when she had gone to look for the drug to send it back to the pharmacy and get a credit, it was nowhere to be found. She didn't recall any physician ordering it. Neither did any of the other midwives or the residents.

She dropped the requisition in the pharmacy pickup box. As she left to see her first patient, she hoped the medication wasn't lying in the wrong drawer. Somebody could get hurt.

Chapter Twenty-Four

Sandy, the oldest of James Madison's security guards, was stationed at the main entrance of the hospital checking ID badges on everyone who came through the door. He hated the new orders to watch for signs of drunkenness in employees coming back from break, so he ignored the policy unless the worker was practically falling down.

The old guard thought that he might get away without having to enforce the new rule when he saw an unpleasant sight on the marble steps. Baby Love, one of Joe West's snitches, was stumbling up the steps. Reaching the landing, she swayed and threatened to fall on her face, but somehow kept her balance.

As the wobbling young woman reached for the front door, a white female visitor came out, bumping into her and knocking her off balance.

Teetering back, Baby Love let out a string of curses. "You piss-ant dick-wad shit-ass bitch! You damn near knocked me on my sweet black ass!"

The visitor stood still, not knowing what to say to the drunken young woman. Finally she blurted out, "I'm sorry, miss, but you really should watch where you're walking."

"There ain't nothin' wrong with my eyes! I got a mind to kick you down these steps and watch your head bounce like a damn bowling ball."

As Baby Love walked toward the woman, Sandy came out

of the lobby and stepped between them. "You watch your tongue, young lady. This is a public place. We can't have that kind of language in the hospital."

"Shut the fuck up," she said. "You don't scare me none."

The old guard shook his head in pity at the drunken young woman. He didn't expect Joe West's snitches to be angels, but this lowlife was too much, even for a guard with thirty years on the job.

"Come with me, miss." He grasped her arm as gently as he could and began dragging her inside.

Baby Love smacked Sandy in the chest with her open hand. "Lemme go, this is police hair-assment!"

Sandy pulled her through the entrance and led her down the corridor, warning her to cooperate or he would have to put handcuffs on her.

"I bet you like your women in cuffs," she said.

As they marched along, Baby Love giggled. She was confident that her mentor, Joe West, would chew out the guard and thank her for giving him the inside dope on Tyrell Hardy. With any luck, he would probably give her money for more drinks.

His shift over, a tired and hot Lenny Moss punched out at the Housekeeping time clock and headed for the lobby. He stopped at the gift shop, where Marissa, a plump Filipino woman with sagging shoulders and drooping eyelids greeted him .

"Hey, Lenny Moss. How's the mayor of James Madison?"

"I hate that name," said Lenny, picking up a *Daily News*. "How are you?"

"Bad," she said.

"What, is your husband sick again?" He handed her the exact change.

"No, he's on a new diet and he wants me to eat the same thing he does. I hate grapefruit!"

"I'd miss my bagel and peanut butter in the morning. How long do you think he'll last?"

"I give him a week. Tops."

Lenny spied some water pistols on a display by the counter. He thought about the trip to the zoo with Patience and her children. Smiling mischievously, he selected four pistols and took out his wallet.

"Going hunting?"

"To the zoo."

"You're going to squirt the animals?"

"Yeah, the two-legged kind."

He headed for the exit, chuckling over the look he expected to see on Patience's face when he and the kids took out their water pistols and began shooting the penguins. Except he was saving his best shots for her.

Patience was driving up Germantown Avenue, the smell of Giovanni's pizza filling the car. Traffic was heavy, it was Friday afternoon, and it seemed as if everybody was out on the road. She looked at the dashboard, saw that the temperature gauge was approaching the red zone. She turned off the air-conditioning, afraid the engine would boil over.

"Hey, why you turn off the air?" asked Malcolm.

"Yeah, mom," said Takia. "It's *hot* outside."

"I'm sorry, kids. I have to give the engine a rest. It's hot, too."

"But it's supposed to be hot, it burns gasoline," said Malcolm.

"Not this hot. See that gauge there?"

"Where?" asked the two children in unison, leaning forward from the backseat to look over her shoulder.

Patience pointed at the temperature gauge. "It's touching the red zone. That's bad. It means the engine could burn up."

She remembered Lenny's advice the last time her car threatened to overheat: turn off anything that drained the power. And put the transmission in neutral when the car was stopped or going downhill. That increased the speed of the cooling fan.

As the car started downhill she shifted into neutral and turned off the radio. The temperature gauge slowly drifted out of the red zone.

"Mom! We're dying back here!"

"Open your windows! And drink more water." She tossed a bottle of water back to them. "I'm not burning up my car and going back to riding the bus."

As the road leveled off, she put the gear in drive and gently pressed on the gas. The engine hesitated, then picked up. She told herself it was only three more miles to her house. Three more hot miles.

"We be taking Lenny's car to the zoo, won't we?" said Malcolm.

"We *will* be taking Lenny's car," said Patience. "Don't talk street."

"Aw, mom. All the kids talk like that."

"Not all of them. Only the ignorant ones who are never going to college. My children are going to college."

She turned a corner, feeling relief that Lenny would be coming by that evening. He could look at the engine and set things right, like he always did.

If she could just get the car to hold on until they got home.

Chapter Twenty-Five

On his way home Lenny stopped at the Acme on German-town Avenue and picked up some fresh fruit, bread and boxes of juice for the zoo trip in the morning. Once he made it home, he took a cold shower. The needle mark on his leg seemed less red to him. He touched it, and it didn't hurt; so he figured that was a good sign.

He changed into shorts, tank top and sandals, and drove over to Patience's. He found the children sprawled out on the living-room rug, the television set and air-conditioning unit running full blast. They waved at him from the prone position and sipped on cold sodas.

Patience was in the kitchen. Lenny kissed her. With one arm wrapped around her waist, he opened the door to the fridge and pulled out a Yueungling.

"I iced a mug for you," she said, retrieving the cold glass from the freezer.

"Great!"

"You want to eat in the dining room?"

"It's too loud. Let's go upstairs."

"Okay." She pulled a plate with three slices of pizza from the fridge and set it on a tray, placed a napkin beside it, and handed it to him.

"Yum, yum," he said. "Pepperoni and onion."

Passing through the living room to the stairs, he called out, "Hey, Malcolm. I thought you were gonna order pizza with liver and pickles."

"Guh-ross," said Malcolm.

The master bedroom was deliciously cool. A new air-conditioning unit hummed quietly in the window. While Lenny was wolfing down his first slice, Patience told him about her car nearly overheating again.

"I'll check the thermostat tomorrow when I get back from my jog with Moose. If it's bad, I'll pick up a new one at Pep Boys."

He told her what Dillie had said about trouble between Mai Loo and Dr. Odom in Saudi Arabia. "Her friend wouldn't go into the specifics. I don't know if she didn't have all the facts or if she didn't trust me with the story."

"Are you going to see Mai Loo?"

"I'd like to, but I have so many things I'm working on." He told her about Tyrell's firing and the new policy about drunk testing. "I'm trying to find Mai Loo a labor lawyer. There'll probably be immigration issues, too. It's going to be a mess. Plus, I have the grievance over working conditions in the laundry."

"Do you *have* to take everything on by yourself? Where are the *other* delegates?"

"They have their own issues."

"No, Lenny. Everyone comes to you because you push so hard."

He grabbed up another slice of pizza and concentrated on eating instead of talking. He was forever surprised at the way Patience supported his frequent evening visits to coworkers in trouble. He knew guys on the job who told their wives bullshit stories and fooled around at night. Patience never seemed to doubt his reason for being out, even on a weekend.

She said he was easy to read. He had developed a pretty

good poker face after years of handling grievances and contract negotiations, but Patience said that she could see through him just like one of her kids.

"What are you smiling at?" she asked him, a bit suspicious.

"It's good pizza," he said, reaching for the last slice. Then he settled back into the bed and turned on the evening news.

Maurice sat at the little folding table in his kitchen and reread the copy of Mai Loo's letter of termination. It was clear that Odom was behind the firing. Maurice's hatred seethed and swelled.

Washing his glass in the sink, he saw his favorite knife: a small paring knife. He liked its sharp tip that could pierce a thick-skinned pomegranate. He liked to keep the blade razor-sharp with a whetstone, the stone now worn into a convex surface after years of use.

Taking the little knife out of the cutlery drain on the sink, he carefully felt the edge of the blade with his thumbnail. With enough pressure it could cut through the nail and split the finger.

He placed the knife on the counter and looked at it, imagining what it would be like to hold it up to Odom's face. He would love to threaten slicing off the arrogant physician's nose. It would be like a scalpel in the operating room. One quick slash and the nose would be lying on the floor.

Drying his few dishes and putting them away, his lips formed the hint of a smile as he thought about different ways to hurt Dr. Leslie Odom.

After reading a good-night story to the children, Lenny tucked Takia in bed. Then he followed Malcolm into his room. As usual, the boy entered his bed from the bottom, burrowing under the top covers until he emerged at the head, grinning broadly.

Malcolm said, "Can you teach a turtle to do tricks?"

"I guess so. What do you want to teach him?"

"I don't know. I guess he couldn't shake hands. Huh?"

"Nope," said Lenny. "And he definitely can't learn to roll over."

"Good thinking," said Malcolm.

"How about we go to the library and see if they have any books about training turtles?" said Lenny.

"Okay."

Lenny kissed him good night, turned off the light, called good night to Takia, and made his way to the master bedroom. He found Patience running an emery board over her nails.

"When you go jogging with Moose," she said, "be sure to bring plenty of water."

"He's gonna throw me in the creek."

"That lead apron I have to wear makes me sweat like a pig. I swear, if this heat doesn't break soon, half the city is going to go crazy. It'll be like one of those horror movies where people rise from the dead and walk around killing each other." She snuggled up beside him. "You can be my hairy werewolf."

"Oh, yeah? Look at it from my side. As men get older, they lose their hair. As women get older, they grow more hair. Eventually we'll be equal."

She pinched him hard in a tender spot.

"Ouch!"

"You better watch out. I hear that as men get older, they lose more than just their hair."

"With you I'll always be horny," he said.

She pulled away from him. "It's too hot to touch."

"I could turn up the air-conditioning," he said.

"And run my electric bill to the moon. No thank you. Go to sleep." She turned off the light.

He closed his eyes and soon felt himself drifting off. In a few minutes he was snoring away.

Lying awake beside him, Patience looked down at Lenny's face, softly lit by moonlight. She felt an upwelling of tenderness tinged with fear. Tenderness for the gentle man who was so good to her and her children. Fear that her problems might drive a wedge between them.

She knew he wanted to have a child of his own. A "little Lenny." And she knew she might never be able to bear him that child. Her desire for him to stay with her forever was tempered by her wish that he not give up his dream of fathering a child.

If it was true that she could not conceive, as the doctor had told her years ago, how could she ask him to give up his dreams of fatherhood?

Chapter Twenty-Six

Mai Loo rose from her bed and stepped to the window. She shut off the air-conditioning and opened a window. Looking down, she saw what a long drop it was to the ground. There was a sidewalk beneath her window and a few trees beyond it in a little fenced-in yard.

She felt nausea overwhelm her. Stepping back, she hurried into the bathroom and vomited. It was mostly bile, since she had eaten very little that day.

The nausea subsided, leaving her trembling and sweaty. When she was at the window, she had an image of herself stepping out and sailing down through the air. She thought the rush of air would feel cool; it would dry her hair and loosen her sticky clothing.

But the impact at the bottom—that would not feel good at all.

She trembled with the thought that she could do it. She could step out into the empty air and end her pain forever.

Cleopatra sat in the medical school library cubbyhole taking notes, a stack of bound journals nearly concealing her face. She found it difficult to concentrate. The *Voice of Africa* would be publishing the article about Odom in the morning. The hospital would retaliate, and she would be the number-one target.

She was determined to get the mainstream news outlets to

cover the story of Odom's butchery. So far, they had ignored her press releases. Even Penn's "alternative" news program on WXPN—another mouthpiece for the white establishment.

She closed the book, placed it on a stack, leaned over to Lincoln, whose face was buried in a textbook.

"I'm going for some coffee. You want one?"

"Sure," he said, not looking up.

As Cleopatra left for the cafeteria, Lincoln jotted down a summary of the article he was reading. He had six more to review. The Attending for his rotation had assigned each med student to review a topic for their rounds, and he wanted to be ready to talk about the topic with confidence.

He looked at his watch: eight o'clock. Plenty of time to finish all the articles before the eleven o'clock closing.

A young library aide came by with a cart and asked if the journals in Cleopatra's cubby could be shelved. He told her to leave them, his friend was coming back.

The library aide moved on with her cart, picking up journals and books, while Lincoln began another article.

Tyrell poured the Jack Daniel's over ice, lifted the glass to his lips, and let the liquor run over his tongue. There was nothing like a shot of Jack to make a man feel better. He hated being stuck in an empty apartment, drinking until he fell asleep. Life had been so much better when Charyse was with him. What a hot little firecracker. Jamming her tongue in his ear. Holding his head down on the bed with two hands while she teased his lips with perfumed breasts.

He took another sip of whiskey, holding the liquor in his mouth. Charyse had loved her Jack Daniel's, too. Especially when they passed it mouth to mouth.

Now all he had were memories and his hatred for that butcher who killed her. Leslie Odom. What kind of preppie name was that for a guy? Probably lived in a million-dollar home and drove a Porsche. Or a Ferrari. He hadn't believed Charyse when she said she had a doctor for a boyfriend. He could believe a dentist, *maybe*. Or a physical therapist. Some weight-lifting guy with long hair. But a doctor? He didn't think so. Although . . .

Dr. Leslie Odom sat in the black leather chair, his face in shadow; the only light a desk lamp bent low over the black cherry desk. Apart from his quiet breathing, there was no sound; the digital clock on the desk made no tick, no tock.

He thought about his enemies, the ones who could damage him, the ones who were merely pests. An irritant from his past had been eliminated, another neutralized. Soon they would all be out of his way, and he could continue his work unhindered.

He glanced at the clock: nine-ten. His appointment was ten minutes late. He would wait five more minutes. If the appointment failed to show, he would apply the punishment. Hesitation was for weaklings, mercy for fools. For him there could be no failure, only triumph. And domination.

The door opened without a knock. His visitor stepped in, closed the door, slowly approached the desk.

"You've kept me waiting," said Odom, contempt in his voice. He glanced at his visitor's hands, saw they were covered by latex gloves.

"Take those gloves off, you're not at work," said Odom.

"Not until justice is done," said the visitor.

Odom waved his hand in dismissal. "Don't be a fool. Are you speaking of those scurrilous accusations being bandied about? Fabrications every one! No one can blame me for what happened to that young woman. Medicine is not an exact science. Even idiots understand that."

"*I* can blame you," said the visitor, "and I *do.* "

"Don't be absurd. In this institution you are less than nothing. One word from me and Joe West will escort you out of here in handcuffs."

The visitor wordlessly reached a hand into a leather bag. The hand came out with a gun. The barrel had a bulge at the end like a cancerous growth.

"You haven't the nerve," said Odom, his teeth bared in an arrogant sneer that concealed a growing sense of danger. He started to rise from the chair.

The hand pointed the gun at Odom's heart, paused, then rose high above the physician's head. The gun descended in a swift arc, striking Odom on the temple. Dazed, Odom slumped back in his chair, disbelief and confusion on his face.

The visitor calmly set the gun on the desk, removed a roll of gauze from the leather bag, and stuffed it into Odom's mouth. Then the assailant peeled off a strip of nylon tape and pressed it across the doctor's mouth.

With slow, methodical movements, the visitor taped Odom's arms and legs to the chair. Next, the visitor took out a scalpel, removed the plastic safety tip, approached the half-conscious victim, and slit his pants and underwear. Peeling the clothing apart and exposing Odom's genitals, the visitor grasped Odom's organ with one hand, pulled it up and out, and stared deep into Odom's eyes. Then the visitor looked back down at the helpless organ and neatly sliced it off at its root.

Bright red blood spurted from the yawning wound. A muffled moan died in Odom's throat. His look of disbelief gave way to a primal terror.

Moving to the scrotum, the visitor dissected it from the perineum with a series of confident incisions. A fresh torrent of blood flowed onto the thick wool carpet, Streaks of crimson obliterated the delicate handwoven design.

Taking up the scrotum and testicles, the visitor ripped the tape off Odom's mouth and pulled out the gauze pad. Prying the slack jaw wide open, the killer felt deep in the back of the throat for the opening of the trachea, found the opening, and stuffed the scrotum and testicles deep into Odom's airway.

Odom tried to take in a breath, found his airway occluded. Already weak from hemorrhagic shock, his eyes bulged with terror as he felt the effects of asphyxiation. Like a drowning man held underwater, he squirmed and fought for air, his limbs straining against the tape, but the reliable nylon tape held them fast.

The visitor stared into Odom's eyes as the physician's face grew dusky. His eyes closed, his head lolled forward, his chest ceased its effort to inspire.

The visitor reached for Odom's neck, felt for a pulse, found none. Peeling off the latex gloves, the killer placed everything in the bag, turned, and left the room.

The growing stain on the carpet glistened in the lamplight.

Chapter Twenty-Seven

Lenny slipped stealthily out of bed and reached for his gym bag. He tiptoed to the bathroom to put on his shorts and T-shirt, not wanting to wake Patience. Realizing he'd forgotten his watch, he tiptoed back in for it.

"Are the kids awake yet?" she asked in a groggy voice, her eyes half closed.

"No, they're still out."

"Good," she said, lying back and closing her eyes. "Leave the door open, I'll get up when they do."

"Okay," he said in a whisper. "See you at lunchtime."

He looked back at her sleeping form, saw the soft curve of her bare shoulder, the outline of her face. As sleep embraced her, he felt a stir of desire. She was so sexy in the morning when she first awoke.

Making a quick cup of coffee—Patience had no cappuccino machine, something he vowed to soon remedy—he slipped out the front door and made for his car.

The air was hot, stagnant and oppressive. There was no promise of a breeze to blow off the thick layer of pollution that hovered over the Delaware Valley. Lenny had a hunch it was just as miserable down the Jersey shore, even at the water's edge. As he opened the door to his car, he spied a neighbor watering his brown lawn despite the city ordinance banning all watering. The neighbor saw Lenny, shrugged, turned his back, and swept his garden with the spray.

Lenny started the engine, opened the windows to air out the car, turned on the air-conditioning, and headed for Fairmont Park.

Lincoln tried to ease out of bed without waking Cleopatra, but she sat up and ran a hand through her thick hair.

"I'm awake," she announced.

"I'll make you some coffee."

"I'll make my own. I know you have to get to work."

He pulled on a set of scrubs, tucked his hospital ID badge in his shirt pocket. "Only one more year working in the OR, baby, and then I'll be a Resident."

"That's when your hourly wage drops by ninety percent."

"Yes, but my credit rating goes through the roof." He bent to kiss her, but found her already busy making the bed, tucking the corners square as a military bed. He gave her a peck on the cheek. She could be so cross in the morning.

As he hurried out to his car and started for the hospital, Lincoln hoped there would be some interesting cases today. Maybe a motor vehicle accident. Or a flail chest. Or an industrial accident that required orthopedic surgery.

He loved working in the operating room. Every case that he assisted brought him closer to becoming the complete surgeon.

Kate ran a brush through her daughter's hair, marveling at its luster. "I have a surprise for you today."

"What?"

"We're going to the zoo!"

"Yippee!" Sarah turned around and gave her mother a hug. "Can we go to the diner and see grandma after?"

"Of course. It wouldn't be a day out without seeing my mom."

"And can I help serve the food and keep my tips."

"Sweetie, you're only ten years old."

"I didn't drop anything the last time!"

"True." Kate put a finger to her chin, pretending to fall into an internal debate. "Oh-kay, I guess if you're really, really careful. And you only serve little dishes."

"Yay! When do we go?"

"Just as soon as you make your bed."

"Aw, Mom."

"And put your dirty clothes in the washer."

"Aw!"

"And give your mother an hour to read. I am way behind in my studies."

Kate smiled to see her daughter drag herself to her bedroom to make her bed. She pictured Sarah meeting Lenny at the zoo. She was certain he would be great with her, he was such a kid himself.

And so dedicated to the things that mattered.

Dr. Singh watched Mr. Darling's chest rise and fall smoothly and rhythmically. The deep sedation had knocked out his breathing reflex, letting the machine do all the work. Better for him to sleep and not hear the discussion on rounds of his evolving pneumonia brought on by the vomitus that had entered his lungs.

A technician came to the bedside with the plasmapheresis machine. Singh hoped that the second treatment would begin to turn the tide on the paralysis. He knew it sometimes took three or four exchanges of blood plasma before enough of the antibodies were removed to begin reversing the disease. If the treatment worked at all.

He was worried that Darling's pneumonia would worsen if they couldn't get him off the breathing machine. The morning chest x-ray showed a new infiltrate on the left side of the lungs. In fact, the whole left lung was whited out. The patient's temperature had reached one hundred and four during the night, and the low oxygen content in the blood confirmed his belief that Darling was developing a rip-roaring pneumonia.

Singh knew that the second treatment had to begin reversing Darling's paralysis. If it failed, they would have to leave the breathing tube in place for days. Maybe weeks. And every mechanical breath blew the thick, brown secretions laden with bacteria deeper into his lungs, spreading the pneumonia.

Patience came down the stairs to the living room, picked up the remote control for the TV and turned off the set.

"Hey!" Malcolm and Takia cried out in unison.

"You have chores to do. Put your dirty clothes in the washing machine and get it started. I'll put them in the dryer when they're done."

"It's so early!" cried Malcolm.

"It's so hot!" cried Takia.

"I won't have my children turning into zombies in front of that thing," she said. "Now get going."

The two children stood up, extended their hands in front of them, looked up at the ceiling in order to display the whites of their eyes and walked stiffly to the stairs. "Must . . . do . . . chores. Must . . . do . . . chores," they chanted.

Patience shook her head and walked into the kitchen to start preparing breakfast.

The OB-GYN fellow was anxious to get the first abortion started. They had twelve cases on the schedule. On top of that, there were eleven in-patients.

"Has anybody seen Dr. Odom?" he asked, looking around the Labor and Delivery nursing station. None of the nurses or residents had seen him that morning.

"Did he leave a message saying he'd be late?"

Nobody admitted taking a message.

"It's not like him. You know what a fanatic he is about being on time." The fellow cast a stern look at the medical student, a blonde man with a hesitant look.

"Aubrey, see if you can find Odom."

"Uh, where shall I look?"

"I don't know. Start with his office. He might be there, dictating chart summaries. You know where that is, don't you?"

"Yes, sir, I know."

While the student was leaving the Labor and Delivery Suite, the fellow told the nurse to page Odom again. "Have the operator page him overhead as well as on his beeper. And tell her to call his cell phone. Christ. Tell her to send out the dogs!"

Chapter Twenty-Eight

Moose jogged easily along the bumpy Forbidden Trail. Although he was a big man, his feet landed lightly and he sprang ahead in a smooth flow of power. The air along the trail was humid, even beneath the park's green canopy. The babbling brook running parallel to the trail had dried to a trickle, providing no coolness.

He glanced at his friend. "Hey, Lenny."

"Huh?"

"You gonna pop the question?"

"What question?" Lenny wiped a rivulet of sweat from his eyes. The moisture glistened on his face and trickled down his neck as he trod heavily on the hard, caked ground.

"You know, the *big* one. You been going out with Patience for almost, what, a year now, isn't it?

"It'll be a year next month." The heat was beginning to sap Lenny's strength.

"When are you tying the knot?" asked Moose.

"I've got a knot in my stomach right now."

"Don't change the subject."

Lenny slowed his pace, the stitch grabbing him in the side. Moose slowed with him, jogging in place to keep his limbs in motion.

"I don't know, Moose. I've thought about it. We get along great. We almost never argue."

"That'll change."

"Probably so. But still . . . we have some things to work out."

"What things?"

"Like if I can adopt her kids. Their father has to give permission, and we don't even know where he is. Things like that." Lenny picked up his pace. "After the third mile, I'll start walking back."

"Three miles is for pussies."

"Give me a break. It's a hundred degrees already."

"Okay. I'm doing the five. I'll pick you up on the way in. Don't stop moving!"

"I know," said Lenny. "Walk it out."

Moose picked up speed, stretching his long legs and pumping his arms like pistons. He turned a corner, ducked under a low branch, and was soon out of sight.

Lenny plodded on. He felt his legs getting heavy and his breath growing short. Two anorexic young women with heads nearly shaved jogged past him, chattering about free radicals and scavengers. Lenny knew they were talking about nutrition, not politics. "They probably have cholesterol levels of ten," he grumbled.

He wanted a drink from his water bottle, but had left it at the car. The stitch came back, forcing him to a walk that was closer to a stumble. He turned around, wishing he could ask Moose to carry him home.

Medical student Aubrey Dickerson found the door to Dr. Odom's office ajar. He knocked timidly. Received no reply. He pushed the door open and stepped into the office.

"Dr. Odom? Are you there, sir?"

Poking his head in, the student saw the physician's tall, black leather chair turned away from the door. An arm dangled down from one side, as if the physician were reaching for something.

Thinking that Odom had fallen asleep, the anxious student stepped toward the desk.

"Aubrey Dickerson here, second-year medical student. They're waiting for you in Labor and Delivery."

Odom ignored him.

Puzzled at the physician's stony indifference, yet mindful that Odom was a man of few words and withering silences, the student stepped up to the desk. His nose detected the unpleasant odor of a GI bleeder passing bloody stool. Feeling a current of fear riding up his spinal cord, the student took one more uncertain step, stopped, and peered down at the floor.

A pool of black blood glistened on the carpet.

Horrified and fascinated at the same time, Dickerson continued around the desk to get a look at Odom. He found the physician naked below the waist. There was a gaping wound caked with black blood where Dr. Leslie Odom's genitals had been.

Dickerson's stomach turned upside down. He rushed out of the room to find a place where he could safely vomit without adding to the mess.

As Lenny walked along a downhill stretch of the trail on his way back to the car, he heard light footsteps behind him. Turning his head, he saw Moose coming down the trail.

Moose came toward Lenny, sweat glistening on his face and arms, and still his feet seemed to barely touch the ground. As he approached, he slowed, like a great bird coming in to land on water.

"Man, I feel great after a good run," said Moose. "Don't you?"

"I feel like I've just been through surgery. Without anesthesia." Lenny walked wearily along the trail, his T-shirt sticking to his chest and back. "I've been wondering about something."

"Like what?"

"You remember one time you asked me if I knew what I would be getting into if I married Patience and adopted her kids?"

"Sure I do. Mixed couples get a lot of shit from ignorant people." Moose pulled off his T-shirt and tied it around his waist. "You had any bad experiences yet with the kids, out in public?"

"I was just thinking about a time a few weeks ago. We were at the movies and this white couple gave us a funny look. I was afraid the guy would say something, and instead, he winked at me. Like Patience and I were cool."

"You two *are* cool."

"I'm not trying to minimize the racism out there, believe me. I hear it all the time on the job. But I see a lot of solidarity, too."

"Look at us. We been friends a long time."

"That's right," said Lenny. He walked beside Moose, wishing a breeze would stir the branches and cool him a bit. "I want to tell you something, but you've got to keep it strictly between us."

"You know I will."

"I'm not sure Patience can have more children. She hasn't used birth control as long as we've been together."

"What's the problem?"

"I think she had an infection after the last time she delivered. To me, we have the tests and work it out. There are lots of ways to get pregnant."

"If you got the money," said Moose. "With *our* ratty ass insurance . . ."

"I know. The HSWU plan doesn't cover fertility treatments. But if I have to take out a second mortgage, fuck it."

"I know you want to have a little Lenny," said Moose. "Though I can't see why."

"Like it would be the son of Frankenstein, is that what you're saying?"

"Heh, heh." Moose smiled at the thought of a baby who looked like Lenny. "Well, if you do get up the nerve to propose, you better be clear on one thing."

"What's that?"

"I'm gonna be your best man."

"My brother won't like that."

"Tough titty. Manny can give you away."

"Great idea. He can walk my mom down the aisle."

They reached the parking lot. Lenny retrieved two bottles of water from the car and gave one to Moose. They were hot enough to make tea, but he didn't care; he drank greedily while he sat on the dead grass beside his friend, happy for a quiet moment.

"Don't drink it too fast, you'll get sick," said Moose.

"Okay," said Lenny, pouring a few drops onto his face.

"You still going to the zoo with the kids?"

"Yeah. I picked up a bunch of water pistols from the gift shop."

"Does she know?"

"Nope. Me and the kids are going to surprise her."

"You can tell me all about it tonight. You're still coming for dinner, aren't you?"

"Of course. She's bringing dessert. I'll bring the beer."

"Good. I'm gonna barbeque a ton o' ribs."

Chapter Twenty-Nine

Returning home from his jog, Lenny took off his shirt and sat beneath the ceiling fan in his living room. His body gave off waves of heat as if it harbored a small reactor. He drank from a bottle of seltzer water, enjoying the tickle of the carbon dioxide as much as the cool water.

"I hate that Moose," he grumbled, feeling the ache in his legs.

He went into the kitchen and took out the bread for sandwiches. He had bought cinnamon raisin. Not his favorite, but the kids loved it. He decided on peanut butter and jelly, there was less chance of spoiling in the heat and making the kids sick. Six boxes of juice, frozen, went into an insulated bag with the sandwiches.

"The hot dogs cost a million dollars," he said to himself.

Next he took out the four water pistols and filled them with water. He chuckled as he thought about the look he would see on Patience's face when he and the kids drew a bead on her and opened fire.

That was one of the things that made their relationship so good. She was not the most playful mom in the world. With formal games like Checkers or Monopoly she was great. But acting like a kid herself did not come easy for Patience. She had been the oldest of seven; a parentified child.

He knew that one of the things she liked most about him

was the playful quality that children loved. Lenny made a vow that one day he would get her to play patty-cake with him. It could be a terrific kind of foreplay.

Joe West was delighted when he got the frantic call from an excited security officer, although he maintained his deadpan demeanor on the phone. Doctor Leslie Odom was dead! Finally West would have something more meaningful than a stolen computer or a drunken employee to deal with. A murder investigation! And he would be the first to examine the crime scene.

"Sir?" the officer continued. "Shall I call nine-one-one."

"No. I will contact the police. Secure the site and let no one enter until I get there."

"Yes, sir."

West allowed half a grin to disturb his implacable visage. He would examine the crime scene thoroughly before calling in the police.

Lenny had his backpack filled with the sandwiches and the water pistols ready for the trip when he heard the laughter of children approaching the door. He found a moment of simple joy in the unadorned sound.

Soon there were four little fists pounding on the door.

"Open, sesame!" called Takia.

"I'll huff and I'll puff and I'll blow you away!" cried Malcolm.

Lenny opened the door. "Who intrudes on the castle of Prince Moss-en-stein?" He stepped aside and let the children tumble into the living room. Patience followed behind, shaking her head.

"You're as bad as the kids," she said.

"I'm in touch with my inner child," said Lenny.

Malcolm and Takia jumped on the sofa.

"How come you got half the wallpaper off?" asked Malcolm.

"It's too hot to finish scraping the walls," said Lenny. "As soon as the weather cools down, I'm going to paint the whole room. Want to help?"

"How much you give me?" said Malcolm, holding out his hand.

"Malcolm!" said Patience. "That is very rude. Lenny is your friend. You don't ask friends for money."

"I don't mind paying him to work," said Lenny. "My dad paid me to help him paint our house when I was a kid."

"How much did you get?" asked Malcolm.

"A dollar a day and all I could eat."

"For real?"

"Honest to god," said Lenny."

"I ain't workin' for no dollar," said Malcolm. He saw his mother glaring at him. "I know. I'm *not* workin' for no dollar."

"For *any* dollar," said Patience.

As Lenny and Patience went into the kitchen, the children drifted upstairs. Lenny showed Patience the sandwiches and the frozen juice cartons in his backpack, but kept the water pistols concealed in another pocket.

"What about snacks?" she asked.

"I thought we'd pick up some soft pretzels on the way down."

"Okay." She kissed him on the cheek. "Thank you for making lunch."

He put his arm around her, enjoying her slim waist and soft curves. She was a head shorter than he, with a button nose and a little mouth. He kissed her gently. At the start of their affair, Patience had been embarrassed to kiss him in front of the children, but now she was happy to let them see affection between them. Besides, the children weren't even in the room, they were upstairs somewhere—

"Ow-ow-ow!"

Patience withdrew her lips from Lenny's.

Upstairs, Malcolm could be heard saying, "What the hell is that?"

Lenny and Patience rushed upstairs. They found the children in the spare bedroom. Malcolm was holding onto his knee and grimacing. Beside him was a long, slim metal pole with a rubber tip on one end, footpads, and a handle on the other end.

"Hey!" said Lenny. "You found my pogo stick!"

"Your what?" asked Takia, looking at the stick from a few steps away as if it were a dangerous animal.

"It's a pogo stick," said Lenny. "My uncle Arnie gave it to me when I was your age."

"It was fun until I fell off," said Malcolm, suddenly recovered and standing up. Picking up the pogo stick, he placed first one foot, then the other on the foot pedals and tried bouncing on it again. He bounced for a minute, then fell off, this time without injury.

"You're pretty good for a first-timer," Lenny told him. "When I was your age, I did all kinds of tricks. Back flips and somersaults and stuff."

"For real?" said Malcolm. "Would you show me?"

"Well, I'm a little out of practice." Lenny grabbed the pogo stick, got on it and started bouncing. Higher and higher, the tip of the stick clearing two, three, then four feet. He let go with one hand like a cowboy on a bucking horse.

"Whoppee!" He bounced out into the hallway. "I was the citywide pogo stick champion three years in a row!" he cried, bouncing in a zigzag pattern across the floor.

"Awesome!" said Malcolm.

"Cool!" Takia said.

"Here," said Lenny, passing the pogo to Takia. "You take a turn."

"I'm not very good with sports," she said.

"You just need to practice."

She bounced a dozen times before tipping over.

"See?" said Lenny. "You're really good."

Patience pointed to the watch on her wrist.

"Yeah, we should go," said Lenny. "I'll put the pogo stick in the trunk. You kids can take it back to your house to practice."

They all tumbled downstairs and out the door. As they piled into Lenny's car, he put on a confused look and turned around to the kids in the back. "I forget. Where are we going today?"

"The zoo!" they cried in unison.

When they were on the Schuylkill Expressway heading downtown, Malcolm said, "Mom, was Mr. Lenny really the Philadelphia pogo champion?"

"He said he was, didn't he?"

"Yeah, I know, but . . ."

Patience remained facing forward, not wanting her children to see the silly grin lighting up her face.

Wearing latex gloves, Joe West bent over Leslie Odom and examined the site of the castration. The security chief admired the work; the incision was neat. He assumed the killer had used a surgical scalpel.

He stood up. All in all, a competent piece of work.

Wondering what had become of the organs, West scanned the room, but found no human tissue. He was not surprised. A murderer as cold-blooded as this one would want to keep a souvenir.

West removed his gloves and pocketed them. He took out his cell phone and called the local police precinct on his speed dial. Hearing the bored voice of the duty officer, West said flatly, "Joe West at James Madison here. I've got a body here you'll want to see."

Chapter Thirty

Lincoln opened the sterile pack with the rod and hammer and placed it where the orthopedic surgeon could reach it. As the physician packed the open wound with dressings, he glanced at Lincoln.

"You're a fourth-year med student, aren't you?"

"Yes, sir."

"What specialty will you be choosing for your residency?"

"I'm going to be a surgeon."

"Good choice." The surgeon reached for the rod. "What type of surgery?"

"I, uh, haven't decided yet. I might choose orthopedics. Or transplant."

"Ever drive a rod into a bone?"

"No, I haven't. I've applied some casts. And I reset a dislocated shoulder in the ER."

"Good. Put on some fresh gloves and take the hammer. I'll show you how we do it."

Lincoln eagerly pulled off his sterile gloves, reached for a new pair, and began putting them on. He took the hammer in his hand, surprised at the weight of it. With the surgeon holding the rod in place, he reached back and drove the first strike at the head of the rod.

The steel rod bit into the bone. Lincoln felt a rush of power as he lifted the hammer to strike again. He couldn't wait to tell Cleopatra what he'd done in the OR.

A Race Against Death

★ ★ ★ ★ ★

Mai Loo crawled out of bed and shuffled into the kitchen to make some tea. She put the kettle on to boil. Her legs were heavy, her mouth dry. With the air-conditioning off, she had sweated heavily in her sleep. Comfort meant nothing to her. Grief squeezed her heart, leaving an unbearable ache.

She knew she had to iron a uniform for the night shift in the nursing home. But she was so tired. She wanted to sleep forever. In sleep there would be no Mother Burgess or Joe West to punish her. No Dr. Odom to abuse her. Only relief from pain and escape from despair.

As the kettle heated up, she laid a towel on the kitchen table and plugged in the iron. She placed her old white nurse's uniform on the towel and ran the iron over it. When a stubborn wrinkle refused to flatten out, she moistened her finger on her tongue and quickly touched the flat of the iron. A brief *ssst* told her the iron was hot.

So was her finger. It was stinging and turning pink. She felt a powerful urge to press her finger firmly against the iron and let the hot steel burn through her skin. Let it sear the muscle and blacken the bone. Let it boil the blood out of the finger.

Trembling and afraid, she put the iron down, pulled the plug out by the wire, and hung the uniform up. The kettle was spewing steam into the air. Slowly and carefully she turned off the heat and poured the steaming liquid into a cup, mindful of the temptation to dip her finger in the boiling hot water, afraid she would be unable to resist the temptation.

At the zoo, Lenny, Patience and the children piled out of the monkey house, the children and Lenny bent over and making monkey noises.

"I don't know how you can stand the smell in this heat," said Patience.

"They smelled worse than diarrhea!" cried Takia.

"Mr. Lenny made a face that looked just like one of them!" declared Malcolm.

"I think the monkey mistook me for his cousin Bozo," said Lenny.

"Mom," said Takia. "Does the monkey really have a cousin Bozo?"

"I guess he could." She turned to Lenny. "I want to go someplace cooler. And less smelly."

"Let's go see the penguins," said Lenny. "They're swimming around in a pond. It should be cooler."

As they came up to the penguin house, Lenny grabbed Malcolm's and Takia's hands and held them back, allowing Patience to enter ahead of them. When the children looked at him, he placed a finger across his lips, then said, "I have a surprise for your mom."

He reached into his backpack with both hands, the children waiting with wide eyes. He retrieved two water pistols, one bright red, the other bright green. He gave them each a pistol.

"Put them in your pocket and don't tell your mom. When we get to the penguin house, I'll count to three, we'll take out our pistols and blast the birds. Okay?"

The kids stuffed the pistols into their pants pockets.

They entered the penguin house together. Patience, at the edge of the pool, was watching a pair of penguins float idly in the middle of the pond. Another bird was sleeping in the shade.

The children found it difficult to suppress their giggles.

"What's the joke?" asked Patience.

"I told them I was going to jump in the pool with the

birds," said Lenny. Seeing the look of horror on her face, he quickly added, "Don't worry; I was only kidding."

"The poor babies," said Patience, staring at the penguins. "They're not used to heat like this. It's usually frigid where they come from."

"A little *rain* would cool them off," said Lenny. "Don't you think so, kids?"

"Yeah!"

"Let's help our feathered friends," said Lenny. "One . . ." He reached into his back pocket. "Two . . ." He pulled out a pistol and crouched in a marksman's stance. *"Three!"* Lenny and the kids blasted the penguins with their water pistols. One of the birds turned its face toward them, as if enjoying the bath.

"Hey, he *likes* it!" cried Malcolm.

"Of course he does, it's a cold shower," said Lenny.

Patience, with her hands on her hips, shook her head. "I don't know which one of you is the child," she said.

Lenny held his pistol pointed up in the air, police-style.

"I think your mom looks awful hot, don't you, kids?"

The three of them began squirting her. She put her hands in a defensive posture.

"Hey, that's not fair," she said. "I'm unarmed."

"Not for long," said Lenny, reaching into his bag. He handed her a water pistol. "Now it's a fair fight. Us against them."

"I don't think so. Children. You love your mother, don't you?"

The kids pointed their guns at Lenny, and began firing, with Patience joining in. He tried to duck for cover behind a pole, but they quickly surrounded him, firing from opposite sides. He gave off shots left and right, but his glasses were dripping with water and he had trouble seeing.

"Wait, I'm out of ammo," he said.

"So am I," said Malcolm.

"Well I'm not," said Patience, and continued firing into his face until she had emptied her weapon. When she was out of water, she looked around and realized that several zoo patrons were watching them. She grabbed his arm and led him away, the kids trailing behind her.

"Ice cream for everybody," she announced.

"Yay!" the kids cried. And no one yelled louder than Lenny.

Chapter Thirty-One

Lenny, Patience and the children were eating their ice cream in the shade of a tree when Kate Palmer and her daughter Sarah approached them.

"Hi," said Kate. "Looks like you know how to cool off on a hot day."

"Hi, Kate," said Lenny.

"I promised Sarah I'd take her someplace fun. I hope it's okay." She looked at Patience and her children.

"It's nice to see you again," said Patience. "Lenny told me he was helping you investigate that creep, Odom."

Kate introduced Sarah to Patience's children.

"I'll get her an ice cream," said Patience. "Okay?"

"Thank you," said Sarah.

As the children sat together eating their ice cream and chattering away, Kate said, "Remember on Friday we talked about how Charyse Desir died from an infection?"

"Sure," said Lenny. "It was that E. coli bug."

"That's right. She died from a highly virulent strain of E. coli o-one-five-seven. Dr. Auginello, one of the ID Attendings, doesn't see how a hospital patient could come down with this infection in the hospital, especially in the OR. It's always a community-acquired bacteria."

"Moose thought that Odom dirtied up his instrument and infected her to make her sterile," said Lenny. "Can it do that?"

"I think so. These infections could scar over the fallopian tubes."

"They should take that man's license away and lock him up," said Patience. "He . . . it's too horrible to talk about."

"Unfortunately, there's more," said Kate. She told them about the missing culture from the Microbiology Lab and that the DNA in Charyse Desir's culture matched the DNA in the missing culture. She added that the Microbiology Lab was easy to enter when no one was around.

"The first specimen *could* have been misplaced," Kate added.

"Or Odom could have taken it and grown more of the bug," said Lenny. "Jesus Christ. Every time I think I get a picture of how low this bastard can go, he gets worse."

"It isn't mysterious to me," said Patience, her voice trembling with anger. "Odom doesn't want black women having babies. And we have to stop him."

Detective Williams strode into Joe West's office and said, "I heard from my officer you corrupted the crime scene this morning. What the hell were you thinking?"

"Hey, don't tell me how to do my job. I have full police powers on hospital property."

"You can handle drunks and petty thieves, but murder is my business."

"Then perhaps you don't want me to share my insights into the case."

"Don't be coy, Joe. Anything you give us on the murder, we'll put to good use." Williams settled into a chair and wiped his face with a handkerchief.

West told Williams that the black medical students had been making charges against Odom. "They called him a racist and demanded that the hospital suspend his privileges."

"You think one of them didn't wait for the administration to act?"

"If I were you I'd look at their so-called president. Cleopatra Edwards. She fancies herself another Winnie Mandela. I have an informant who's heard her threaten to get rid of Odom if the hospital didn't take action."

West slid a file toward the detective. It contained copies of Cleopatra's student application, her photo, copies of the M-SOC newsletter, and a summary of her speeches before the medical students association.

Williams glanced at the reports. "Is she a Muslim?"

"She's a politician, not a minister. Her religion is accusing the hospital of racism."

"I'll interview her first."

"She lives in the student housing. I'll send a security officer to bring her to my office. We can interrogate her there."

"*I'll* do the questioning," said Williams. "You can listen if you keep your mouth shut." He stood up, taking the folder. "I'll need to talk to some of Odom's colleagues."

"I'll arrange it." West held open the door. "I recommend that you obtain a search warrant for her student organization before she can remove any forensic evidence. I can padlock her locker until the court gives up the paperwork."

Annoyed, Williams looked hard into West's eyes. Cold steel met dead shark. "Don't tell me how to run my investigation. And don't do anything unless I tell you to do it."

That stupid bastard was a lousy cop, and now he's a lousy detective, Williams thought, as he set off to examine the crime scene.

Cleopatra found little satisfaction as she read the article on Odom in the *Voice of Africa*. The racist was dead, escaping her accusations and her opportunity to force the hospital to

admit its part in his butchery. The description of his genocidal acts would be lost in the news about his murder.

The news of the death had spread quickly through M-
SOC and student housing. As much as she regretted the loss
of her nemesis, she was glad that James Madison's abortion
mill would be stopped, at least temporarily. With more publicity and pressure from M-SOC, they might even close it
down for good.

Only then could she take credit for the liberation of her
people from the genocide.

Seeing that the children had finished their ice cream,
Lenny said to Kate, "Let's hook up Monday morning. I'll
take my coffee break in the sewing room in the basement at
ten o'clock."

"Great," said Kate.

"I'll be there," said Patience.

Kate called to her daughter. They said good-bye to Patience and her children, then headed for the birdhouse.

"It's awfully hot, I think we should, go," said Patience.

"Okay," said Lenny.

As they made their way out to the car, Lenny found Patience to be unusually quiet. His efforts to engage her returned one-word replies and distant looks.

"What's up?" he asked as he drove onto the Schuylkill.
"You look a little off."

"It's the heat," she said.

Driving back to Patience's house, he wondered if she was
upset to see Kate at the zoo. Was Patience worried he might
take up with other women? Surely she knew that his relationship with Kate was strictly professional.

So why was Patience in a mood?

Chapter Thirty-Two

Dr. Singh snapped Mr. Darling's x-ray into the light source while Dr. Auginello stood by. The dark region in the right and left bases were worrisome. They confirmed the diagnosis of pneumonia. The patient's temperature was hovering around a hundred and three, and his white count was creeping up.

"Was there any sign of aspiration when you intubated him?" asked the ID Attending.

"Yes, he vomited. We irrigated and suctioned out his airway; but there was very little stomach contents present."

"His lungs still may have been inoculated with bacteria," said Auginello.

"Do you think I should cover him for fungal infection as well?" asked Singh.

"Let's hold off for now. I'll go down to Microbiology and look at the sputum. I'll let you know if you need to change the antibiotics."

They stepped to the bedside and watched Darling's chest rise and fall. The steady movement was almost hypnotic. Auginello listened to the chest with his stethoscope. "A few crackles in the base, but he's otherwise clear."

After the ID physician completed his note in the chart, Dr. Singh said, "Auggie, have you heard about the E. coli o-one-five-seven that was cultured from Charyse Desir?"

"Yes, and I am very concerned, Samir. It is never, I state categorically never, a hospital-acquired pathogen."

"Then should there not be an outbreak in the community?" asked Singh. "A shipment of contaminated processed meat?"

"That is the usual finding, but there have been no reports. I checked with the Department of Health yesterday."

"What do you make of it?"

"My good friend, I am a not a clairvoyant. I cannot see into the mind of the physician who cared for the unfortunate young woman."

"Do you suspect that her infection was not merely an accidental occurrence?"

"Yes," said Auginello, his face darkening. "I do."

"I find it hard to believe that Odom could have been such a monster."

"Why not? You know the stories of the Nazi physicians." Auginello rose to go. "It's too bad he's dead. We'll probably never know if the infection was intentional or not."

"Perhaps it is just as well," said Singh. "An investigation would have created many problems for the hospital."

"True. But I'd still like to know what happened."

Cleopatra and a couple of junior students were in the M-SOC office when two big security guards came through the door.

"Cleopatra Edwards?" the bigger of the two asked her.

"Yes?"

"They want you in the security office."

The students rose from their chairs as if to protect her. "What is this about?" asked one of them.

"A detective wants to talk to her."

"It's all right, I'll go," Cleopatra said. "You stay and finish the newsletter. We have to explain how Odom's death helps the hospital bury their racist crimes."

She walked around the security guards, opened the door, and stepped into the hall, her head held high, her eyes blazing. She was ready to demand of the racist police: *Where were you when Odom was murdering black babies and butchering poor black women?*

Lenny, Patience and the kids stepped up to Moose and Birdie's house, in East Mt. Airy. As soon as Birdie opened the door, Malcolm and Takia raced into the living room, looking for Sakira and Tyrone. Patience went to the kitchen while Lenny continued on to the backyard to hang with Moose.

"How was the zoo?" Moose asked, his head shrouded in blue smoke from the burning charcoal.

"It was a blast," said Lenny, pulling a can of beer from a cooler. He told Moose about the water pistol fight and how Patience and the kids ganged up on him.

"Kids always stick with their mothers," said Moose, moving upwind of the smoke.

"I disarmed them before they left the house to come here," Lenny said.

"Good thing. We don't allow guns in our house."

Inside the kitchen, Patience found Birdie standing over the stove. She wore a long red apron and an oven mitt on one hand. She was testing the sweet potatoes with a fork, the aroma of the savory syrup making the room smell like a candy factory.

"What can I do?" asked Patience.

"Taste this," said Birdie, dipping a spoon in the sauce and holding it out.

"Mmm-mm," said Patience. "I want your recipe."

"Brown sugar, maple syrup, butter and molasses and ground cloves."

"But how much of each?"

"Hell, I don't know. I just use what I have until it's all gone." Birdie turned off the heat beneath the saucepan. "Hey. Come and see what Moose gave me for my birthday."

They walked upstairs. In the master bedroom, Birdie pulled the cover off a new sewing machine.

"What a beautiful machine," said Patience. "Is that a little computer screen?"

"Yup. It's got a computer chip and software and everything. I just put in the pattern I want, and it sews whatever is on the screen. I only have to change the thread for each color, is all."

"That's amazing. Look at the little dog with the eyes and teeth. The machine did all that?"

"It sure did. Right now I'm working on sewing one of Moose's cartoon characters."

Out on the back terrace, Lenny watched while Moose moved the ribs to the edge of the grill and threw on some burgers.

"The kids get the burgers, we get the ribs," said Moose. "Is the beer cold enough?"

"It's great," said Lenny.

Moose basted the meat with a sauce that smelled of hot peppers and lemon. "What do you think about that bastard Odom ending up dead? Somebody sure did the world a favor, didn't they?"

Lenny's hand with the can of beer froze halfway to his mouth. "Odom is dead? Since when?"

"You mean you ain't heard? Somebody killed him last night, right in his office. The police are all over the hospital. I'm surprised you didn't know about it."

"I haven't had the radio or TV on. We played CDs on the drive over." Lenny held his beer up. "Here's to good old American justice," he said, clinking his can with Moose's.

"It's kind of nice, the racist getting lynched instead of the black man," said Moose.

Lenny smiled, picturing the physician on a gurney in the morgue freezer. "This means I can quit that investigation into his abortions. What a relief. Although I would have liked to nail his ass."

"You and a whole lot of other people," said Moose.

Birdie and Patience came out to the yard.

"Lenny, did you hear about Doctor Odom?" asked Patience.

"Moose was just telling me."

"What goes around comes around," said Birdie.

"Amen," said Patience. "May he burn in hell for all eternity."

Moose told Lenny to open some buns for the burgers. Together they made a pile of hamburgers on a platter. While Lenny carried the platter inside, Moose loaded the ribs on another platter and poured the last of his sauce on top of them.

As Patience helped Birdie carry the salads and sweet potatoes into the dining room, the children came tumbling down the stairs. Moose placed a huge platter of ribs on the center of the table, their blackened surfaces glistening with sauce and giving out a sweet, tangy aroma.

Lenny set the plate of burgers on the table and said, "Okay, who's ready for a burger?"

"I want ribs," said Malcolm.

"Me, too," said Takia.

Moose's two children echoed the sentiment.

Lenny looked at Moose, who shrugged his shoulders and said, "I guess you and me are having burgers."

Chapter Thirty-Three

After the dishes were washed and the leftover food put away, with a generous doggie bag for Patience and her kids, the children went upstairs to watch television while the grown-ups sat in the living room over cold drinks: iced tea for the women, beer for the men. Lenny told them how he was glad he wouldn't have to investigate Odom's abortions.

"At first I wasn't willing to look into it, but when I heard Mai Loo, this young nurse on my floor, was fired and that Odom had a hand in it, it tipped me over."

"Did you see what they wrote about him in *Voice of Africa*?" said Birdie.

"No," said Lenny.

"I meant to show it to you," said Moose, while Birdie left to get the article. "My neighbor brought us a copy. She knows we both work at James Madison."

Lenny and Patience read the article together.

"Damn!" said Lenny. "They don't hold anything back. Racist health care in the southern United States was never as blatant . . . Dr. Odom's abortion practices do not meet the most basic standards of safety or medical care. It says that M-SOC has data proving that his infection rate is eight times as high as any other obstetrician."

"If that's true," said Birdie, "they were probably gonna kick him out. Don't you think?"

"Maybe not," said Lenny. "Even if they were going to suspend his privileges, any lawsuit brought against him would also be brought against the hospital that hired him."

"You thinking what I'm thinking?" said Moose.

"I'm thinking that M-SOC was trying to get his ass kicked out so they wouldn't have to kill him."

"I thank God he won't be doing any more of those abortions," said Patience.

"Are you against a woman terminating her pregnancy?" asked Lenny.

"No. I just want every child to be wanted."

Birdie said, "I think stopping abortions would just make more kids grow up without homes."

"I don't know," said Patience. "Isn't it all the same thing?"

"How do you mean?" asked Birdie.

"Let children go hungry. Let mothers get pregnant without thinking about the consequences. Let fathers walk away from their children. It's all part of the same indifference to suffering."

"But a woman who makes a mistake shouldn't have to bear a child she doesn't want," said Birdie.

Her face drawn, Patience said, "Maybe they should be grateful for being able to even *have* a child." She got up from the table. "Maybe they should cherish the child they created and not toss it away!" She picked up her glass and carried it back to the kitchen, with Birdie following her.

Moose looked at Lenny, who shrugged and said nothing.

Lenny was sure that Patience was bothered by more than Odom's racist abortions. The surprise visit from Kate Palmer at the zoo had soured her mood. The talk about wanting babies was the nail that anchored the coffin lid.

"Maybe it's time we headed home," he said to Moose.

"I'll drag the kids away from the TV. You and Patience have got some talking to do."

Lenny walked to the kitchen, where he found Patience already packing their leftovers for the trip home.

During the short ride back to her house, Patience was silent. After the children were washed and put to bed, Lenny put fresh sheets on their bed and settled in. Patience spread lotion on her legs. Her skin was often dry. She often awoke in the middle of the night, itching and scratching, waking Lenny from a deep sleep.

"Do you want me to do your back?" he asked her.

"Okay." She dropped the straps of her nightgown and lowered it.

As he ran his fingers gently over her back, marveling at her smooth, soft skin, he said, "Do you want to talk some more?"

"No."

He rubbed more lotion into her skin. "You sure?"

"Yes."

He finished with the lotion and kissed her bare shoulder.

She pulled her nightgown up and turned to face him. "I'm sorry. I know I was testy tonight. I do want to talk about this whole thing. But not tonight. It's hot and I'm tired and I just want to go to sleep. Okay?"

"Fine," he said. He kissed her gently on the forehead and the nose. He loved her pug nose.

She turned away from him, snapped off the light, and pulled the sheet up to her shoulders. When he put his arm around her, she told him it was too hot and curled up along the edge of the bed.

He lay awake for a long time, wishing he could ease her mind and take away her pain. He reminded himself that often the best strategy was to wait and watch and listen. And to be available when she was ready to open up.

A Race Against Death

★ ★ ★ ★ ★

Mai Loo stood in her white nursing uniform, a little bag with her dinner of rice and fish in a plastic container on the dining-room table. Stethoscope. Bandage scissors. Pocket calculator. Drug book. She had all her tools in another zippered bag.

The sheer curtains on the open windows hung sadly. No breeze stirred them. No hope lifted Mai Loo's heart. She thought of the eight-story drop from her window to the sidewalk below. Considered the relief she would feel from the grief that squeezed her heart. It would be so good to not feel so afraid. To not feel so much despair.

But Dillie would be disappointed if Mai Loo didn't show up for work. And the nice woman at the agency would not be able to replace her. The elderly patients in the nursing home would not have a nurse to care for them.

Her fear of disappointing others won out over her desire to end the suffering. She picked up her bag and left for work.

Chapter Thirty-Four

While Patience squeezed oranges, Lenny cut a hole in the middle of a slice of bread and dropped it onto the buttered skillet. He cracked an egg on the side of the pan and dropped it into the hole in the bread. The egg sizzled and popped, the yellow yoke looking like a cartoon eye.

"My mom used to make these for me and my brother when we were kids," he said. "She called them 'Shirley Temple' eggs."

"Who's Shirley Temple?" asked Takia, seated at the breakfast table.

"She was a big movie star when she was, like, six years old."

Malcolm jumped off his chair and ran into the living room. He came back a moment later with an armful of action figures, which he dropped onto the kitchen table and began arranging in strategic positions.

"What're you doing that for?" asked Takia. "We gonna eat our breakfast."

"They're re-con-oiting."

"*Reconnoitering*," Patience corrected him. To her daughter she added, "And say, 'we are going to eat,' not 'we gonna eat.' I won't have my children talking street in my house."

"But we live on a street," said Takia.

"You know what I mean."

A Race Against Death

Sitting at the table, Patience said to Lenny, "What do you want to do today?"

"I want to run your car one more time to make sure the new thermostat is okay."

"Thank you for fixing it," she said, pouring juice for everyone.

"Then I'm going home. The block club is going door-to-door to check on the shut-ins." He flipped the egg and bread combo. "I've got to catch up on my laundry. And I have to review some past cases for Tyrell's appeal on that drinking-on-the-job thing."

"I guess I won't see you until Monday at work."

"Is that okay?" he said.

"Fine." She drank her juice and didn't look at him.

Lenny began cooking another egg. He reminded himself to be patient. She would tell him in her own good time.

Ray Darling sat at his brother's bedside, reading aloud from John Rousemaniere's sea stories. As he read, Rupert bent one leg and lifted his knee a few inches.

Ray waved to a young resident passing the bed with a bag full of blood tubes. "I thought my brother's legs were paralyzed."

The resident looked at the patient's leg. "The plasmapheresis has washed out the antibodies from his blood. His paralysis is resolving nicely."

"That's wonderful!" Ray leaned over his brother's head. "You hear that, Rupe? You're on the mend. That tube will be out of your throat in no time."

The resident went off with his specimens. He didn't want to tell the brother that although the paralysis was improving, the patient's pneumonia was worsening. They might have to keep him intubated another couple of days. *If* the antibiotics turned the tide.

217

★ ★ ★ ★ ★

After returning home, Lenny went door-to-door with his neighbor Legrand, checking on the shut-ins. All but one had good fans or air-conditioning, or both. However, Mrs. Holland was sitting in a darkened room with her air-conditioning turned off. Asked why, she explained that she feared if she turned on the air-conditioning unit, she wouldn't be able to pay the electric bill. She lived with her retarded daughter, who didn't work, and her granddaughter.

Legrand, the block captain, reassured her that PECO could not, by law, turn off her power during the heat wave. Lenny turned on her air-conditioning. Then he took out the filter, found it filthy, and cleaned it. They made sure she had plenty of juice in her fridge before leaving.

Finishing the rounds on the block, Lenny had his key out and had climbed the steps to his porch when he felt a tap on his shoulder. Thinking it was Legrand, he turned, only to find himself looking into the familiar face of Philadelphia detective Bill Williams.

"Mr. Moss. You got a moment?"

Lenny sighed. He was hot and tired and didn't want to have to spar with the detective. He hoped the interview would be short and simple. After all, Lenny wasn't involved with the murder investigation. How much could he tell?

"Yeah, sure, come on in. You want a beer?"

"That would be fine," said the detective.

"You can drink while on duty?"

"It's Sunday," said Williams.

Lenny settled the detective on the couch, turned on the ceiling fan, and walked into the kitchen. He took a pair of mugs from the freezer and poured a couple of Yeunglings.

Accepting one mug from Lenny, Williams asked, "When are you going to get some new furniture?"

"I have a living-room set on order from L.L.Bean."

Williams took a long pull from his beer. "I'm here about the Odom murder."

"I figured," said Lenny. "Why come to me?"

Williams shot Lenny a skeptical look. "Don't kid me, Moss. I know everybody in James Madison confides in you."

"I pick up a little gossip. I'm sure it can't match the troves of information you find."

"Are you telling me you don't have any information about the murder victim?"

"I haven't even been to work since he was killed. Besides, I'm not sticking my nose in it. I've got plenty of stuff to deal with without worrying about who did the world a big favor."

"That's what I want you to tell me about. I understand a lot of people hated him."

"Thousands. Me included. Am I a suspect?"

"Everybody's a suspect," said Williams. "Tell me about this nurse he reported. Mai Loo."

"Give me a break. She's the sweetest, gentlest woman I've ever known. You can't be looking at her for Odom's murder."

"Just answer my questions."

"She's great. She wouldn't hurt a fly." Lenny thought of the autopsy report that Regis had given him. "I did hear something about how Charyse Desir died."

"Who?" Williams kept a poker face, but Lenny had a hunch the detective knew all about her.

After briefly describing the death of the young woman, Lenny said, "How about this? I'll tell you what I know, but you've got to promise to look into Charyse Desir's death."

"Dying from an infection. That's not in my bailiwick."

"Bailiwick? Isn't that an old English castle?"

Williams didn't smile.

"Listen," said Lenny. "If you saw the pictures of the autopsy report, you'd be sick."

"I might be interested in her case as a motivation for the murder."

"Really?"

"I'll keep an open mind about the girl's death; best I can do. Now give me everything you have."

Lenny told him what he knew of Charyse Desir—that she had been infected with a bacteria that usually struck people in the community, not the hospital, and that Odom may have been responsible, either intentionally or through negligence.

"Interesting," said Williams.

Lenny added the information about the E. coli culture missing from the Microbiology Lab, leaving out his source. He finished with the charges from M-SOC over Odom's butchering poor women from North Philly.

"I know about Cleopatra Edwards. She's been trying to get coverage from K-Y-W and the other news media. It looks like she's finally going to get her fifteen minutes."

"If she's a suspect, she'll definitely be in the news," said Lenny.

Rising from his chair, Williams said, "As far as I'm concerned, you're my number one suspect."

"Me? Why would I want to kill a racist butcher like Odom?"

"Who knows? Maybe you're moving up from hospital gadfly to killer bee."

As Lenny watched the detective walk down the steps to his car, he couldn't decide if the cop's parting comment was a compliment or a dig. Either way, he liked it.

Chapter Thirty-Five

Dillie was seated at the kitchen table in Mai Loo's apartment. She sipped her tea and watched as her friend buttered some toast.

"The nursing home was not a nice place to work," said Mai Loo. "The smell—it was horrible. And this one poor lady, her legs and arms were contracted so bad. I worked with her, but I couldn't straighten them. And she had a huge decubitus that was draining pus. I still can't get the smell off me."

"They are the hardest places to work," said Dillie. "They should pay the best, not the worst."

"At least I have a job." She set a plate of toast in front of her friend.

"You can build up your references again. It won't be forever." Dillie noted that Mai Loo was not putting more bread in the toaster. "No food for you?"

"I'm not hungry."

"But you must eat. You will waste away. Here!" She divided the toast and gave Mai Loo half. "If you have no appetite, eat because you know you must. Make a schedule and put something in your mouth, like passing out your medications."

As Mai Loo took a small bite from the toast, Dillie said, "You should be happy, now that Odom is dead. It might help your case."

Mai Loo put down the toast, her eyes wide with surprise. "Dead? Doctor Odom? What do you mean?"

"Haven't you heard? That evil man was murdered Friday night. In his own office."

Mai Loo sat stone-faced and quiet, ignoring her tea and toast.

"What is the matter with you?" Dillie asked. "Aren't you relieved?"

But Mai Loo could not answer. How could she explain to her friend that she herself felt dead? She imagined meeting Doctor Odom again in the afterlife, after she ended her own pitiful life and went down to hell, where she was sure Odom was waiting for her.

Tyrell poured Jack Daniel's over ice, settled into a stuffed chair, and flicked on the TV. It was too early for the Phillies to start their home game. Golf was on ESPN, but he didn't play the game and didn't care if Tiger Woods racked up another win.

Wrestling was on. He wondered if they would have a female bout. He loved to see the women beating up on each other. Pulling hair, throwing a sweaty body down on the mat, legs wrapped around the other's head and squeezing the opponent's face between her thighs—now that was a sport he could watch for hours.

He turned up the volume and waited for the men to finish their bout, wondering if he had any chips and salsa. The apartment was a mess. There were empty beer bottles on the floor and dirty dishes in the sink.

It hadn't been like this when Charyse was around. She always had music playing, swaying to the beat and singing along. Not that she had much of a voice, but the girl could move like nobody else.

She had been such a pistol. When he came home after work one day and found her clothes gone, no note, no message on his answering machine, he had been stunned. Okay, maybe he wasn't going to med school or law school. But he was studying mechanical engineering at Community College. He was bettering himself. He was going places.

He couldn't help but think that if Charyse had stayed with him, she never would have had the abortion, and she would be alive and dancing to the music today.

But she *was* dead. And Odom was dead. And he was out of a job for a couple of lousy beers at lunchtime. The whole world was going to shit, and he was going down with it.

In his efficiency apartment Maurice sat at a plastic folding table, reading the *Daily News*. He read the lead article about Odom's murder a third time. The story didn't have a lot of details about the actual crime, but it covered his abortions and the controversy. There were quotes from Cleopatra Edwards and the *Voice of Africa*.

Maurice was relieved that there was no mention of Mai Loo and her troubles with Odom. He was worried that the police might suspect her of the murder. It was a crazy idea, but there was no telling with the police. She had reason enough to hate Odom; that much was clear, and the police might not look beyond that.

He knew she hadn't a single mean bone in her body. She was an angel with a pure heart. She wasn't capable of such a violent act.

If the police did arrest Mai Loo, he vowed that he would do everything in his power to help her. He would testify on her behalf. He would tell them of her goodness and sweetness. He would say that she was a loving nurse who lived to heal and comfort the sick.

Timothy Sheard

If the police refused to listen to him, he would confess to the crime. They would have no choice but to release her. He would write to her from prison. They would not be together in the true sense, but she would be closer to him than she was now. And she might visit him on Saturdays. Her visits would make prison worthwhile.

Chapter Thirty-Six

Monday morning Lenny was in the little pantry across from the nursing station when he spied Moose. Lenny stepped out into the hall and stood, feet slightly apart, hands at his sides, a weapon tucked in his belt. He curled his lip in a wicked sneer and said, "This town ain't big enough for the two of us."

Moose grinned, held his hands up. "I'm not drawing against you, Lenny. No way Jose."

"You sure?" Lenny placed his hand lightly on the butt of his water pistol.

"I been shot three times already," said Moose. "Some of the guys down the kitchen are carrying automatic weapons. It's out of control."

Lenny walked toward the housekeeping closet, his friend walking beside him. "They better be careful. Having fun on the job is a major infraction."

"You can't blame them. With a heat wave like this, a man can always use a shower."

"I'm thinking of planting cactus in my front yard," said Lenny. "Even the weeds are toast."

"Good thing the hospital air-conditioning is finally blowing a little bit o' cool air. We were dying down in the kitchen."

"It does feel better on my ward," said Lenny. "I'll take some readings and see how good the system is."

They reached the housekeeping closet, where Lenny tucked an envelope on a high shelf.

"What's that?" asked Moose.

"Some research I did for Tyrell Hardy. I'm hoping to get him an expedited hearing. I can't let them keep doing these drunk tests. There's nothing in the contract about it."

"A lot of the guys in the kitchen enjoy a cold one on their lunch break. You got to shut that Joe West down."

"I'll let you know as soon as I get a hearing," said Lenny. "Did you bring us any more lemons?"

"Sure did. Betty's making lemonade right now."

"Thank God," said Lenny. "I'll see you in the sewing room for break."

"Count on it," said Moose, who hurried off.

Lenny braced himself for a sweltering eight hours on the ward.

After a weekend off, Gary was anxious to learn if the treatments had reversed Mr. Darling's paralysis. He looked down the row of beds, saw that Darling was still on the ventilator. Crestfallen, he checked to see that he was assigned to the patient and walked to the bedside. He found Darling clean and fresh-smelling. The night nurse had used a fragrant soap and plenty of perfumed lotion after the bath. Darling's hair was damp and combed straight back. His chin rested on a neatly folded blue pad that acted as a bib for secretions.

"I gave him a good bath and rubbed him down with lotion," the night nurse said. "He really likes the hands-on treatment."

Gary thought it better to not tell her about all the time Darling had spent in whorehouses.

He learned that the paralysis was better. Darling was beginning to move his legs, but his lungs were worse. He was producing copious amounts of thick, brown secretions, his temperature was one hundred and two, and his blood oxygen levels were borderline.

Taking charge of the patient, Gary began his physical assessment, listening to the breath sounds as the ventilator inflated the lungs, examining the urine in the catheter for sediment, feeling the strength of the pulses, and, most important, noting the level of paralysis, which was now localized to the lower legs and feet—a huge improvement.

He trapped some thick secretions in a specimen container and showed it to Dr. Singh, who was rounding with his team.

"Shall I send off another specimen for culture?" Gary asked.

"Always a good idea," said Singh. Turning to the residents, he said, "Should we also request a Legionella culture?" No one answered. "The Legionella bacterium does not grow in normal culture media," he explained, "so we miss it on routine culture. Mr. Darling's sputums have all been negative, so . . ." The team understood: no growth in a culture did not mean there was no infection.

Gary mixed rubbing alcohol with water in a washbasin and wet the patient's arms, legs and chest, letting the alcohol cool the skin as it evaporated. Mr. Darling seemed to smile as the cool liquid drew off his fever.

Kate was on her way to a lecture when she saw Lincoln coming toward her, a grim look on his face.

"Kate, may I have a minute?"

She saw the worry in his eyes. "What is it, Lincoln? You look upset."

"I am very worried for Cleopatra. I . . ." He glanced down the hall, saw several employees approaching. "Perhaps we could find a quiet spot?"

"Of course."

Inside a small alcove with chairs for visitors to sit and wait, Lincoln pulled a chair close to Kate, leaned forward, and spoke in a whisper. "You have heard, no doubt, that Dr. Odom has been murdered."

"Yes, of course. I can't say it caused me much grief."

"My sentiments were the same. Unfortunately, the relief I felt on hearing the news was soon replaced by a fear that the police will arrest Cleopatra for the crime."

"I don't see why—"

"She was questioned by a detective on Saturday."

"That's outrageous. Just because she criticized his practice?"

"The police believe her hatred constitutes a convincing motive. To make matters worse, she hasn't much of an alibi. Only one person can vouch for her at the time of the murder."

"You?"

"Yes, unfortunately. Since I'm her fiancé . . ."

"The police don't think you're a credible witness."

"Exactly." Lincoln took in a big breath, let it out slowly. His eyes grew moist as if he were holding back tears. "Today she received a letter from the Dean, suggesting that she complete her medical school education at another university."

"They can't force her out of the program!"

"So far they have only made it a 'strong suggestion.' They are very upset over the article in the *Voice of Africa*."

"It did have some strong language in it."

"Terrible crimes demand sharp accusations. Kate, I don't know where to turn. I don't know what I can do to help her. I'm afraid of what will happen."

Kate heard her beeper go off. She checked her message, saw that Jennifer was waiting at the lecture hall.

"I have to get to class," she said. "But I have an idea. I've got a friend who knows everybody in the hospital. A lot of people confide in him. Why don't we talk to him?"

"What is he, a senior Attending?"

"No he's . . ." She stood up, hefted her backpack on her shoulder. "I'll explain it all later. Do you know where the sewing room in the basement is?"

"No, but I'll find it. What time shall we meet?"

"Ten o'clock. My friend takes his break then."

"I'll be there," Lincoln said, stopping to catch an elevator. "And, Kate, thank you."

As she hurried off to class, Kate wondered if the imperious Cleopatra Edwards, so busy with her political agenda, appreciated what a lucky woman she was.

Chapter Thirty-Seven

Detective Bill Williams knocked on the door of the second-floor apartment. He heard feet shuffling, a chain scraping. The door opened.

"Tyrell Hardy?" he asked.

"Yeah. Who are you?"

"Detective Williams, Philadelphia police." He flashed his badge, took a step into the doorway. "Mind if I come in?"

"No, I guess, not." Tyrell moved aside. "What's it about?"

"I want to ask you a few questions about your relationship with Charyse Desir."

Williams stepped into a tiny living room. A bottle of beer stood on the dining-room table. The ring of water around its base and the drops formed on its side told him the beer was cold.

Tyrell sat on a wooden chair with rope crisscrossing the legs, holding it together.

"Why do you want to know about Charyse?" he asked.

"I understand that you blamed Doctor Leslie Odom for her death. You were angry with him."

"Why shouldn't I be pissed? He killed her. Everybody knows it."

"The Medical Examiner hasn't made his ruling yet," said Williams.

"I don't need no ruling. I heard the doctors in the Emergency Room wanted him to take her to the operating room and he refused. He fucking wanted her to die!"

"Which is why I want to know where you were on Friday evening," said Williams.

The detective studied Tyrell's face as he waited for the young man to answer. Waited and watched for a change in the inflection in his voice, a tendency to look away from him, a vagueness in his answer. He watched and listened for one of a hundred signs that the young man was lying.

Lenny knocked once on the door to the sewing room and entered. A rotating fan blowing over Birdie and her industrial sewing machine made the room almost cool. Moose sat beside her, drinking lemonade.

"I made a pot o' lemonade," said Moose. "Grab yourself a cup."

Lenny poured a drink, letting several cubes of ice plop into his cup. He unfolded a chair and sat beside his friend.

"Hey, Birdie, you keeping cool?"

"Could be a whole lot worse," she said. "I could be working down the laundry."

"I took some readings there this morning. The ironing room is still over a hundred."

"They'd be better off picking cotton down in Georgia," said Moose. "They should all call out sick."

"Yeah, but if all the laundry workers call out, the hospital will shut down the department and outsource the service. They want to prove a private company will save money with newer, more efficient machines."

"They could upgrade the machines they got," said Birdie.

"All their capital goes into things that bring in money," said Lenny. "Like the lobby upgrade and the new open MRI unit. Stuff they can show off to the press."

"I seen the ads on TV," said Birdie.

"Those ads are bullshit," said Moose. "Saying they got the 'best' doctors in the Delaware Valley. Five'll get you twenty Odom was on that list."

The door opened and Gary Tuttle walked in, carrying a plate with a soft pretzel and mustard.

"Hey, Tuttle," said Lenny. "Things must be quiet in the ICU."

"My patient is stable. I wanted to see you, Lenny. Have you been in touch with Mai Loo?"

"No. She hasn't answered her phone. I was going to stop by her apartment after work today."

"Please tell her I want to help." Gary settled into a chair. He spread spicy mustard on his pretzel. "I've been worried about her all weekend."

"I will." Lenny filled Gary in on their conversation about the hospital's threat to shut down the laundry if the workers walked off the job. "Human Resources isn't in a mood to compromise. This murder of Odom is a public relations disaster. The article in the *Voice of Africa* didn't help, either."

"It was almost a shame his getting murdered," said Moose. "I was kinda looking forward to us taking him down."

"Doctor Odom could have saved the life of his abortion patient," said Gary. "He told the ICU Attending that he was busy, but he could have sent her to the OR and told his fellow to begin the case. He let her die."

"What goes around comes around," said Birdie.

Lenny took an ice cube from his drink and rubbed his forearms. "I'm happy about it. With all the union issues I have to deal with, I don't have time to investigate some racist doctor like—"

The knock on the door interrupted Lenny in mid-sentence. The door slowly opened and a familiar face poked in.

"Hi," said Kate, coming into the room with Lincoln behind her. "Are we interrupting things?" She introduced Birdie, Moose and Lenny to her colleague.

Lenny pulled out two folding chairs while Moose poured two cups of lemonade.

Kate turned to Lenny. "You remember Wednesday when I asked you to help me investigate Odom for his racist medical practice?"

"Yeah, but that issue is moot now that the bastard's dead."

"Not exactly," said Kate. "Lincoln is worried the police will arrest his fiancée, Cleopatra Edwards, for the murder."

Lincoln said, "You must be aware that accusing an innocent black man, or a black woman, is one of the oldest tactics the police use."

"I know it happens," said Lenny. "You can go back to the Scottsboro Boys. But what makes you think they'll do it in this case?"

"The police have already interrogated my fiancée, Mr. Moss."

"Call me Lenny."

"Lenny, Cleopatra has caused the hospital a great deal of trouble. Putting her in jail would take the spotlight off James Madison and onto her."

"I know what it's like to earn the hospital's wrath," said Lenny. "But I don't see how we can help you."

"You already agreed to investigate Odom's abortions, right?" said Kate.

"Yeah."

"Lenny, we need your help finding out who killed Odom," said Kate.

"Wait a second. I can talk to a few people, sure. Poke around the trash looking for evidence. Fine. But a murder investigation is out of my line."

Lincoln leaned forward, his hands clasped together almost like in prayer. "We in M-SOC believe that Odom did not stop with butchering our sisters from North Philly. We think he contaminated his surgical instrument with the bacteria and caused the infection that killed her."

"That's a medical investigation," said Lenny. "I don't know squat about infections."

"Lincoln and I can help with the medical issues," said Kate. "We already know that Charyse Desir died from a highly virulent strain of E. coli that usually appears in a community outbreak, not in a hospital."

"How can you be sure she didn't just eat some contaminated lunch meat?" said Lenny.

"There would be reports of infections from emergency departments all over the Delaware Valley if that was the case," said Kate. "Doctor Auginello would know about it."

She put a hand on Lenny's arm. "You've already got the hospital chart and the autopsy report. You'll just be continuing something you already started."

"For which we are deeply grateful," said Lincoln.

Lenny looked at Moose, who had that sly smile of his that meant he was ready to get into the ring and mix it up.

"I have so much to do," said Lenny. "Joe West is busting my balls with the crackdown on drinking." He looked at his friends and wished he could be nothing more than a simple custodian keeping the hospital clean.

Chapter Thirty-Eight

Lenny looked into his cup of lemonade as he considered Kate's plea for help. Looked into himself. He wanted to help her; she was a solid friend who had once put her career on the line to help him save an innocent hospital worker from jail. But he knew only too well that crossing swords with Joe West and the administration would bring him an unbelievable amount of grief. Grief he didn't need when he had his hands full with a dozen union issues.

"I don't know," he said. "A part of me thinks we should let sleeping dogs lie."

"What do you mean?" asked Lincoln.

"I mean, whoever killed Odom did the world a big favor. Maybe the killer shouldn't *be* brought to justice."

"I'm with that," said Moose. "Give him a medal. Don't arrest him."

"Or her," said Birdie. She saw the surprised look on the others' faces. "You don't need to be a big strong man to cut somebody's privates off and let him bleed to death. You just have to have guts and a sense of righteous indignation."

Kate said, "The hospital allowed Odom to keep on butchering those young women. Couldn't the trial bring out the truth about what he did?"

"That's a dangerous idea," said Lenny. "It means I'll have to ask where Cleopatra was when Odom was killed."

"She was in the library with me, studying," said Lincoln.
"The whole time?"

"Yes. From just after seven until it closed at eleven." Lincoln looked worried when Lenny's face remained skeptical. "Cleopatra is very passionate, but she'd be a fool to kill Odom."

"Why is that?"

"He made great copy for M-SOC's newsletter. She was building a reputation with it. Lose him, you lose your campaign."

"I can believe that," said Lenny. "But what I believe doesn't count for squat with the cops." He looked at his friends. "How about this? We need to know who had a reason to kill Odom. That means we have to get to know as much about Odom as we can. Maybe he wasn't killed because of his abortions."

"He could've been screwing somebody's wife," said Moose.

"He could've been phony-ing up insurance claims," said Birdie. "Some of these doctors have all kinds of scams."

"Which is why we need to learn as much as we can about him," said Lenny.

"I'll talk to my friend in Medical Records," said Moose.

"I'll talk to my girlfriend in Purchasing," said Birdie. "She hears lots of things."

"I'll follow up on Charyse Desir's cultures," said Kate. "I might be able to get an idea how she contracted the infection."

"Good," said Lenny. "Let's get together after work. How about we meet at the Cave at four?"

Everyone agreed to the meeting. As Kate and Lincoln rose to leave, Lenny said, "You should know one more thing. I'm going to follow my nose wherever it leads me. If the evidence comes up against your friend Cleopatra, I won't sit on it."

"I'm not worried," said Lincoln. "I know she's innocent."

Lincoln shook everyone's hand, thanking them profusely for agreeing to help, then reached for the door. As he hurried off, Lenny grasped Kate's arm and held her back.

Once they were alone he asked Kate if she trusted Lincoln.

"Of course. He's not like Cleopatra. Lincoln doesn't have a political agenda. He just wants to be a damn good physician."

"So you think he's being honest when he says he was with her all evening on Friday?"

"Lincoln had the highest pre-med score of any non-white applicant to James Madison Medical School. His father is a minister, his mother a social worker."

"All right, he's a saint," said Lenny. "But can we trust him?"

"He volunteers at a woman's free clinic in North Philly. And he works weekends in the OR here at James Madison. You're not going to find a more honorable man than Lincoln Jones."

As Kate hurried off to class, Lenny looked at the clock, saw he had five minutes to get to the hearing for Tyrell Hardy. He said good-bye to Moose and Birdie and headed for the Executive Suite.

Entering the outer office of Human Resources, Lenny found Baby Love sitting on a chair, reading a glamour magazine and popping her bubble gum. She was wearing tight black Calvin Klein jeans, a black top with a deep V-neck, and gold chains around her neck. There was no sign of Tyrell.

"This meeting is stoo-pid," she said as soon as Lenny entered. "I was *supposed* to be drinking in the Cave. I was watching for guys getting drunk."

"So you were a snitch for Joe West?"

"I sure was, and I ain't ashamed of what I done. Drinking on the job is stoo-pid. Anybody that does it don't deserve to have a job in a hospital."

Lenny bit his tongue, not wanting to waste his words on Baby Love's twisted logic. He hated her and everything she stood for. Not because she was a snitch for West and a drunk, but because she was so fucking "stoo-pid."

"You gonna get me my job back, ain't you, Lenny?" she said.

"I don't know. You flunked the breathalyzer test. It's pretty hard to argue against that."

"But I was supposed to be drinking!"

"Drinking, not drunk," said Lenny.

"Mr. West gave me ten dollars. That buys more than one beer."

Again Lenny decided not to challenge her contorted thinking. He was worried that he might have to beg the appeal board for a postponement if Tyrell didn't show up. He checked his watch again. Sighed. Picked up a computer magazine from the desk. He had just started reading a review when Tyrell came sauntering into the office.

The young man had a wobbly stride and a glassy look in his eyes.

Stepping close to him, Lenny whispered, "Have you been drinking?"

"I ain't on duty."

"I appreciate that, Ty, but, Christ, it's nine o'clock in the morning."

"Fuck the time of day. Let's get this show on the road. Who do I have to see?"

"Just sit tight. Both of you. I'm going to go into the room and talk to the Appeals Board. I'll let you know when you should come in."

"Don't forget to tell them Joe West gave me money," Baby Love called after him.

Lenny knocked once on the heavy oak door. Hearing permission to enter, he stepped inside. He found three familiar faces: Warren Freely, Director of Human Resources; Lance Jacobson, Vice President for Hospital Affairs; and Stephen Myles Waterman, Esquire, James Madison's rabid legal beagle.

Of the three, Lenny had the most intense loathing for the lawyer. He hated the way Waterman used his entire name and title in such a pretentious manner. He hated the way the lawyer always had a smug look on his face, as if everyone in front of him was a pathetic joke. Mostly he hated him because Waterman never answered one of Lenny's questions without a lot of shifty, prevaricating bullshit.

"Are your people here?" asked Freely.

"Yes."

"Do you have witnesses?" asked Waterman.

"Uh, no."

"Then you intend to offer statements of support for your people," the lawyer added.

"No, not at this time."

Waterman looked confused and a little annoyed. "Do I understand you to mean that you intend to argue against the validity of the terminations based solely on contractual rights and past precedents? Is that your game?"

Ignoring the dig, Lenny looked at the three pairs of eyes staring at him. He knew he was playing to a hostile crowd. Knew he would almost certainly lose his case here and have to take it to binding arbitration. So he decided to try a surprise maneuver.

"Look. We're going to appeal the breathalyzer test since the hospital has no written policy on it. It'll end up in the courts or before an arbitrator. Agreed?"

"That is our expectation," said Freely.

Lenny looked from face to face. "It's hot and we're all beat. Let's not waste everybody's time. I'll give you Baby Love if you give me Tyrell."

Lenny stopped there and waited, letting the simplicity of the proposal sink in.

"You aren't going to offer an argument over the testing?" asked VP Jacobson.

"I could take an hour to do that," said Lenny. "Maybe two. I could talk about case law and past arbitrator decisions. I could speak at length about civil liberties, due process, and the divine right of kings. But it's too fucking hot and we all have a job to do. Let's split the charges down the middle and get back to work."

As Jacobson and Waterman leaned over to speak privately to Freely, Lenny wished he could read lips. He didn't like the look on the lawyer's face, but that guy always looked unhappy. Jacobson looked equally unhappy. Freely's poker face told Lenny nothing about how he would rule.

Freely picked up a pencil and made a little doodle on a legal pad. The other two men leaned into him and spoke in whispers. Freely mumbled something back, then turned to Lenny. "Mister Moss, you have a deal. Tyrell Hardy is reinstated. Miss Love's termination stands."

Lenny stood up. "I'll tell them they can expect a letter postmarked today. I suggest that Mr. Hardy take the rest of the day off. He wasn't expecting the case would be settled so quickly."

Smelling an issue, Waterman demanded to know why Tyrell couldn't begin work immediately.

Lenny ad-libbed. "It's his scheduled day off. He was supposed to work the weekend."

Freely instructed him to be sure that the young man was

back on duty on time Tuesday morning, advising him that if Tyrell had one more drink on the job he would be out for good.

Freely stood up, indicating the meeting was over.

Stepping out into the waiting room, Lenny found Baby Love looking at the pictures in the magazine while Tyrell had his eyes closed and was nodding his head as he listened to a DiscMan.

Lenny tapped the young man's shoulder. "Ty, we lucked out. They're taking you back."

Tyrell pulled off his earphones and stood up. He swayed slightly, then steadied himself. "Fucking great!" he said. "I can go back to work? Today?"

"I told them you were supposed to work the weekend and this was your day to be off. You start back tomorrow."

Tyrell gave Lenny an exaggerated wink. "Smart. Very smart."

Lenny stepped closer. "You can't come to work when you've been drinking. And you can't drink on your break. West will test you all over again."

"I thought you beat that testing shit."

"The issue has to go to an appeal board. That part isn't settled. But your case is. Go home, go to bed, come back tomorrow cleaned up and sober. Okay?"

"Yeah, I will." Tyrell shook Lenny's hand. "You can count on me, Lenny."

"I hope so."

"What about me? When am I goin' back to work?" asked Baby Love.

"I'm sorry," said Lenny. "They wouldn't budge on your case."

"What the fuck you talking about?" Her hands balled up in fists.

"They wouldn't take you back."

"But I wasn't any more drunk than he was."

"Your drunk test was quite a bit higher than Tyrell's," said Lenny. "You can't argue against the test. It's objective evidence."

"But I was *supposed* to be drinking. West *told* me to do it."

"You'll never get him to admit that. But I don't think it was the test alone that turned them against you."

"What was it? Was it 'cause I'm a girl?"

Lenny had to use all of his self-control to not tell her it was because she was a slut. Instead he said, "I just don't think they *like* you."

"That's no reason to shut me out!"

"You're right. Justice ought to be blind. But judges are human. When they don't like a defendant, they usually rule against him."

"This is fucking *bullshit!*" Baby Love threw down the magazine and stormed out of the room. "They can't do this to me! I'm getting me a Jew lawyer and sue their asses!"

The two men shook their heads as they watched Baby Love stalk down the corridor.

"Come on, I'll walk you out," said Lenny. "I can use the fresh air."

Patience stepped into the sewing room. She smiled at Birdie, who was repairing hospital gowns, their sleeves cut open to allow quick removal when the patient's arm was connected to an intravenous line.

"Hi, Birdie. How are you doing?" she said in a weary voice.

"I'm cool. Nobody bothers me down here. How about you? You okay?"

"I'm all right." Patience pulled a chair up beside Birdie.

"That was a fantastic meal on Saturday. The kids had a great time, too. Thanks."

"You and Lenny are always good company." Birdie snipped a thread and folded a gown before starting up the sewing machine. "What's the matter? You not feeling right?"

Patience's eyes lost their focus as she stared at something in her mind.

"Is it about Lenny?" Birdie asked.

"Of course."

"He's a fine man. Good as Moose, just not as handsome."

"Oh, Birdie, I know he's a great guy. That's not the problem. I'm happy with him. I think he wants to marry me. It's just, I know he wants to have a child of his own, and I'm never going to have any more."

"How can you be so sure?"

"I haven't used birth control in years."

"That don't mean you can't. It just means you ain't. Yet."

"No, I went to a gynecologist a year after Malcolm was born. He did all the tests. The doctor said my fallopian tubes are blocked. I must have had an infection after my last delivery."

"But they got lots of ways of getting you pregnant. Scoop out your eggs, open up your tubes, start a baby in a test tube. You can get pregnant nowadays six ways to Sunday."

"I don't think so."

"It's just gonna take a little extra effort, that's all."

"What if all that doesn't work? What if I can't give him a little Lenny?"

"If I know Lenny, and I *do* know Lenny, he'll marry you, baby or no baby. He'll take the chance, and if the dice come up craps, he'll never complain about it. Not for a minute."

Birdie ran another gown through the machine. When she

was done, she looked up, saw that Patience was crying. "What's the matter?"

"Oh, Birdie. I don't want Lenny to give up his chance to be a daddy!"

Chapter Thirty-Nine

As Lenny and Tyrell walked out of the main entrance into a blistering sun, Tyrell said, "Man, how'd you get me off? I was sure the verdict was in."

"You were lucky they didn't insist on interviewing you, drunk as you are," said Lenny.

"Hey. You can't blame me for starting my day with a little Jack. The cops come over this morning asking me all kinds of questions about the doctor that was killed. Like I had something to do with it."

"Wait a second!" Lenny grabbed Tyrell's arm. "Why did the cops question you about Odom's murder?"

"You didn't know? Charyse was my girl."

"Odom's patient was your girlfriend? Aw, I'm sorry, Ty. I didn't know."

"I still can't believe she's dead. She was so alive. Even when she was asleep she was always talking and giggling in her sleep."

"You must be devastated."

"We were supposed to get married. I bought the ring and everything, and then she went and dumped me a couple of months ago. She said she was moving up. That she had a professional for a boyfriend."

"You think it was true?"

"I don't know. I think it was on account of her being light-skinned and pretty. She figured she didn't have to settle for somebody works in maintenance like me."

"That's a bite." Lenny stopped on the driveway leading to Germantown Avenue. "Did you know she was going for the abortion?"

"Not until after it was over. I went to see her. She was having cramps and stuff. I told her to go back to the doctor."

"Did she?"

"She said her doctor told her to stay in bed and get plenty of rest and drink a lot of fluids and she would be fine."

"He didn't prescribe an antibiotic?"

"It didn't sound like it. That motherfucker Odom *wanted* her to die. That's why he didn't give her a prescription."

Lenny shook his head sadly. "The more I learn about that bastard, the less I'm surprised at what he was capable of." He put a hand up to shield the sun. "I hope you have a good alibi."

"For Friday night? Nah, I was drinking alone, at home. I fell asleep on the couch."

"Great."

"Hey, I ain't worried. I got Lenny Moss on my side!"

"Now I know you're in deep shit. Listen. It's too hot to stay out here. You need to go home, get some rest, and show up tomorrow. *Sober.*"

While Lenny hurried back into the building, Tyrell made his way out to the street. He crossed Germantown Avenue and entered the Cave, figuring a shot and a beer would be just the right thing to take the edge off being out of work and out of love.

Kate left morning report and hurried to the Infectious Disease office, hoping to find Dr. Auginello. Punching in the code on the door lock, she was relieved to hear jazz playing softly. Auggie had to be nearby.

She found him in the next room, staring into a microscope and humming along to the music, his glasses propped on top of his head amidst the curly black hair.

"Hi, Auggie," she called.

"Kate! Did you hear about the guy on Five North with pulmonary TB?"

"No, I didn't. I'm on endocrine this month. Is he homeless? Does he live in a shelter?"

"Nope." Auginello grinned like a cat with a pair of baby mice trapped under both paws. "This crazy guy has a parrot."

"Okay . . ."

"You remember that birds can acquire mycobacterium tuberculosis, don't you?"

"Sure. You told me the first week of my rotation. But how was it transmitted?"

"Aha! That's the fun part. This guy put the birdseed in his mouth, right on his tongue. He trained the bird to peck the seed off his tongue."

"That's disgusting!"

"Isn't it? The bird transmitted the mycobacterium to the pet owner's mouth, the bacteria multiplied, and inoculated his lungs."

"Giving him TB."

"Precisely."

Auggie pulled a stack of magazines off a bar stool and gestured for Kate to sit down. "No doubt you're here about that young abortion patient, Charyse Desir."

"Yes."

"I became curious about Odom's infection rates after studying her culture. Especially when I found the E. coli isolate missing from the lab."

"I was curious, too, but I couldn't get my hands on any data."

"I asked Infection Control to fax me physician-specific infection rates for obstetric procedures. They crunch that data as part of their hospital surveillance."

"His rates were high?"

"Off the chart. I called back and asked them what had they done about it? They said they forwarded the data to the chair of OB-GYN and the head of Surgery. They also sent it to the Q-I people and the Chief of Staff."

"Dr. Slocum knew about Odom's infection rates?" asked Kate.

"He got the reports."

"Then why didn't they suspend Odom's admitting privileges?"

"The Infection Control people didn't want to say too much. I got the impression that Odom was under investigation. I'm sure he was told to lower his infection rate."

"This is a great system," said Kate. "They slap his wrists and he kills Charyse Desir. The public should know about what's going on."

"You are undoubtedly right," said Auginello, handing Kate a sealed manila envelope. "And what you do with the line listing of Odom's patients is entirely up to you. Just be sure the trail doesn't lead back to me."

Kate held the envelope in two hands. It was explosive material. M-SOC would be a logical place to drop it. But first, she wanted to look at it herself.

Lenny was mopping the floor on Seven South and talking to Betty when he saw her mouth drop open. Before he could turn, he felt a spray of water playing a tattoo on his back.

Expecting to see Moose with his water pistol, he was surprised to see Regis, the young morgue attendant, standing with his legs spread apart and his two hands clasped over the barrel of a long, lethal-looking, rifle-style water gun.

"God damn," said Lenny. "Even Dirty Harry didn't have a gun that big."

"I got you good, didn't I?" Regis cradled the weapon in a holster and sauntered up to Lenny in his best bad-ass gunslinger style.

"You better be careful showing that weapon in public. West will call the ATF on you."

"He can kiss my black ass," said Regis. "Hey, I thought you'd like to know, Doctor Fingers talked to the Medical Examiner about Odom."

"Yeah?"

"The ME said Odom died from hemorrhagic shock and asphyxiation due to airway occlusion. Sweet, eh?"

"I'm impressed," said Lenny. "You've learned a lot in your year down the morgue."

"The best thing about the report is that the airway obstruction was on account of his balls were stuffed down his trachea."

For the first time since becoming involved with the racist butcher, Lenny found something to smile about.

Chapter Forty

Lenny ran the buffer over the floor in the Seven South hallway. Making graceful arcs as he ran the machine side to side, he found the rhythm soothing. Plus, it didn't add moisture to the heavy air.

He spotted Maurice coming up the hall with his messenger cart. The young messenger was walking with his usual lurching step and mumbling to himself. Lenny noted that his clothes were badly wrinkled and stained. He recalled Betty telling him that Maurice had looked badly shaken the day that Mai Loo was fired. He was obviously crazy about her, the operative word being "crazy."

Lenny turned off the buffer and hurried to catch up. "Hey, Maurice, I bet you could use a cold glass of lemonade."

Maurice looked blankly at Lenny. "I guess so."

"Betty made a whole pitcher. Follow me."

Lenny led Maurice to the tiny pantry across from the nursing station. He poured them each a cup, noting that Maurice's hand trembled as he picked up his lemonade. Lenny wondered if the young man was on drugs.

"I feel so bad about Mai Loo getting fired," said Lenny. "She's such a nice kid. It was a raw deal."

Maurice slowly nodded his head. "It was a crime," he said.

"The way they treated her was barbaric," Lenny went on, trying to bring Maurice out. "I hear you were real upset about it."

Maurice held his cup in two hands and kept silent.

"I know getting fired can do a number on your head," Lenny said. "It's always a shock. You lose your paycheck and can't pay your bills."

"She has another job," said Maurice.

"Oh, yeah? Great. How did you hear about it?"

"I hear stuff." Maurice took a sip of lemonade. "Can you help her get back in James Madison?"

"I'd like to," said Lenny, "but I'd have to know more about her case. I don't even know why she was fired."

"It was Odom. He told the Human Resources a pack of lies."

"Are you sure? It would help a lot if I knew exactly what went down."

Maurice stared at Lenny as if weighing a decision.

"Listen," said Lenny. "If you have any information about her case, it could help clear her of the charges."

Maurice slowly reached into a back pocket and came out with an envelope folded several times. He handed it to Lenny. "I got this from Human Resources. They always send one out when somebody gets canned."

Lenny recognized the termination letter. He also noted the glossy surface of the paper. "You copied it on your fax machine?"

"Yeah. In our office."

"Fantastic! I can get it to a lawyer as soon as she hires one. He can check it out with the hospital in Saudi Arabia."

"Odom's dead. Shouldn't they drop the charges?"

"It doesn't work that way, my friend. It's not about justice."

Lenny asked if he could keep the letter; Maurice told him okay.

"There's something else I have to talk to you about," said

Lenny. "Have the cops questioned you yet?"

"Me? Why me?"

"Because you're a logical suspect. You're crazy about Mai Loo."

Maurice said nothing.

"They're gonna ask you where you were Friday night," Lenny said.

"I was out."

"Out where?"

Maurice looked at his feet.

"Look, I'm trying to help. You and Mai Loo both hated him. The cops are going to suspect both of you."

"That's nuts! She was home Friday night!"

"Yeah? How do you know?"

"Because I saw her. I was watching her window."

Lenny arched a single eyebrow.

"I like to watch until she turns out her light and goes to sleep, so I know she's okay."

"I see. What time was that?"

"She had trouble sleeping. She was up until past midnight."

Lenny studied the young man's face. This was love. Twisted, but love. It was also a powerful motive for murder.

"All right," said Lenny. "When the cops talk to you, don't tell them about the letter. Tell them where you were Friday night. It gives you both an alibi of sorts. I'll do what I can to try and find out who really did kill the bastard." He studied Maurice's face. "Can you do that?"

"Yeah. Nothing about the letter; okay about watching her apartment."

"Right." Lenny threw their cups in the trash, then went back to buffing the floor. He needed time to think. And to talk to Moose and Kate about the suspects, who seemed to be growing in number by the minute.

By noon, Mr. Darling's fever had broken, or as Dr. Singh described it, "deporvessed." Gary loved the sound of that word. After checking with Crystal, the charge nurse, he stopped the sedation and reminded the patient to keep his hands off the breathing tube.

"Doctor Singh will remove the tube as soon as your lungs are strong enough to support your breathing," said Gary. "Okay?"

Mr. Darling gave Gary a thumbs-up, then made rings with his thumb and index finger and placed them over his eyes.

"You want your glasses?" asked Gary.

Darling nodded.

"For the newspaper?"

Now the patient made two thumbs-up. Gary was retrieving his copy of the *Daily News* when he saw the patient's brother come into the unit.

Ray Darling walked to the nursing station and asked Gary how Rupert was doing. Gary told him that his brother's paralysis was greatly improved, but he had contracted pneumonia. "He's on double antibiotics. His fever broke this morning. Doctor Singh feels that's a good sign."

"You've got the infection on the run. Is that it?"

"We hope so," said Gary, handing Ray the newspaper and asking him to give it to his brother.

Ray gave his brother the paper. "You're looking mighty good there, bro."

Rupert picked up a pad on a clipboard with a pencil attached to it by a rubber band and wrote, BASTARDS HAVEN'T KILLED ME YET!

Ray chuckled. "Listen, Rupe. I know you're gonna get

better, so it's not like you're on your deathbed or anything like that. The thing is, I've had something sticking in my craw for a lot of years, and, well, it's about time I got it off my chest."

Rupert put the pad on his chest and cupped his hand behind his ear.

"Here's the deal. When we were young and I went to college and you went into the merchant marines, I know I sometimes made out like I was the smarter brother. Like I had my act together and you were the screw-up. And I know that a couple of times I more or less told you that, which was wrong. It was stupid. But I was full of myself and I didn't think about what I was saying."

Ray leaned closer to Rupert, looked into his brother's eyes. "I just want to tell you that I'm sorry if I hurt you back then. I'm really truly sorry, and I'd really like it if you'd forgive me."

Rupert picked up the pad and wrote furiously. When he was done he tore off the page and passed it to Ray.

I KNOW YOU ALWAYS LOVED ME AND I DID FUCK MY LIFE UP. SO WHAT? WE'RE BROTHERS. FORGET ABOUT IT AND DON'T LOOK BACK.

Ray smiled to read the words. "Can I keep this?" he asked.

Rupert nodded his head. Ray folded it carefully and put it in his shirt pocket. Then he said, "I got to use the head. I'll be right back. Don't go anywhere."

Rupert made a gesture of dealing out cards.

"A game of gin rummy? You're on!"

As Ray walked out of the ICU toward the bathroom, Gary noticed tears in the man's eyes and a sweet smile on his lips.

Chapter Forty-One

As soon as Kate finished afternoon rounds with her Attending, she hurried to the library. Finding a computer terminal in a corner away from the foot traffic, she took out the list of infected women who had undergone abortions by Dr. Odom. She also had a list of Odom's patients who had carried their babies to term.

Kate discovered that nearly a third of the women who aborted their babies became infected. She looked for a cluster of the same bacteria that might suggest a common reservoir, but there was no such grouping. Charyse was the only one infected with the deadly E. coli.

The lab data shed no light on how she had become infected.

Next Kate looked over the labs of the women who carried their babies to term. Very few of them had developed infections. When this group of women became pregnant again they did not develop infections or have abortions. The lab reports were all normal.

Something in the data nagged at her. She had a sense that she was missing something important, but she couldn't put her finger on it.

Maybe it was something that *wasn't* there. During her ID rotation, Dr. Auginello had often told her, "A negative culture can tell you as much as a positive. Ask yourself why nothing grew. Did the patient receive antibiotics before the culture was collected? Do you suspect a pathogen that requires special growth medium?"

Suddenly she sat forward. Calling up an infected patient's lab results, she realized that there was a positive pregnancy test recorded *before* she terminated her pregnancy, but there were no pregnancy tests posted *after* the abortion.

She opened another abortion patient's file and clicked on the urinalysis section. She found a positive pregnancy before *her* abortion, no pregnancy tests after.

Kate felt goose bumps on her arms and chest, recalling the medical term for it: *piloerection*. A horrible thought formed in her mind. What if *all* the women who had undergone abortions at Odom's hands were rendered sterile? Could he have been such a monster?

She checked the other labs. The math was easy: fifteen percent of the abortion women had pregnancy tests some time after their abortions, and all but two of those negative. Among the full-term mothers, fifty-eight percent had later pregnancy tests, and more than half of those tests were positive.

She took out her calculator and fed in the numbers in a Chi square. The probability that the differences between the two groups happened by chance alone was less than half of one percent—a statistical near impossibility.

Her hands were trembling when she shut down the computer and put away her notes. She had to get to Lincoln and Lenny to tell them, Cleopatra was right, Odom *had* been sterilizing the women. The world had to know the depths of Odom's crimes, and the complicity of James Madison University Hospital.

When Lenny walked into the laundry room, he held the digital thermometer at eye level and waited for it to equilibrate.

Big Mary said, "You don't need that thing to tell you that."

"We have to have documentation, Mary. Otherwise it's just griping to the boss."

"Just griping? My oven doesn't get this hot, and it's self-cleaning electric!"

"We should just walk out!" said Little Mary. The other women supported the idea.

"If we walk, it has to be all of us," said Lenny. "Myself included. But I have to tell you, if you walk, they'll bring in an outside contractor and close the department. They'll fire everybody who refuses to come back to work, and they'll lay off the ones who report for duty."

"We're screwed frontward and back," said Little Mary.

"Sounds like my first honeymoon!" said Susie, a widow of many years.

Worried that a job action would backfire, Lenny said, "The room is six degrees cooler than Friday. The engineer told me he's working on putting in a temporary air-conditioning unit, hopefully next week."

"We'll all be feeding the worms in a week," said Big Mary. "Look at my scrubs. I look like a girl in a wet T-shirt contest."

Little Mary threw a bundle of dirty linen onto the floor. "You smell that? That's shit! In this heat the smell is worse than a Georgia pigsty."

"There is something they can do," said Lenny. "They can switch the work to nights until the heat wave breaks, and pay everyone a shift dif."

"I'm not leaving my kids home alone at night," said Little Mary.

"I'm not leaving my *husband* alone at night," said another woman.

Amid the laughter, Lenny said, "It's better than suffering

in the heat. Plus, you could wash everything in cold water and dry them on a low temperature."

The women looked at each other and nodded their heads. Big Mary said, "What if the temperature in the laundry doesn't come down?"

"The hospital safety officer and I will take readings every day. We agreed the average temperature has to come down by at least ten degrees over the next couple of days."

"And if it don't?"

"Then we turn off the machines and tell them to use paper linen until the heat wave breaks, or they fix the problem permanently."

"This heat wave could go on the *whole* summer," said Big Mary.

"If Human Resources doesn't agree to the night work and the shift dif, everyone reports to Employee Health and tells them they're dizzy from the heat."

"Even if it means they shut the department down?"

"It's a chance we have to take."

"We're ready," said Big Mary. "Even a dog gets to sleep in the shade. We deserve no less."

Chapter Forty-Two

Detective Williams stepped into the Messengers' Office. A tired-looking woman was at the desk manning the phone. She entered a request in a ledger book, keyed in a page to one of the messengers.

Williams flashed his badge. "You have a Maurice Peltiere on duty?"

"Yeah. He's taking a patient to X-ray."

"I want to see him." When the woman only looked at him, he added, "Now!"

"Sure, sure," she said. "I'll get Wyneva to cover for him. His shift is just ending anyway. He'll be punching out in fifteen minutes."

When Maurice entered the office and saw the detective, his stomach began to churn and he felt light-headed.

"Maurice Peltiere?"

"Uh-huh."

"Detective Williams, Philadelphia police. I need you to come down to the station."

"You do?"

"That's right. We have some things to talk about."

"I'm not supposed to punch out until three-thirty," said Maurice.

"I already told your boss. Let's go."

As Maurice followed the detective out of the office, he repeated Lenny's advice over and over in his mind: *Watching the window, okay. Copying the letter, not okay.*

Lenny was making his way down the broad marble steps of the main entrance when he heard a voice call out, "Lenny! Wait!"

Kate Palmer hurried to catch up. "I was afraid I was late," she said.

They walked past the employee parking lot, where Sandy, the old security guard, was seated on a little electric cart. Sandy winked at him, making Lenny think the old guy had the wrong idea about him and Kate.

They crossed Germantown Avenue and entered the Cave. Going to the back, Lenny saw Gary Tuttle and Moose at a table in the corner.

"Whoa, Tuttle, you beat me to the bar. That's a first."

"It's one of the few advantages of being the new nurse in orientation. I only work eight hours." Gary made room at the table for Lenny and Kate.

Lenny ordered a Jack Daniel's on the rocks; Kate, a wine cooler. Moose wasn't ready for a second Yuengling; Gary drank Coke with a twist of lemon.

Once the drinks were served, Lenny said, "It looks to me like Odom's murder is a response to the way he performed his abortions at James Madison, and especially how he treated Charyse Desir. Agreed?"

"Definitely," said Moose.

"The autopsy says she died from an infection she got from her abortion," Lenny continued. "Right?"

"Exactly right," said Kate, who brought out a printout and handed it to Lenny. "You remember the microbiology report showed she was infected with a very virulent pathogen, E. coli o-one-five-seven."

"It's a scary bug," said Gary, picking up the report. "It

causes kidney failure and shock."

"That's the one that grows in contaminated meat," said Moose. "But it didn't come from our kitchen. Trust me."

"If a bunch of hospital workers got sick from the food, I'd hear about it from Employee Health," said Lenny.

"If there was an outbreak in the community, Doctor Auginello would have heard about it," said Kate.

Lenny repeated the story Kate had told him at the zoo about a specimen with the same lethal bacteria mysteriously disappearing from the Microbiology Lab.

"It matches the DNA of Charyse Desir's culture perfectly," Kate added. "The frozen specimen *could* have just gone missing."

"How secure are the specimens in the lab?" asked Lenny.

"Not very. The access code for the door is one that's used all over the hospital."

"Three-two-one," said Moose. "We got it in the kitchen."

"We use it in the ICU lounge," said Gary.

Lenny said, "So anybody could have gone in, taken the frozen culture, thawed it out, and used it to infect a patient."

"It was Odom," said Moose. "Had to be. The bastard dirtied up his equipment and infected her on purpose."

Gary said, "Why would a physician intentionally infect his patients?"

"Simple," said Moose. "To a racist like Odom, black people aren't human. Killing us isn't even a sin."

Gary continued to look skeptical.

"Think about it," said Lenny. "Any time you label a group inferior, they end up slaves or in gas chambers. It's an easy step from aborting black babies to infecting the mothers."

"There's one thing that puzzles me," said Gary. "You haven't established a connection between Odom's murder and the death of Charyse Desir."

"Come on, we have to make a *few* assumptions. You don't kill somebody without a motive."

"You think the murderer was punishing him for his crimes?" Gary asked.

"It makes sense, doesn't it?"

"In that case, wouldn't it have to be somebody who can read the lab reports the way that Kate did and come to the same conclusions?"

"Someone like Cleopatra Edwards," said Kate.

"We can't ignore the fact that she hated his guts and wanted to see him punished," said Lenny.

"Cleopatra is a deeply principled person," said Kate. "She would never stoop to murder."

"You feel the same way about her friend, Lincoln," said Lenny. "Don't you?"

"Lincoln only wants to be a good physician. He couldn't possibly do such a thing."

"Well," said Lenny, "if Odom wasn't killed for his racism, it must have been personal."

"A crime of passion," said Moose.

"It could have been linked to the way Odom got Mai Loo fired." Lenny told them about Maurice's twisted love for the nurse, leaving out how the messenger had copied Mai Loo's termination letter.

"Has he got an alibi for Friday night?" asked Gary.

"It's a screwy one. He says he was watching her window until she put out the light."

"That boy's got serious problems," said Moose.

"He certainly has sufficient motive," said Gary.

"There's also Charyse Desir's boyfriend, Tyrell Hardy."

"Lemme guess," said Moose. "No alibi."

"He was home alone drinking till he passed out," said Lenny. "He also told me Odom didn't put Charyse on an antibiotic, even though she was complaining of pain and a fever."

Draining his glass of soda, Gary said, "It looks as if we still need to determine if there's a connection between Odom's murder and Charyse Desir's death. If there's no connection, we have to consider Maurice or Tyrell."

Lenny clinked his glass against Gary's. "Tuttle, once again you are the master and I but the learner."

Kate raised her hand in a stop-sign gesture. "There's one more thing I have to tell you. It's so horrible, I can hardly say the words."

Lenny and Gary put down their drinks and looked at her.

"I was looking over the lab reports on the women who had the abortions and . . ." She stopped in mid-sentence. A figure coming through the door to the bar had caught her eye. Lincoln Jones was rushing toward them, a look of panic on his face.

As he raced up to the group at the bar, he said, "Kate, it's so terrible. The police have searched the M-SOC office. They took the computer and the files. They took everything!"

"Oh my God," said Kate. "Did they arrest Cleopatra?"

"No. Not yet, at any rate. But I doubt very much that they believed what I told them."

Lincoln thanked Kate for paging him and inviting him to the meeting in the Cave. Then he explained that he and Cleopatra had been in the library together at the time of the murder. "The fact that we are engaged to be married weakens our credibility in the eyes of the police, I'm afraid."

"Your working in M-SOC together doesn't help, either," said Lenny, grabbing a chair from another table and making a place for Lincoln.

Once Lincoln had ordered a drink, he said, "It's only a

matter of time before they arrest her." He gratefully accepted a bottle of beer from the waitress. "Have you uncovered anything that will help us?"

Lenny said, "We were just talking about that. So far we have two kinds of motivations. Guys who hated Odom for personal reasons—Charyse Desir's boyfriend, for example—and people who were angry over his racist abortions. Kate was about to tell us something else."

She sighed. "I can hardly bring myself to say it. I discovered that a significant number of the women who had abortions from Odom never again became pregnant."

"Their post-procedure infections must have damaged their fallopian tubes," Lincoln said.

"That's what I was thinking," said Kate. "I'll ask Doctor Auginello what he thinks."

"He is a fine teacher," said Lincoln. A beeper sounded. Lincoln looked down at his belt. "It's Cleopatra," he said, taking out a cell phone. He dialed a number, said "It's me," listened, said "Okay, I will," and hung up the phone.

"I have to go," he said. "The police want to talk to me. They're at our apartment in the med school."

"Have you got a lawyer?" asked Lenny. "I know somebody."

"We have resources, thank you." He stood up and shook everyone's hands. "I can't thank you enough," he said. "When this is all over we'll throw a big party and I will express my gratitude." He turned and hurried away.

Kate finished her glass of wine and picked up her backpack. "Lenny, you don't really think that Cleopatra or Lincoln could have killed Odom, do you?"

"She did hate his guts."

"Don't forget they're a couple," said Moose.

"What does that prove?" asked Kate.

"Simple. You got one to hold the bastard down, one to cut him up." As he held up his empty bottle for the waitress to see, he added, "Ain't nothin' like teamwork."

After Gary and Kate left the Cave, Lenny and Moose lingered over their drinks.

Moose looked into the throat of the beer bottle in his hand. "Tell me something. You still want to leave your millions to your firstborn son? Like you was royalty?"

Lenny took a moment to study the label of his own bottle. "Yeah, I do. A son, or a daughter of my own. Maybe I'm being selfish."

"There ain't nothin' selfish about it. I got one of each."

"I worry sometimes that Patience's kids won't look at me like their real dad."

"You're nuts," said Moose. "I've seen those kids with you. They couldn't love you any more than if you nursed them at your own tit."

"I guess. But my being white. Down the road they might want to have a black father to identify with. I don't know . . ."

"You don't *know?* Man, you're forgetting the most important part of being a parent."

"What's that?"

Moose poked his friend in the chest. "Kids need to see a man and a woman love and respect each other. What matters is how they share the load."

"You think?"

"Trust me." Moose cocked his head and looked at his friend. "For a smart guy, you don't know jack about families. The kids see how happy you make their mother. As long as you do that, it don't matter if you're white, black, or three shades of purple. You're their A-number-one superhero."

Chapter Forty-Three

After leaving Moose at the Cave, Lenny drove to Mai Loo's apartment building. He had promised Dillie he would try and help Mai Loo. At the same time he wanted to check out Maurice's alibi. It would clear both of them.

He buzzed her apartment, but got no answer. She hadn't answered her phone, either. Lenny knew that a job termination can knock someone into a well of despair. He suspected that she was home, trying to shut out the world.

He waited with his keys in his hand on the sidewalk until he saw someone coming out of the elevator. He wanted to look like a tenant coming home from work. As he approached the front door, the resident coming out saw Lenny's hospital ID, smiled, and thanked him for holding the door open for her.

Lenny wished her a pleasant evening and stepped into the elevator. Finding Mai Loo's apartment, he rang the bell and listened at the door. Silence. He knocked gently and called out, "Mai Loo? It's me, Lenny. Are you there?"

He heard a clippity-clop of feet on the hardwood floor. *She's wearing those nursing clogs,* he thought, recognizing the patter from her days on Seven South. A chain slid on its track. A lock turned. The door opened a crack.

"Hi!" said Lenny. "Remember me? Your friendly neighborhood custodian?"

"Hi," said Mai Loo in a low voice.

"Can I come in? You don't want all the neighbors listening to me run my mouth, do you?"

"Okay." She opened the door wide and let him in. "I was making a cup of tea. Would you like one?"

"Sure."

He followed her into a tiny kitchen, noting the dirty dishes in the sink. A quart of milk standing on the counter would soon be sour in this heat, if it hadn't turned already. The termination had hit her hard.

"How are you doing? I heard you got work. Is that right?"

"Yes," she said, pouring him a cup. "Dillie has a friend. She gave me work in a nursing home. I started Saturday night."

"That's great. How did it go?"

"It's not a very nice place to work. It smells bad and some of the patients are very dirty. They have giant bedsores. When I came home I still smelled them, even after a shower."

"Still, you must be relieved, knowing you'll have a paycheck coming in."

"Yes. To not have a job is very scary." She offered him milk for his tea, which he declined.

"What was all that about Odom complaining about you? Something about a job in the Middle East . . ."

He watched her silently stir her tea, though she had put no sugar in it.

"You can tell me, you know I don't pass stuff on. Anything I hear gets lost in the waste disposal of my mind."

She put down her spoon. "A long time ago I worked in a hospital in Saudi Arabia. A lot of us Filipino girls get jobs there. Doctor Odom was working in the hospital. He did bad things. I complained about him. It was foolish, but I was young. I thought the hospital would make him stop."

"They fired you instead."

"Yes."

"If you knew how many times I've heard that story."

"Really?"

"Really."

He waited for more. She offered nothing. They sat for a moment letting the tea cool. After a while, Lenny asked, "Did you do the same thing at James Madison? Complain about him?"

"No, not this time. I didn't want to lose my job. But I did speak to him. I told him I knew what he was doing, and God knew what he was doing. I shouldn't have said anything."

"Did you threaten to take it further?"

"No. I never said anything like that!"

"Still, he must have felt threatened." Lenny sipped his tea. "I know Odom was butchering women with his abortions. Is that what you meant by the 'bad things' he did in Saudi Arabia?"

"Not exactly," she said.

"What, then?"

She stared into her tea cup. Her eyes were growing moist, on the verge of tears. "I was foolish to talk to him." Her voice was tremulous.

"Maybe it wasn't the best way to handle it, but you had to tell him how you felt."

"It was stupid."

"Come on, look at me. I've made lots of dumb mistakes as a union steward. Some of those mistakes hurt the people I was trying to help. But you do the best you can and move on. You only hurt yourself when you dwell on the mistakes."

"My friend Dillie says the same thing. She tells me I have to look to the future and not think about what can't be undone."

"She's right. She's a good person."

"Dillie is strong; not like me."

"But look what you have. You're working. You have friends. Odom is dead. He's the one who lost out in the end."

She didn't look cheered up by his remarks. He decided to try and get one more piece of information from her and then call it quits.

"Are you working the night shift at the nursing home?"

"Yes."

"That's a rough shift. Have you been sleeping okay?"

"I don't sleep much."

"What about Friday night? Did you sleep okay?"

"Not really. I was awake until midnight. And then I woke up many times. When the sun came up, I felt like I had been up all night."

Satisfied that Maurice had told him the truth, Lenny took his tea cup to the sink and ran some water into it. "I should get going. But listen. You have a right to appeal your termination. Do you want me to help you find a lawyer?"

"I don't know."

"Or I can help you prepare your case. And I can be with you when you go in front of Human Resources."

He saw that she was unconvinced.

"You only have ten days to request an appeal. If you want, I could pick up the form and give it to Dillie for you. You want me to do that?"

"I guess so."

Lenny looked at the downcast eyes and the sagging shoulders and knew she felt her case was hopeless. "I'll get the form and give it to Dillie. She can help you fill it out. If you decide not to go through with it, that's okay. But at least you'll have the option if you want to take it. Okay?"

She looked up into his face and nodded her head once, fighting back tears.

He wanted to put his arms around her and hug her; to

comfort her and tell her things would be all right. But he knew that things might, indeed, end up much worse. Especially if the police arrested her for Odom's murder.

Chapter Forty-Four

Lenny was only half awake as he took his turn punching in at the housekeeping time clock. "What's with the air-conditioning?" he said to one of the night custodians who had just punched out.

"PECO had to drop their voltage, or some shit. The system's overloaded."

"Christ," said Lenny. "Just when the hospital had the AC upgraded they have to turn it down?"

"Life is full of ironies," said the fellow, a skinny guy with big ears and a shaved head.

Lenny dropped his time card back in its slot on the wall and was about to go to his locker when he felt an iron claw squeeze his shoulder. Turning, he found himself looking into Joe West's gray dead man's eyes. The security chief released his grip, handed Lenny a piece of paper.

"Read it and weep," said West, who brushed past Lenny and walked off without waiting for a response.

Robbed of an opportunity to give West a pithy reply, Lenny read the document as he wearily climbed the stairs to his ward. The memo from Human Resources said: GUIDELINES FOR OBJECTIVELY DETERMINING ALCOHOL IMPAIRMENT OF HOSPITAL EMPLOYEES.

First, it stipulated that whenever a supervisor or a hospital security officer (Lenny mentally inserted the phrase *prison guard*) notes behavioral signs of drug or alcohol impairment, as listed below, that representative shall require the employee to report to the Security Office for the purpose of submitting to an alcohol level test by measurement of exhaled breath.

Who writes these memos? Lenny wondered.

The paragraph was followed by a list of "behaviors" that indicated alcohol use, being careful to stipulate that the list was not exhaustive, and that the hospital representative *may use professional judgment and prior experience in order to identify alcohol-related impairment.*

The memo went on to state: *Refusal by the employee to submit to testing will constitute admission of alcohol ingestion and result in immediate dismissal. Alcohol level above the guidelines stated below will also result in dismissal.* The memo used the same blood-alcohol levels that the Commonwealth of Pennsylvania employed.

Lenny suspected that the hospital would be on strong legal ground by using the Pennsylvania guidelines. He worried that the heat wave gripping the Delaware Valley would continue driving the workers to the Cave to slake their thirst, and West would have new snitches watching everyone who took a drink.

It was beginning to look like high noon at the James Madison Corral.

Kate was leaving Morning Report on her way to her assignment when her beeper went off. Calling the number, she heard the midwife McSweeny saying they needed to talk again.

"I have rounds in a half hour, but I can stop by now," said Kate.

"Good. Come to my office. I can't speak about it over the phone."

"Okay," said Kate. "Is it about Odom and—"

The midwife hung up before Kate could finish her question.

Dr. Singh told Gary, "It is time to extubate the patient."

Mr. Darling tapped the breathing tube, giving Gary a questioning look.

"Yes, we're taking the tube out," said Gary. He peeled the nylon tape off the patient's face, revealing gray stubble where the electric razor had been unable to reach. Gary told Darling to take a deep breath and cough. As he pulled the breathing tube out of the airway, Darling let out a forceful cough, bringing a wad of thick mucous up to his mouth.

Gary held out a gauze pad for Darling to expectorate. Then he placed an oxygen mask over the patient's face. "How does that feel?"

"Great," said Darling in a hoarse voice.

Dr. Singh listened to the breath sounds as he moved his stethoscope over the front and back of the chest.

"He has a few crackles in the bases, but otherwise he is clear," said Singh. "I believe his pneumonia will resolve very well."

Dr. Singh noted the oxygen level reading on the monitor. Satisfied, he added, "Gary will show you how to do the breathing exercises. If you fail to perform them, we will have to put the tube back. Do you understand?"

"No way I'm swallowing that sucker again," said Darling. "I'll blow down a barn door if I have to."

Singh went on to examine other patients.

As Gary made a note in the chart about the extubation, Darling said, "I'm hungry as a hyena. What's the chance you can get me some steak and eggs for breakfast? And coffee? I want a big, hot, steaming cup of coffee."

"I can get the coffee and the eggs," said Gary. "I'm not sure about the steak."

"What a cheap-ass place. I bet you serve powdered eggs and instant coffee."

"I assure you, the eggs are collected fresh from the hen house each morning."

Darling adopted a more conciliatory tone. "I don't suppose there's any chance you could bring me a little whiskey to go in the coffee, could you?"

"No, I can't. You'll have to make do with sugar and milk."

"It's a sorry crossing when a man doesn't get his daily pint of grog."

Darling sat back and closed his eyes, as if to shut out the room and return to the long slumber he had enjoyed while under sedation. Gary went to the phone to call for a late breakfast, happy to be hearing his patient's voice once again.

Cleopatra walked with Lincoln to the medical school lecture hall. He had a lecture, she had to go on rounds with an attending physician. At the door, Cleopatra placed a folded piece of paper in his hand.

"What's this?" he asked.

"It's the password and ID code for the hidden files at the free clinic."

"Baby, you don't need to—"

"Lincoln, I need you to take charge of the files. All our information about Odom is in their computer. After I'm arrested, you have to make sure the information gets to the press."

Lincoln looked into her face, saw her pride and her strength. He was moved by the fierce conviction in her eyes. He never loved her more than when she was in the heat of battle.

"You will have to hold M-SOC together," she said.

"Cleopatra, I can't fill your shoes."

"I know you don't like politics, but there's no one else."

She held his hand up and looked at it. "You will be a fine surgeon one day, Lincoln Jones."

"Hey, don't talk like that. We're gonna be in practice together. We're going to make Africa House a real clinic. The police haven't got any evidence."

"They don't need evidence to convict a black woman."

She released his hand, turned and walked on to her appointment, her shoulders square, her head held high, her arms swinging like a soldier.

Chapter Forty-Five

Lenny fished out a wad of bloody gauze pads from the regular trash and threw it in a red bag, being careful to look for sharps. A twinge of regret ran through his mind as he recalled the needle that had stuck him on Wednesday and his decision to not take the HIV prophylactic drugs.

Fuck it, he thought. The needle didn't have any blood in it. He vowed to put it out of his mind and focus on the problems at hand: the situation in the laundry and the alcohol testing.

He spotted Maurice coming onto the ward with his messenger cart.

"Hey, Maurice. How're you doing?"

Maurice shrugged his shoulders, his face a mask. "Okay, I guess."

"You look tired."

"I don't sleep good. I worry about Mai Loo. And I'm afraid to stand outside her building since the cops talked to me."

"The police questioned you? Why didn't you tell me?"

Maurice gave another shrug. "I didn't want to bother you."

"Come on, we're friends. I don't want you in trouble with the cops. How'd it go?"

"Okay, I guess. I did like you told me. I said I was outside her window Friday night. I didn't say anything about the letter from Human Resources."

"Good." Lenny stood in front of the big pedestal fan, letting the breeze cool him. "Did the cops ask what you knew about Odom?"

"Uh-huh. I told them I heard around the hospital that he complained to Miss Burgess. Gossip. You know."

"That was smart."

"They asked me if I ever worked in the operating room or any place where I handled sterile instruments and stuff. I told them I never did."

"Have you ever worked with sterile instruments?"

"No, never. I worked in a butcher shop one summer when I was in high school, but I didn't tell them about that."

Again, Lenny told Maurice he had done well. He made the young man promise to page him if the cops came back with more questions. As Lenny picked up the trash, he pictured Maurice in a butcher shop, slicing filets from a side of beef hanging on a hook in a big refrigerated storage locker.

The image was not reassuring.

Kate arrived in the Labor and Delivery Suite a few moments after getting the call from McSweeny. She found the midwife in her office. McSweeny shut the door and pulled a pile of magazines from a chair to make room for her.

"Maybe I shouldn't talk to you about this," said McSweeny, sitting on the edge of the bed. "But I worked with you last year and I know you are a good person. And I know Doctor Odom was pure evil."

"Thank you," said Kate, settling back in the chair. "What is it?"

"It all started about six months ago. I was going over our monthly unit costs for Q-A. We are on strict inventory rationing."

"Everyone's feeling the budget crunch," said Kate. "They don't even serve coffee at Morning Report anymore."

"The administration sent out a memo telling us to reuse paper clips and rubber bands."

"The little things."

"You said it. Anyway, there was an antibiotic on the pharmacy cost summary that caught my eye. I didn't remember us ever using it. So I called the pharmacist to tell him they made a mistake, and Mike checked for me. Do you know Mike DiPietro?"

Kate shook her head.

"A very nice man." McSweeny thought she heard a sound at the door and stopped to listen. Satisfied it was nothing, she went on. "The drug is Doxycycline."

"An antibiotic."

"That's right. We would ordinarily dilute it in normal saline and give it IV. But some doctors use it for a sclerosing agent."

"Like a pleurodesis," said Kate. "It triggers an inflammatory response in the lung."

"Right. Or in GI to shrivel up a varices or a hemorrhoid."

Kate's mind drifted back to the lab results she had been studying. Her stomach tightened as she waited for the news.

"The thing is, I saw that somebody was requesting the Doxy for the past year, but none of the physicians were ordering it for their patients. And I know that Odom was a monster who was capable of anything."

"My God! Odom must have ordered the drug and injected it in the women he was aborting."

"It makes me sick to even think it," said McSweeny, her eyes welling with tears. "I wanted to tell you, since you're investigating that monster."

Fighting back her own tears, Kate explained how she had discovered that many of Odom's abortion patients had never gotten pregnant again. "Odom must have injected it directly into the fallopian tubes."

"I'm glad that he's dead, God forgive me," said McSweeny. She reached for a box of tissues and dabbed at her moist eyes.

As Kate stood to leave, she remembered something the midwife had told her days before. "Miss McSweeny, remember that resident who had a fight with Odom and left in the middle of his rotation?"

"Sure I do. The one who went to Women and Children's."

"Do you recall his name? I'd really like to talk to him."

In the dirty utility room Lenny washed down several rolling IV poles and intravenous pumps. His sweat-stained shirt stuck to him as he worked. He asked himself why Odom would purposely infect his patients. The idea that he was sterilizing women was too far-fetched. It would trigger an investigation of his practice. Lenny knew that when doctors had too many complications, the Department of Health looked at their practice.

But if Odom hadn't infected Charyse Desir, who had? And how was that connected to Odom's murder?

Lenny looked at his watch. He had just enough time to nose around the library and check out Lincoln's and Cleopatra's alibis before he met Moose for break. After getting Betty to cover for him, Lenny made his way to the medical library.

When he entered, he felt a familiar sense of peace and calm. The cool, hushed atmosphere of a library had long made it one of his favorite places. He could turn off his beeper, and turn off the world, while he hunted for an interesting book or used the computers for research on a union issue.

When he had studied history at Temple University, before

his dad died, he loved to pile up a stack of books and journals in a quiet spot and read until his eyes grew blurry. His father had said that the free public library was one of the great reforms of the American democracy, unlike the exclusive libraries of Europe or Asia.

Walking among the stacks, he saw a young white woman with a nose ring and orange hair pushing a cart loaded with books and journals. She was wearing a blue apron with the James Madison Library logo written in bold letters. He walked up to her. "Hey, Gwen. How's it going?"

A broad smile with a missing tooth formed on her face. "Oh, hi, Lenny. Wow, I haven't seen you in, like, six months or more." A dark cloud briefly swept away her joy. "I'm not in trouble, am I?"

"No. I came by on an errand and I saw you."

"Thank the Lord. I can't afford to lose this job. They're paying for my classes at Community College."

Lenny recalled the battle he had waged the year before over the hospital's hiring welfare workers for below-minimum wage. James Madison had argued that the fierce competition forced them to cut labor costs. In the end, the union caved on bringing in the welfare workers, but won on the minimum wage issue. And the hospital submitted a side letter promising to hire any welfare worker who completed their work period with a good evaluation.

Lenny knew what the "good evaluation" meant. Most of the welfare workers received bad write-ups. Without a union steward to challenge the evaluations, only three of the fifteen welfare workers were given regular jobs when their work contract was completed. Gwen was one of them.

Leaning against the stack, Lenny watched as she read the spine and hunted for the appropriate slot. "Did you work last Friday?" he asked.

"Sure did," said Gwen. "The librarian offered me a double. Time and a half. There's no way I'm turning that kind of money down."

"So you were here until closing. What is that on Friday—ten o'clock?"

"We close at eleven every night but Sunday."

"Gotcha."

Gwen put the last of her books on the shelf. She turned to Lenny. "Has this got to do with that racist that was murdered last Friday?"

"Yeah, it does. But you have to swear you'll keep this to yourself. I can't have anyone know I'm even involved."

"Okay."

"I mean it, Gwen."

"I'll put Krazy Glue on my lips. Ask away."

Lenny peered through a space in the stack to be sure that nobody was listening. "Do you happen to know who Cleopatra Edwards is?"

"Sure I do. She's the one who writes all those leaflets for the black medical students. I heard her speak one time."

"That's great. Did you see her here studying Friday night?"

"Yeah, she was here. She had on this great leopard-skin robe and a really cool hat."

Lenny silently thanked heaven for female fashion. "Okay. Did you notice if she was with a tall black male student? He has dreads."

Gwen lowered her voice. "I see him with her all the time. That man can park his shoes under my bed any time."

"His name is Lincoln Jones. Did they both stay in the library until closing?"

"She went out for a while. I remember I was tempted to pick up her stack, but Lincoln told me to leave them."

"Hmm. What about him? Did he leave?"

"I don't think so. He was always there whenever I went through."

Cleopatra's alibi was now in doubt, but Lenny wanted to be sure of Lincoln's before he went any further. "What time was your dinner break?" he asked, thinking that Lincoln might have left the library while Cleopatra was gone.

"Friday I didn't take no dinner break. My supervisor lets me skip my breaks and leave an hour early." In a hushed voice, she added, "He punches my time card. Am I in trouble?"

"No, Gwen, you're okay. But you're better off taking your break. The supervisor might not cover for you if you're caught."

As he exited the library to meet Moose, Lenny realized that Gwen's leaving early had left both of the medical students without an alibi. They were well aware of Odom's butchering poor women. If they knew about his sterilizing them . . .

Getting Lincoln to open up to him was going to take some real finesse.

Tyrell told the supervisor he needed to go to the storeroom for some packing and nylon tape. On his way he decided that he couldn't face a whole day sticking his head up in the ceiling checking the air-conditioning ductwork. The heat was giving him a headache already.

Leaving the hospital, he crossed Germantown Avenue and entered the Cave. The bar was cool and dark, and the smell of beer and last night's sweat still hung in the air. He ordered a Colt 45 and took a long pull, the cold liquid soothing his dry throat and instantly relieving his headache.

He looked at his watch, decided he had—no, he *deserved*—

a solid half hour to himself. He had the whole day to get his work done. One cold beer to the memory of Charyse. A man who had been through so much shit deserved no less.

Oblivious to the hot sun and the sweltering humidity, Joe West stood on the steps of the main hospital entrance. Two young security officers beside him sweated profusely, but West, his eyes protected by reflective sunglasses, seemed to not sweat at all.

As hospital employees came up the steps, the two guards observed them for signs of alcohol intoxication. If there was any sign at all, they stopped them and smelled their breaths.

West was annoyed. He had lost his best snitch, Baby Love. It was going to take time to recruit somebody who could sit in the Cave and watch people drinking without attracting attention.

However, there were many ways to shoot fish in a barrel, even if he was temporarily without a fish-finder.

Chapter Forty-Six

After leaving the library, Lenny picked up an iced coffee from a vendor in the lobby and made his way to the sewing room in the basement. He found Moose seated beside Birdie and chewing on a soft pretzel with spicy mustard. Lenny sat down beside his friend, pried the lid off the coffee, and stirred it with his straw.

"This murder investigation is a big headache," he said, trying to get the sugar to dissolve in the cold coffee.

"Who you trying to kid? You love it," said Moose. "It feeds your sense of injustice."

"That's what Patience says. She's surprised I'm not religious. I have such a strong sense of righteous indignation."

"Did your sense find out anything new?"

"I found out that Cleopatra's alibi isn't worth shit." Lenny explained that the library aide told him Cleopatra had left the library for some time. On top of that, the aide went home over an hour before the library closed.

"Either one of them could've done it," said Moose.

"That's what I was thinking."

"Does it really matter?" asked Birdie. "Whoever killed Odom did us all a favor. As long as the cops don't arrest anyone, you should drop the whole thing."

"We made a promise," said Lenny.

"We can't go back on our word," said Moose.

"You men just like to run around and play detective," said Birdie.

Kate stuck her head in through the doorway. "They told me on Seven South I'd find Lenny here," she said. "You won't believe this, but I think I found out how Odom sterilized his patients. That man was worse than Dr. Mengele."

She told them about the Doxycycline that was missing from the Labor and Delivery Suite, and how it was used as a sclerosing agent when administered full strength. "Odom doesn't deserve a burial," she said. "They should throw his body on the beach and let the crabs pick at him."

"They'd have to close the beach for the smell," said Lenny.

"You see?" said Birdie. "I was just telling them they should let the investigation drop. The murderer did everyone a favor."

"Lincoln is certain the police will arrest Cleopatra soon," said Kate. "That would be a travesty."

"If she's innocent," said Moose.

Now it was Lenny's turn to fill Kate in. He told her that Cleopatra's and Lincoln's alibis were thin.

"I don't care," said Kate. "I know them both, and they're committed people. They volunteer at a free clinic in North Philly. M-SOC has an agenda, not a death squad."

Lenny said, "We haven't ruled anyone in or out yet. We have to keep digging."

Moose tossed his paper plate in the trash. "We find the killer or we don't. Either way, the people have a right to know how the hospital covered for him and let it go on for years."

"They should arrest all the suits," said Birdie.

"Don't worry," said Lenny. "I have no doubt M-SOC is planning a press release. And if one of their members goes to trial, I'm sure they'll use Odom's crimes in their defense."

Popping an ice cube into his mouth, Lenny added, "They may even come off as heroes."

★ ★ ★ ★ ★

When Will Wheat, a clerk from Central Stores, left the hospital by the main entrance, he saw a security guard sniff around a guy in scrubs like a beagle at the airport checking for drugs, while Joe West stood watching.

In the parking lot, Will asked Sandy, an old security guard, what was going on at the entrance.

"West is looking for people to test for alcohol," said Sandy. "He's hot to use that breathalyzer test. You best tell people to keep the drinking down for a while. He's not playing."

Will crossed Germantown Avenue and ducked into the Cave, where he picked out several liters of soda to bring back to the department. He saw Tyrell sitting alone at the bar.

"Hey, Ty. You on duty?"

"Yeah, I'm hard at work. Can't you tell?"

Seeing the bottle of beer in Tyrell's hand, Will said, "Man, you better be careful when you come back. West is gunning for anybody with alcohol on their breath."

"I'll hold my breath," said Tyrell.

"I'm serious. You better slip in through the loading dock."

"O-kay, thanks," said Tyrell, his eyes half closed.

The clerk hurried back to the hospital. At the entrance, he pulled out a bottle of soda and held it up to the guards. "See? I'm a vegetarian," he said and passed through the entrance.

Inside the sewing room, Lenny was rubbing an ice cube from his iced coffee on his forearm. "I wish they could bring that bastard back to life so I could kill him myself," he said.

"I heard his balls were stuffed down his throat," said Moose.

"How long do you think he suffered?" asked Lenny, turning to Kate.

"It depends on how complete the obstruction was. If it was partial, he might have starved for air for several minutes."

"I hope so," said Lenny. He took a last sip from his coffee. "How hard would it be to inject that Doxy-whatever without anyone seeing him? I mean, during an abortion?"

"The vacuum abortion is a blind procedure. I guess it's possible he instilled the drug through the tube before starting up the suction. That would scar over the uterine lining."

"You were going to ask the nurse and the residents who were there if they saw anything suspicious," said Lenny. "What were their names?" He opened the copy of Charyse Desir's chart and turned to the procedure record.

"The nurse's name was Munios, but she was out when I went to L & D. Doctor Margolis clammed up pretty tight when he thought he could be found negligent for the infection and the death."

"C-Y-A time," said Moose, as he looked over Lenny's shoulder at the surgical record.

"I got hold of Doctor Dobkin yesterday," Kate continued. "He swore Charyse's procedure was completely successful. There were no problems."

"What about the other one, Doctor Johnson?"

"The midwife didn't know him. I'll get a list of all the residents and fellows and track him down."

"Mind if I borrow this page?" asked Moose, picking out the surgery record.

"Be my guest," said Lenny.

"Speaking of residents," said Kate. "The midwife told me there was an OB resident who left in the middle of his rotation."

"Odom canned him?"

"Sweeny thought he quit over a disagreement he was having with Odom."

"Interesting," said Lenny. "You think you can find him?"

"He's working at Women and Children's. I could try and talk to him."

"That would be great," said Lenny. "Since he's out of the program, he might be more willing to talk."

"I'm not defending the residents or students because I'm one of them," Kate said.

"I'm not writing off Tyrell and Maurice just because they're in my union," said Lenny.

"But Cleopatra and Lincoln would never knowingly kill a human being. They're committed to saving lives."

"I'll tell you one thing," Moose said. "A doctor has the power to pronounce you dead. How tough is it to go from pronouncing you dead to making you dead?"

Kate stood up to go, folded her chair, and leaned it against the wall. "I still think it's important to remember that Maurice or Tyrell were both angry enough to kill Odom," she said.

"I agree we can't cross them off the list," said Lenny. "But I'm not sure either one of them would castrate Odom."

"Tyrell works with plenty of sharp tools," said Birdie.

Kate said, "And Maurice was obsessed with Mai Loo. Someone who harbors secret feelings is capable of all sorts of wild revenge fantasies."

Lenny reminded them that Maurice knew what time Mai Loo turned off her bedroom light.

"He could've killed Odom and rushed over to her apartment in time to see her go to bed," said Kate.

"I say a man that stands outside a woman's bedroom window is creepy," said Birdie.

"He is a weird guy," said Moose. "He's got those wild eyes. And that face that's like a mask."

"A mask?" Kate said. "That's interesting. Is he on medication?"

"I don't know his medical story," said Lenny. "Why?"

"Some medications can affect the nervous system. Steroids can cause a psychosis, for example. And there are several diseases that can alter your mood and behavior."

Lenny folded his chair and leaned it against the wall. "I don't know if he's taking any medication, but I know somebody who does. I'll see what I can find out."

Kate said good-bye and left the sewing room.

As Lenny and Moose walked toward the kitchen, Lenny said, "I'd really like to know if Cleopatra and Lincoln had the same kind of data you did about the women not getting pregnant after their abortions. It would give them even more reason to cut him up."

"They'll never tell you what they knew."

"True," said Lenny. "I might be able to get a little information from a detective, but he's gonna ask a stiff price for it."

"The cops won't give you squat. They'll just pump you for information and throw you in a cell if you clam up on 'em."

"Unfortunately, I don't see any other way of getting what I need." Leaving his friend at the entrance to the kitchen, he added, "I'm going to have a chat with Detective Williams."

On his way to the elevator—it was too hot to walk the stairs—Lenny passed by the Central Receiving Unit. Will, the clerk, called out to him, "Hey, Lenny. You got a minute?"

"I'm kind of in a hurry. What's up?" He followed the clerk toward his office.

"Joe West is checking everybody coming in the main entrance. He's pulling people down to security and giving them that breathalyzer test."

"Shit! The bastard!"

"There's somebody I think you better talk to," said Will, leading Lenny into his office.

"Who? I've got a million people pulling on me right now. I—" Lenny stopped short when he saw Tyrell Hardy seated at the desk, his face resting on a cardboard box.

"I saw Ty at the Cave," said Will, "and told him to come in through the loading dock."

"You did right," said Lenny.

"Hey! How's my little buddy," said Tyrell, lifting his head off the box.

"I can't keep him here. The front is all glass. Anybody can see him."

"I'll take care of him," said Lenny.

He hauled Tyrell up by the arm and led him to the sewing room. Depositing him in a chair in the corner, he said, "Stay out of sight until you sober up." He thanked Birdie for covering for him, and hurried back to his ward, thinking that with all the bullshit he had to deal with, he didn't need to play hide and seek with Joe West over a drunken worker.

Rupert Darling sat up in bed, a kidney-shaped spit basin in one hand, a fist full of tissues in the other, while Gary watched him take deep breaths and cough. Gary had warned Darling that if he didn't cough up the mucous in his lungs every hour, Dr. Singh would put the breathing tube back in his throat.

"I'm never going through that torture again," Darling said. "You can let me die and bury me at sea, I don't care. I'm not taking the tube. Not ever."

When Gary pointed to the little paper bag taped to the side rail, Darling dropped his dirty tissues into it. He settled back in his bed, thinking about the week he'd been through. It had begun with his legs getting numb and then giving out. There was his decision to call the paramedics. *Big mistake,* he told himself. But had he stayed at home and not been treated by Dr. Singh and that plasma-whatever-you-call-it, he would have quit breathing and that would have been the end of it.

And he had a lot of living left to do, of that Darling was certain. There were plenty of single women out there looking for a companion: widows and divorcées. Even some spinsters who weren't half bad looking. He was determined to find one.

As Gary started to leave the bedside, Darling said, "Can I ask you something?"

"Sure." Gary stepped closer to the bed.

"This is gonna sound real weird," said Darling, a nervous laugh in his throat.

"You're in a weird place. How bad can it be?"

"Well, I know I've been real sick and I was attached to the breathing machine for the last couple of days, but . . ."

"But," Gary encouraged.

"I didn't leave the hospital any time the last couple of days, did I?"

"Do you mean, did we send you to another facility for tests or a procedure?"

"No. I mean, I have this very clear memory of me and you going out to this club. There were lots of beautiful women there. We each picked out a girl and went up to the rooms and we had sex with them. In separate beds. I know it's not possible, but it was *so real.* I remember the music and the taste of the liquor and the smell of their perfume. I even remember the feeling of her hair on my chest."

Gary put a hand on Darling's shoulder. "It was the medication we gave you to make you sleep. It's an aphrodisiac. The drug caused you to have very pleasant dreams."

"*None* of it was real?"

"No. None of it."

"Damn," said Darling. "Can you get that stuff in a pill?"

"Unfortunately, it's only available as an intravenous solution. And it's not safe to use unless you're on the ventilator. The drug makes you stop breathing."

"That's a damn shame. If you could bottle it you'd make a fortune."

Chapter Forty-Seven

"Where can I find Lenny Moss?" Detective Williams asked the security guard at the hospital's main entrance.

"He works on Seven South. Should I call Mr. West and let him know you're here?"

"Don't bother. I'll page him when I need him." Williams walked to the elevator and rode it to the seventh floor. Striding down the hall, he caught sight of Lenny hauling two bags of linen to the laundry chute, a pregnant nurse's aide walking beside him.

"Moss, you got a place we can talk?"

Lenny heaved the linen bags down the chute, then led the detective to the conference room down from the nursing station. He opened the door a crack, saw the room was empty, and led the detective inside.

"You have information for me. Right?" Williams took out his Palm Pilot.

Lenny weighed the pros and cons of trading information and decided he had no other access to what he needed. "Maybe . . . but you've got to promise me something in return."

"Like what?"

"I need one piece of information from your investigation."

"You're the guy who hears everything in this place."

"Not everything."

The detective leaned toward Lenny. "I have a mind to arrest you for obstruction of justice and haul your ass to the precinct. If you've got information relevant to my case, you can spit it out or park your butt in a cell."

"The precinct is air-conditioned, right?"

"Yeah. So?"

"It's got to be a better place to hang out than the hospital. And I'll get free food. TV in the day room. A court appointed lawyer. Fresh linen."

"Cut the crap, it's too damn hot."

"Look, I'll show you everything in my hand. All I ask is that you show me *one* little card in yours."

Williams drummed his fingers on the table. "What's the little bit of information you need?"

"It's M-SOC. You got a look at their records and computer files. Did they have data that strongly suggested the women were sterilized when they had their abortions with Odom?"

"They were *what?*"

"By the look on your face I can see you didn't know. And since you've seen M-SOC's files, it means Cleopatra and Lincoln didn't know, either. Am I right?"

"There was nothing specific in their files about sterilization. Just a lot of stuff about abortions and infections and talk of genocide. What's with the sterilizing?"

Lenny explained how almost none of the women got pregnant after their abortions. He told Williams there was evidence Odom had injected a caustic drug called Doxycycline into the fallopian tubes of women who underwent caesarian sections, and that the OB department had stocked the drug, but nobody remembered a doctor actually ordering it for a patient.

"What a son of a bitch," said Williams. "If he were alive, I'd shoot him."

"You'd have to wait in line."

"I take it your interest goes to motive. This discovery adds to the reasons the two medical students had to off Odom."

"Except they didn't have the statistics."

Lenny didn't tell Williams how Cleopatra's and Lincoln's library alibis didn't quite hold up. He wanted to determine for himself if they were guilty before giving Williams even more evidence against them.

The detective eyed Lenny for a minute. "Is that all you got?"

"Yup."

"You're holding out on me."

"You want me to take a lie detector test?"

"What's the point. You flunk the test, the machine can't read your mind." Williams walked to the door. "You ever consider going to the academy? You're pretty good at pulling stuff out of people."

"Nah. Guns scare me."

Williams shook his head. "I have a feeling there are damn few things in this world that scare Lenny Moss."

Moose stepped into the Information Services Department and found his friend, Ali. Ali had a cubbyhole crammed with computer parts, disks, and tools.

"Hey," said Moose. "What's shaking?"

"Hello, Mister Moose. It is good to see you. What brings you to my cave?"

"Can I use one of the scanners for a minute?"

"Of course. My home is your home. Come with me."

Moose followed Ali to a workbench crammed with computer equipment.

"This scanner has a very high resolution," Ali said. "What are you scanning—a film strip? A photograph?"

"No. It's an operating report."

Moose placed the report on the scanner while Ali called up the program. In seconds the image of the report was visible on a nineteen-inch, flat-panel computer screen.

"Great bit depth," said Moose, admiring the image. "Scroll down to the signatures. There. That one."

Ali aligned the signature in the middle of the screen and tapped the magnification command. The signature spilled over the edges of the screen.

"Show me the middle of the name, where the *N* and the *S* meet," Moose said.

His friend magnified again, bringing the two letters into sharp relief. Moose leaned closer to the screen and scrutinized the letters. "Just like I thought," he said. "The letters are the same *color*, but they're a different *width*. The *H* started out as a small *N*. See?"

"Yes, you are right. And look at the *N*. It was a small *e*. You can see the horizontal line, still. I think the original name must have been—?"

"Jones," said Moose. "Lincoln Jones was in the OR when Charyse Desir had her abortion."

"What does this mean, Mr. Moose?" asked Ali. "Why did this person forge a name? He wanted to escape blame for something he did?"

"This fucker doesn't want anybody to know he helped Doctor Odom kill a woman."

"Ah, his license would be in jeopardy."

"That ain't it," said Moose. "It was something much more basic." He folded the paper and tucked it in his pocket. "Jones didn't want his woman to know what he did, 'cause she'd cut his balls off if she knew."

Chapter Forty-Eight

Joe West stood ramrod straight and watched while one of the junior security officers administered a breathalyzer test to a man from the kitchen. Two more employees were sitting in the hallway waiting their turn.

"This is bullshit," said one of the waiting men, a wiry black man with a long scar on the side of his face, who had worked as a transporter for twenty years. "A man's entitled to wet his whistle, hot as it is in this rat-ass place."

His companion, a big Irish-American with ruddy brown hair and freckles along the backs of his arms agreed. "A man should be able to enjoy a pint on his lunch. It's in the Constitution. Am I right?"

"You right."

The employee who had taken the breathalyzer test came out of the room and winked at the two who were waiting. The guard at the door signaled to the white man.

"I'm on medication," said the custodian. "For diabetes. That can affect the test."

The security guard rolled his eyes and fitted the breathalyzer with a new mouthpiece.

Joe West took out his walkie-talkie and called the guard covering the main entrance. "Are you staying sharp, Lewis?"

"Yes, sir," said the guard. "So far everyone's walking a straight line. No sign of inebriation."

"Don't go soft on me. If they're blue collar, stop them and smell their breath."

"Yes, sir!" said the guard. "Did that police detective get ahold of you?"

"What detective?"

"The black one. He came through a little while ago."

"You should have paged me."

"He said he was going to page you after he made his appointment."

"Oh? Who did he come to see?"

"That union guy. You know. Lenny Moss."

Steaming with fury, West stalked out of the room. He wondered why the police were willing to talk to that troublesome custodian and leave *him*, the chief police agent in the entire James Madison facility, out of it.

Feeling a powerful urge to hurt the shop steward who was always getting in his way, he took out his key ring and summoned the elevator, determined to silence the pest once and for all.

Kate shifted the Subaru into second and slowed as she entered the driveway of Women and Children's Hospital. The hospital occupied a grassy hill in East Falls, with a beautiful view of downtown Philadelphia. She parked the car in the doctors' lot and crossed quickly to the main entrance, showing her James Madison ID as she entered the building.

Inside, she made her way to the Labor and Delivery Suite. At the nursing station a nurse in dark green scrubs and a lavender cap looked up. "What can I do you for?" she asked in a frosty tone.

"I'm Kate Palmer, from James Madison. Is Doctor Ishmael here?"

"I think he's in the on-call room. Let me page him." The nurse dialed the phone.

A moment later a young resident came to the station. He was lean and athletic-looking, with a strong jaw and a two-day stubble. Kate wondered if he ran the Philly marathon.

"Hi," she said. "I'm Kate Palmer. I'm a fourth-year med student at James Madison."

"Sámi Ishmael."

"I rotated through OB-GYN two years ago. You probably don't remember me."

"Sure I do. You didn't let the Attendings intimidate you. I admired your courage."

Kate stepped closer. "Can you give me a minute?"

"Well, I just delivered and the mom is having some bleeding problems." He paused while the nurse at the station rolled her eyes and walked away. "What is it about?"

Kate leaned even closer and said in a very low voice, "It's about Odom. And his OB practice."

Ishmael made a silent "O" with his lips. He led Kate to an on-call room. The two unmade beds were rank with body odor and littered with empty Styrofoam containers from the local Chinese takeout.

Kate declined a seat, noting the chair seat had a dark stain that she feared might not be coffee.

"I heard about the murder," said Ishmael. "I can't say I was shocked. He was a bastard. Everyone in OB knew it."

"Yes, he was a cold-blooded monster. He got what he deserved."

"He's dead. Why do you want to talk to me?"

"I know about Odom's high infection rate. How he used the vacuum method because it's fast and efficient, even though it isn't safe."

"Everybody knew his vacuum method was inappropriate

for a second-trimester termination. I asked him about it once and got my face chewed off."

"That was Odom's way," said Kate. "Did you know one of his patients finally died from sepsis? I was there when they coded her."

"It was bound to happen. That was why I got out. There was no follow-up. Terminate and out the door." Ishmael picked up a rubber ball and started bouncing it off the wall.

"You probably didn't know that he was injecting the uterus with Doxycycline?"

The resident's hand froze. "Are you serious?"

"L & D has pharmacy stock requisitions for the Doxy, but it was never ordered for a patient. And a majority of the abortion women never had a positive pregnancy test again."

Ishmael had a sorrowful look. "Some of his postpartum women came to the clinic. They were having trouble getting pregnant. I thought it was due to infection."

"The old pelvic inflammatory disease diagnosis," said Kate.

"My God, he was practicing Nazi medicine! It makes what he forced us residents do look comparatively modest."

"He forced you? Do you mean he forced you to do vacuum abortions?"

"You don't know about the dates?"

Kate shook her head.

"How about that? There's one crime you overlooked, Miss Palmer. One big, ugly, conspiracy."

Kate settled into the chair, forgetting the stain. She looked into the young resident's eyes, wondering what other evil Leslie Odom had been capable of perpetrating on the poor women of Philadelphia.

The young resident took a long, deep breath and let it out slowly, like a patient undergoing examination by a physician.

"That bastard Odom sometimes forced the residents to alter the due dates."

It took Kate a few seconds to realize what he was talking about. "He was shortening the period of gestation?"

"That's right. He didn't do it often, but once in a while a woman would come to us very late in her pregnancy. We couldn't legally do the abortion because the fetus was *viable*. So he made us advance the date of conception."

"Making the conceptus appear younger," said Kate.

"That's why I left the program. I refused to alter the date of my patient. He was practicing infanticide!"

Chapter Forty-Nine

Lenny had barely said good-bye to Detective Williams when Celeste, the ward clerk, called him to the phone. As soon as he picked up the receiver Big Mary's voice came screeching into his ear.

"They're fucking us in the ass! You got to do something, Lenny, they're fucking us in the ass!"

"Calm down, Mary. Tell me what the problem is."

"They won't turn down the temperature on the driers and the heat's got bad again and we're all about to fall out!"

"Okay. I'm coming right down."

"You comin' down now?"

"I'm coming down now."

"Lenny's coming down!" she yelled out to her coworkers, nearly deafening him.

He hurried down to the basement. When he entered the laundry room, he found the housekeeping supervisor surrounded by five sweaty women, all talking at once. Miss Battle kept trying to make herself heard, but was drowned out.

"Excuse me," Lenny said, stepping into the circle. "What's this I hear about your not turning down the temperature on the driers? I thought we had an agreement."

Miss Battle said, "I wanted to turn them down, Lenny, I really did. But I had to run it by my boss, and he called engineering, and they said we needed the high temperatures to disinfect the linen."

"Doesn't your detergent do that?"

"To some point, yes, but the high heat provides a final killing."

"The heat is killing *us*," said Big Mary. "I'm getting dizzy from the heat. I can't take it no more!"

As the other laundry workers joined in, Lenny told them that anyone who felt dizzy should go to Employee Health.

He said to Miss Battle, "I'll follow up with engineering about the driers. If they won't let you turn them down, you have to move the work to nights."

"I got no problem with that, Lenny, but Human Resources hasn't authorized the shift dif."

"We're not working nights without no bonus!" cried Little Mary.

"I'll talk to Mr. Freely. When he gives you the word, you move everybody to nights until the heat wave breaks. Okay?"

He turned to the laundry workers. "Are you willing to go to nights? Temporarily?"

They all nodded their heads, except for Big Mary. Lenny gave her a questioning look.

"I don't b'lieve it'll help me, Lenny, swear to God. I'm feeling so punk, I don't know if I can work any kind of way."

"I'm taking you to Employee Health." He turned to Miss Battle. "You're okay with her going?"

"Of course."

"Good. I'll walk Mary over. Then I'll call Freely and tell him the laundry workers are turning sick and they have to get the shift dif for nights."

"What if he turns you down?" said Little Mary. "What do we do then?"

"We won't take no for an answer," said Lenny, feeling less confident than his words suggested. But he was running out of ideas, even as the women were running out of patience.

He took Big Mary by the arm and led her to the elevator. He didn't know much about medicine, but he thought that the fact her skin was *dry* and not sweaty was a very bad sign.

Tyrell got up from his chair in the sewing room, tried to fold it, but had difficulty figuring out which way to pull the seat.

"You better stay put a while longer," said Birdie. "You're not ready to go back to work yet."

"I got to get back or my supervisor's gonna want to know where I've been."

"Why don't you drink some coffee?"

"I don't need any coffee. I need to get back."

He gave up trying to fold the chair, put it down, and stumbled to the door. He looked out into the hall, saw nobody around, and walked out, letting the door bump him in the ass.

He was walking toward the maintenance department, weaving a bit and talking to himself, when he nearly collided with the security guard who stood in the middle of the hall.

"Hey! You're in my way!"

The guard leaned forward, sniffed, shook his head, and grabbed Tyrell's arm. "You're coming to the office."

"Fuck," said Tyrell, his mind beginning to clear. "Fuck. Fuck. Fuck."

Lenny brought Big Mary to the Employee Health service, where he told Margie about the working conditions and Mary's dizziness. "Her skin is dry. I thought that was a bad sign so I brought her here."

As Margie placed her fingers lightly on the laundry worker's arm, her eyebrows rose in alarm. "She's hot and she's dry, Lenny. It's heat stroke. Let's get her in an exam room and cool her down. She'll need intravenous hydration."

While Lenny helped Mary lie down on an examination table, the nurse went for ice. Returning, Margie ran cold water into a bucket with ice cubes. She dropped in some towels, got them saturated with ice water, took them out, and handed them to Lenny.

"Wrap these around her arms and legs." Margie pulled down Big Mary's scrub pants. "I'll start an IV."

"Okay." Lenny apologized to Mary for lifting her leg as he wrapped the cold towel around it, but found that she was paying very little attention to him. "Is she okay?" Lenny asked.

Margie waved her hand over Mary's eyes, saw that she was very slow to blink. "She's got a droop. See how her mouth is twisted? She may have had a stroke. I'll get Doctor Primeaux."

While Margie hurried away to notify the physician, Lenny patted Big Mary's shoulder. "Hang in there, Mary."

Doctor Alex Primeaux entered the examination room and nodded to Lenny. "Let's take a look," he said, pulling a penlight from his pocket and shining it in Mary's eyes. "The left eye is a little sluggish, but it's not dilated. The facial asymmetry suggests a left-sided event." He rubbed her breastbone vigorously. "Can you feel that, ma'am? Does that hurt you any?"

"Oww," said Mary. "Stop!"

"She's got fair pain sensation." The doctor placed his fingers in Mary's two hands. "Squeeze my hand, dear. Squeeze real hard."

Mary slowly put pressure on Primeaux's fingers.

"Her right hand is weaker than the left." To Margie he said, "Call the ER and have them send somebody with a stretcher and a portable monitor. She's going to be admitted. And pull her employee file and find out what medical conditions she's got. How old is she?"

Lenny said, "Actually, there's a story behind that question." He explained how Mary had lied about her age in order to get hired, and that only Lenny knew she was ten years older than her stated age.

"Ah see," said Primeaux, his North Carolina accent coming out. "Well, she sure can't keep on working in that laundry at her age. Not in this heat."

"I've tried to get the hospital to switch the laundry staff to nights until the heat wave breaks, but they've been fighting me. They don't want to pay the shift differential."

"Well they're goin' to be paying through the nose for workman's comp if they don't rectify the situation."

"Will you talk to Freely in Human Resources?"

"Just as soon as I get Mary off to the ER, you bet your sweet Aunt Molly I will."

Primeaux wrote out a quick note. By then Margie had the intravenous fluids running and was speaking to the charge nurse in the ER.

"The ER is sending someone right over," she said.

"Very good," said the doctor. "Tell CAT-scan we have an emergency head CT. Be sure and tell them she's an employee."

"Right away," said Margie.

A few moments later, Napoleon, an Emergency Room nurse, and a nurse tech came in with a stretcher and a monitor. They transferred Mary to the stretcher and had her out the door in short order. As she was wheeled away, Mary stared blankly at the ceiling, her mouth half open and slack, her body listless, even as the stretcher bumped along.

Lenny's fear for his coworker was tinged with fury. The hospital *had* to let the laundry workers switch to nights. He was tired of their excuses and their poverty protests. This time there was no room for compromise.

A Race Against Death

★ ★ ★ ★ ★

Moose brought the lunch cart to Seven South. Before handing out the first tray, he went looking for Lenny. Not finding him, he ran to the desk and asked Celeste where Lenny was.

"They had trouble in the laundry again. He went down there to see what was what."

Moose called down to the laundry and was told Lenny had gone to Employee Health.

"Damn," said Moose, hanging up the phone. "I really need to talk to him."

"Is it about the murder?" asked Celeste.

"Yeah. I was looking over the record of Charyse Desir's abortion on the scanner and I realized that one of the names was altered." He showed her the magnified report with the name Johnson circled in red.

"Shoot," said Celeste. "Look at that signature. You can see the original name if you know to look for it."

"It was a black medical student in M-SOC," explained Moose.

"I better page Lenny. You go on handing out the trays. I'll call you when he answers."

Moose returned to the lunch cart and began distributing the trays, all the while listening for Celeste's voice and watching the hallway for Lenny, eager to tell him what he found.

Lenny stood in the Employee Health office while Dr. Primeaux spoke on the phone with Mr. Freely in the Human Resources office. As the doctor was explaining that one woman had been sent to the Emergency Room for heat stroke, Lenny's beeper went off. He saw it was Seven South and decided to call as soon as he finished with Primeaux.

307

Timothy Sheard

"Ah understand from their union steward that there's a
proposal on the table to move the laundry work to the night
shift as long as this heat wave lasts. I can tell you categorically
that that would be in everyone's best interests."

He listened for a moment, then added, "Ah won't have
our people being subjected to prison camp conditions. If you
don't move them to nights, I will be forced to notify the Department of Health."

Primeaux listened for one more moment. "Ah expect to
have your answer before my office closes today." He hung up,
looked at Lenny. "Well, I told him like it is. I don't know
what more I can do."

Lenny thanked the doctor and was about to go back to
Seven South when he thought he might ask his friend for one
more favor. They had fought together to save the jobs of several James Madison employees, and the struggles had forged
a solid friendship.

"Alex, I know you're busy, but can I ask you one more
thing? It's kind of private."

"O' course. Sit down," said Primeaux. "Are you in
trouble?"

"No, nothing like that. I'm investigating Doctor Odom's
murder."

"Ah thought you might," said Primeaux, a twinkle in his
eye. "How can I help?"

"I need to know about Maurice Peltiere. He works in the
messenger service." As he spoke, Lenny saw a look of recog-
nition on Primeaux's face.

"What is it you want to know?"

"Well, he's odd. He's not, I don't know, responsive. It's
like he's wearing a mask. Does he have a condition that makes
him like that, or is it some twisted psycho thing?"

"Is Maurice a suspect?"

"When the police find out he was in love with a young nurse Odom got fired, yeah, he'll be a suspect."

Primeaux tapped a pencil on his desk. "You're asking me to divulge privileged medical information, here. You understand that?"

"Yes. But I'd like to know so I can get the police to eliminate him as a suspect."

The doctor settled back in his beat-up leather chair, folded his arms across his chest, took on a pensive look. "There's no one else in the hospital I would do this for. You know that."

"Don't do it thinking you owe me anything, 'cause you don't."

"Maybe not, but I do want to help you." Primeaux gestured to the door, which Lenny closed. "Whatever I tell you must be in the strictest confidence."

"Of course."

"I won't show you his chart. You wouldn't understand most of it anyway. But I will tell you one thing. Maurice Peltiere has a form of early onset Parkinson's disease."

"The same disease as Mohammed Ali?"

"And Richard Pryor. And many other poor souls," said Primeaux.

In Lenny's mind all the rumors and anecdotes suddenly made sense. "He must be on some heavy medicine."

"He is. Could his medications cause psychological changes that provoke murderous rage? I'm not a psychiatrist, but there are reports of these drugs producing hallucinations, paranoid ideation, and changes in personality."

"So he's not crazy. He just has a disease that makes you a zombie and he takes drugs that make you nuts."

"That's about it."

Lenny looked glum. He slowly stood up and thanked Dr. Primeaux.

"Ah guess my information didn't help him much, did it?"

"I guess not. Still, I'd rather know it now than after they arrest him."

Chapter Fifty

Lenny left the Employee Health Department and made straight for the Human Resources office. His anger rising to a boil, he cursed himself for not having confronted Freely days before—Big Mary might have been spared the stroke—and for holding back for fear the hospital would close the laundry for good.

Maybe the heat has been sapping my strength, he mused. *Like Superman exposed to kryptonite.*

Entering the Human Resources office, he walked briskly past the secretary with the frilly blouse buttoned up to her throat and the face like a KEEP OUT sign. Or maybe a BEWARE OF ATTACK DOG.

"Freely in?" he asked, not pausing to hear her answer.

Rising from her chair, she said, "He's in but you have to make an appoint-"

Lenny gave the door to Freely's office a shove and barged in. He saw Freely, on the phone, stop in mid-sentence.

"This crap has got to stop," said Lenny, striding right up to Freely's big cherry wood desk. He slammed the memo about the drunk-on-duty guidelines on the table, jabbed the middle of the paper with his index finger. "You can't enforce a new rule until you've instructed the staff about it. The *whole* staff. You know that as well as I do."

Freely told the party on the other end he would call him back, hung up the phone, and looked into Lenny's angry face.

"You have a lot of nerve barging in on me, Mr. Moss. I was speaking with Mr. West about this very issue."

"Joe West is doing the drunk test on workers coming back from their lunch break."

"I'm aware of hospital policy and its enforcement," said Freely.

"If you don't cut it out, there's going to be a lot of nasty shit hitting a very big fan."

"The hospital notified the union this morning of our practice. You received a copy of the new guidelines yourself."

"It's not my job to in-service everybody. Yes, I'll raise it at the next general membership meeting. And yes, I'll tell people on a case by case basis. But it's *your* job to see that *everyone* is informed of a new rule *before* you enforce it. It's a little thing called 'due process.' Remember?"

"Don't lecture me about the law, Mister Moss. Our attorney has reviewed the practice thoroughly. We have a solid legal right to identify and remove from service anyone who is impaired due to drugs or alcohol."

"There's something else you have to deal with. The laundry. The temperature is up again. It's over a hundred and five."

"I received a call from Doctor Primeaux in Employee Health, and I'm very concerned. But you have to understand, PECO has cut voltage across the city. You cannot expect the hospital to perform magic. The city is facing an energy crisis."

"Then shut down the laundry," said Lenny. "Give them the shift differential and put them on the night shift until the heat wave breaks."

"That's a very costly proposal."

"So is paying out workman's comp. One of the laundry

workers was taken to the ER. It looks like she had a stroke. *From working under inhumane conditions!*"

"I certainly hope she recovers," said Freely.

"I have temperature recordings that go back weeks. If you don't give the laundry workers a break, I'll file them with the Department of Health. There'll be an investigation. Publicity."

"Don't threaten me. It will only blow up in your face."

"Oh, yeah? How about this? Your former salaried employee, Dr. Leslie Odom, was sterilizing women while performing abortions in your fucking Labor and Delivery!"

Freely stared at Lenny. "That's impossible."

"I have irrefutable evidence that he was injecting them with a drug that made them sterile. If this gets out to the press, there's going to be a lot of angry women suing you for millions of dollars."

Freely removed a lavender handkerchief from his jacket pocket and wiped his brow. "You are confident in your information?"

"Totally confident."

"I will have to ask the Chairman of the Obstetrics department to look into the matter. In a confidential internal review, of course."

"Good," said Lenny.

"If you will give me your word that you will not release any information of any sort regarding this alleged sterilizing practice, I will ask Joe West to suspend the alcohol testing until the notices are distributed with the employee checks and reviewed at the monthly staff meetings."

"I want it stopped."

"Out of the question. But I will restrict security to testing individuals who are grossly impaired."

"Okay. What about switching the laundry work to nights, with a shift dif?"

"I'll review the situation with the payroll department. I'm confident that we can come up with the differential for your people as long as the heat wave lasts."

"No shutting down the laundry and privatizing it?"

Freely wiped his brow again. "Not in the foreseeable future. No."

"Deal."

"Now if we can all get back to work," said Freely. "This heat wave is making everyone a little crazy. If you knew how many—"

Suddenly, the lights in Freely's office dimmed and went out. The sunlight streaming through the blinds cast striped shadows across his desk.

"What in the world," he said.

"It's PECO," said Lenny. "They must be having a power failure."

A second later the overhead light began to slowly brighten.

"Thank God the backup generators have kicked in," said Freely.

"I better get back to my ward," said Lenny.

He hurried out the door. In the corridor, only one in four small lights spaced far apart illuminated the hall. The stairwell was dim as well, the glowing strips along the wall leading upward. The air was stifling as he made his way up to the seventh floor. Without the air-conditioning the wards would soon become an oven, and the patients, poached.

Chapter Fifty-One

Cleopatra was in a lecture hall, listening to a talk on risk factors for stroke, when the lights flickered and went out. The digital projector's white bulb faded, the image of the slide on the screen dissolved. The hall was as dark as a movie theater.

When the power came back, the hall was only dimly lit; the projector had no power, and the audio system for the lecturer was out as well.

"I suppose we will have to cancel the lecture," the professor told them. "Watch the bulletin board for the date to be rescheduled."

Lincoln leaned close to Cleopatra and said, "I'm gonna go to the gym and work out."

"The air-conditioning won't be on."

"That's okay. I'll sweat out my troubles."

"I'm going to the office. I have an article to finish for the M-SOC newsletter."

Lincoln's face sank with worry. "Do you *have* to release the statement about how Odom sterilized his patients?"

"Of course."

"But the police are getting ready to arrest you! Maybe you should lie low for a while and see if this mess blows over."

"Even if I have to spend the rest of my life in prison, I am going to see that the whole world knows of Odom's butchery and the hospital's complicity."

"I'm afraid for you, baby."

She threw back her head and laughed. "Dear, sweet, Lincoln. When the racists threaten, you have to show strength or they'll tie you up and hang you from a tree."

As she walked out of the lecture hall, she added, "I'm going to print the letter from the Dean asking me to leave in the next M-SOC newsletter."

Lincoln watched her walk confidently out of the hall, a radiant smile on her face. She was a queen going into battle, bathed in fire and passion, anticipating glory. He wished he had her strength and her conviction. All he could do was support her when she faced the punishment that came crashing down upon her, as he knew it would.

The ICU was a cacophony of alarms and anxious voices as the many electrical devices shrieked in response to the loss of electric power. The six ventilators were whooping like cranes, and the heart monitors were clanging like church bells. Crystal, the charge nurse, was calling to the other nurses and aides to check that all the ventilators were plugged in the red emergency outlets. All but one was properly powered. The staff soon had the ventilator alarms reset and all machines operating properly.

Cardiac alarms were silenced and a dialysis machine was restarted. The over-the-bed lights were without power and the fluorescents in the ceiling were dim. Gary suggested opening the blinds. Crystal smiled at the simplicity of the solution and helped him bare the windows.

Rupert Darling watched the frantic activity with interest and awe. He had always believed that the majority of people working in the hospital were lazy or ignorant or both. The whirlwind of purposeful activity surprised him.

When Gary returned to his bed, he said, "I'm gonna have to eat my words, son."

"How's that, Mister Darling?"

"You people really *do* know what you're doing."

"Some of the time, sir. Some of the time."

Inside the security office, the man at the radio was receiving a chaotic burst of calls from the officers in the field. Hearing the confusion, West grabbed the microphone and barked into it, "Take your finger off the button and shut up." Once the airwave was quiet, he began yelling out instructions.

The guard about to administer the breathalyzer test to Tyrell was uncertain what to do next. He realized chaos was erupting around the hospital, but West hadn't told him to leave Tyrell and take up a post.

Seeing the indecision, Tyrell said, "I don't know, man, but I don't think the backup generator is up to the load."

"How's that?" asked the guard.

"See how low the light is in here? The voltage is way below standard. They'll burn out all the computers in the hospital if they can't raise their amperage."

"For real?"

"Fuck, yeah. I gotta get down to engineering. I'm their number-one guy on power generation."

"I don't know . . ." The guard looked from the breathalyzer machine to the dim light. "Mr. West told me to give you the test."

"If every fucking computer in the hospital crashes, you'll have a lot more to worry about than an engineer who had a lousy beer on his lunch break. Remember Y-2-K?"

"Sure," said the guard, baffled by Tyrell's explanation, but not wanting to look like a dummy. After chewing his lip for a few seconds, he opened the door and gestured to Tyrell. "I should be out there helping anyway. Go on."

Tyrell, sober and focused, hurried out of the office.

* * * * *

Regis opened the thick, insulated door to the big fridge, stepped in, and checked the thermometer. It was thirty-eight degrees Fahrenheit. Perfect. He listened for the sound of the fan to be sure that the unit was receiving proper power. The pitch of the fan told him it was running smoothly.

The young morgue attendant was relieved that the bodies wouldn't end up lying in a hot room. The stink that would rise from the bodies would be unbearable.

Little Mary was dumping a laundry bag into one of the big washing machines when the lights went out, pitching the room in darkness.

"What the fuck," she said.

A few seconds later the lights came back, only dim. She looked around the room.

"It's a power failure," said another woman. "That stupid PECO probably let their system get overloaded."

The women gathered in the middle of the room. As the supervisor came out of her office, one of the women said, "What do we do?"

"I don't know," she said. "I suppose it depends on how long it takes for the electric company to restore the power."

"The washing machines and driers don't run on emergency power," said Little Mary. "There's no way they can get them going any time soon."

"I guess that's so," said Mrs. Battle.

"We should get the day off," said another woman. "We can't wash any laundry without power."

"Less'n you want us to find some old washboards and buckets and have us rub the sheets on them," said another, raising howls from the others.

"I can't authorize giving you the rest of the day off."

A Race Against Death

"But it's suffocating down here," said Little Mary. "The air-conditioning's out. I'm gonna have an asthma attack and die because you can't authorize me breathing fresh air? I don't think so!"

The others all expressed health problems that were being exacerbated by the heat.

"Let's all go to Employee Health," said a woman.

They looked at the supervisor, who shrugged her shoulders. "I'm not staying down here," she said.

The women linked arms and walked out, laughing and shouting and eager to be in the open air. It was just a little past noon. The hours remaining on their shift promised freedom form the laundry, and the hospital was paying.

Chapter Fifty-Two

After leaving Freely in the Human Resources office, Lenny found the nurses and aides on his ward hurrying from room to room, checking the patients. The air was still and suffocating. The big pedestal fan stood silent at the end of the corridor.

He asked Betty what was going on.

"They're checking to see if anything needs to be plugged in the emergency outlets." She mopped her face with a towel. "The Lord knows they best get the air-conditioning running soon. Hard as it is to work in this kind of heat, the patients will be falling out before too long."

"Let's see how much ice is in the machine. We can help give out ice water."

They went to the pantry. Lenny opened the top of the ice-making machine. It was one of the new types, without a large reservoir of ice.

"It's not much," he said. "Let's take what we can."

As he was scooping the ice out of the machine into a bucket, Celeste walked in. "Lenny! Moose was looking for you. Didn't you get my page?"

"Shit, I forgot. I was in Employee Health with one of the laundry workers, and then I had to deal with Freely."

"Moose had the report from Charyse Desir's abortion. He scanned the signatures on a computer, and you could tell one of the signatures was faked." She handed him the copy.

"Really?" In a flash, the name of the resident Kate had

been unable to find came to mind. All at once, Lenny knew who killed Odom and who introduced the deadly E. coli into Charyse Desir's body. "It was Johnson, wasn't it? He altered 'Jones' to look like 'Johnson.' "

"Uh-huh. You know how sloppy doctors' signatures are. That's what fooled everybody."

"Here," Lenny said, handing the bucket and scoop to Betty. "I've got to see somebody about a crime."

"You goin' to tell the cops?" asked Celeste. " 'Cause the killer is still a hero to me, and a whole lot of other black folks."

"I've got to call the M-SOC office," Lenny said, hurrying to the phone. He dialed the number.

"Yes?" said a low-pitched woman's voice.

"This is Lenny Moss. Can I speak with Cleopatra?"

"I am she."

"I need to talk to you. Will you be in the office for a while?"

There was a moment of silence. Lenny wondered if she would hang up on him.

"What is it concerning?"

"It's about the investigation we're both working on."

"I really don't see the use of—"

"Did you know that Odom was sterilizing women when he performed his abortions?"

"I have always suspected that he—?"

"He injected a drug into their womb. Doxy something or other. That's why so few of them ever got pregnant again."

"This is extremely useful information."

"That's not all. I have something else I need to tell you about. Is Lincoln with you?"

"No, he's gone to the gym."

"Good. I'll be over as fast as I can."

Hanging up, he hurried to the housekeeping locker and retrieved his copy of Charyse Desir's chart, then left the ward. He wanted to lay out all the facts before Cleopatra. After that, they could decide what, if anything, to do with them.

Kate was half listening to the Fellow report to the Attending on a new patient with Graves's disease. The Attending had not missed a beat when the power failed. Rounds were sacred. Not even acts of God could interrupt them.

Her mind turned to an issue that had nagged her all day. The students in M-SOC didn't have access to the data Dr. Auginello had given her about the fertility of Odom's patients. Without that data, they wouldn't have the sterility of the women as a motive for killing Odom.

The Fellow cleared his throat. Kate found his gaze on her.

"I'm sorry," she said. "My mind was somewhere else."

Frowning, the Fellow answered his own question as he led the team away. As the group walked along, Kate remembered that Cleopatra and Lincoln both volunteered at the North Philly free clinic. That would involve caring for the women who underwent abortions at James Madison. In time those women would ask why they weren't conceiving. The clinic would run tests.

They would see the pattern. Post-abortion patients . . . infertility.

But would Cleopatra's fury over such heinous acts drive her to murder? Wouldn't she use the information to advance her cause?

Then a chilling thought struck Kate. It could be Lincoln, the loyal helpmate. Hard to believe, he was such a caring young man, but any man had his limits. Sterilizing women might have pushed him past his own.

Kate broke from the group of physicians and students.

"Where are you going, Miss Palmer?" the Fellow called after her.

"To turn in a murderer."

Lenny made his way along the corridor of the medical school basement, which was lit by small lights near the floor, like the walkway of a theater when the house lights have been dimmed. He found the door to the M-SOC office, knocked once, and entered. With no windows or emergency lighting, the student office was very dark, illuminated only by a dim glow from a laptop computer on a desk and a small battery-powered lamp.

A dark figure was seated at the desk, her face backlit by the lamp. Lenny was struck by the regal outline of Cleopatra's face—the high cheekbones, the broad forehead, the strong chin and forceful mouth.

"Mr. Lenny Moss," she said, making the name sound almost like a compliment.

"That's me," said Lenny.

"Many of the women in the hospital that I speak with talk of you," she said. "I would not agree to this meeting were it not for their praise."

He pulled out a chair from another desk and sat, facing her. It was as dark and intimate as a nightclub. He decided that the best way to win her trust was to lay all his cards on the table. From what he'd heard, Cleopatra liked people who were direct.

"I guess you didn't know that a high number of women that Odom did his abortions on never got pregnant again."

"What I do and do not know is not your concern," she said. "Tell me what evidence you have."

He explained how the Labor and Delivery Suite stocked an antibiotic called Doxycycline, but it was never ordered for a patient. Nevertheless, month after month, the drug was re-ordered for floor stock.

"It's apparently okay to use if it's diluted," said Lenny. "But if you inject it full strength, it can tear up whatever it comes in contact with."

"Yes, Doxy is sometimes used to create an inflammatory response. In some settings the inflammation is therapeutic."

"That's what I understand."

"And you believe that Odom injected the drug directly into the uterus during the abortion?"

"I don't have any witnesses or anything like that, but the circumstantial evidence is pretty strong."

"It fits his genocidal practices," said Cleopatra. "Abort as many black babies as you can, prevent conception after-ward." For the first time an edge of weariness came into her voice. "I expect the police will arrest me shortly. The hospital has tried to suppress my voice for four years. They are deter-mined to eliminate me."

"I know the feeling," said Lenny. "Being on the short end of the stick, I mean. But you don't have to worry about them arresting you."

"Oh? Why not?"

"I know you didn't kill Odom."

"How can you be so sure? I am a dangerous woman. The Dean is afraid of me."

"Your *ideas* are dangerous, but you couldn't have killed Odom because the murder was committed by someone else."

"Who?"

Lenny had to admit she kept a beautiful poker face. He was sure that she knew the answer to her own question. The one thing he doubted was whether she knew why.

Chapter Fifty-Three

Moose was at the Seven South nursing station, standing beside Patience. He had gone up and down the ward, looking for Lenny. He dialed Lenny's pager, added a "911" to the number to be called, hung up, and waited.

Turning to Patience, he said, "Lenny was supposed to meet you here when his shift was up. Right?"

"That's right. My car's overheating. He was going to take me home."

"Betty's punched out, so we can't ask her."

"It's not like him to forget an appointment. If he says he'll meet somebody someplace, he's there. He never forgets."

"I wonder if his car is still in the lot," said Moose. "Sandy's covering the parking lot. I'll see if he can check it out." Moose picked up the receiver and asked the operator to connect him with the parking lot attendant. Then he asked the attendant to put Sandy on the phone.

Moose explained to the old guard that they were trying to learn if Lenny had left the hospital. "Could you check and see if his car is still in the employee lot? He likes to park it under the trees."

"I know that old Buick," said Sandy. "I never did understand why he's willing to leave his car where the birds can shit all over it. Hold on and I'll check it out. Where're you at?"

"I'm up on Seven South."

"Call you right back."

Moose hung up the phone. "All we can do is wait, I guess," he said.

Patience took another look up and down the hall, hoping to see her man coming toward her, and feeling a rising sense of fear that he was in trouble.

In the M-SOC office Lenny looked into Cleopatra's dark, defiant eyes. "I think you know who killed Dr. Odom," he said.

"You must fancy yourself a mind reader," said Cleopatra.

"No, I don't read minds, just the evidence. Lincoln Jones left the library in time to kill Odom. You know he left because you were seated right beside him."

"Even if Lincoln did leave me for a short time, it doesn't prove anything. Why would he kill Odom? Odom was worth more to M-SOC alive than dead. We were about to launch a whole campaign against him and the hospital. His murder pulled the ground out from under us."

"I know that," said Lenny.

"Then your suspicions are groundless."

"On the contrary." Lenny reached into his pocket and took out the report of Charyse Desir's abortion. He handed it to Cleopatra. "You didn't get a chance to see the report from the operating room. If you did, you might have recognized the signature right away."

Cleopatra's gaze fell on the signature of the assistants. She squinted in the dim light, then picked up the lamp and shone it directly on the paper.

"You thought he was working in the main OR that morning," said Lenny.

"He works there every Saturday."

"You didn't realize that sometimes they pulled him to the

operating room in the Labor and Delivery Suite. I made the same mistake, even though I've cleaned both areas more than once."

"Good God almighty," said Cleopatra as the depth of Lincoln's guilt sank in. "He assisted with the abortion that killed Charyse Desir."

Tears glistened on her ebony cheeks. Her hand trembled as she put the paper down on the desk, along with the lamp.

"I didn't doubt that Lincoln had killed him," she said. "I understand the castration was done with great precision." A smile began to form on her lips, before it became a look of despair. "Will you be notifying the police?"

"That's the tough part, isn't it? The cops are bound to charge you as an accomplice, if not concealing evidence or hindering prosecution. I don't want you arrested. That would be a travesty."

"I agree. If they charge Lincoln, they will charge me as well."

"I don't want any of my coworkers charged, either. Giving Lincoln up seems like the only way to prevent that."

"And if no one is charged? If the case just remains open and unsolved?"

"Let the guilty one get off?"

"There are many shades of guilt, aren't there, Mr. Moss? Levels upon levels."

"Street justice."

"Street justice, people power, divine retribution. It wasn't entirely a selfish crime."

"I had the same thought," said Lenny. "I could walk away and forget the whole thing. But how do I know he won't do it again?"

"You think that killing may become a habit?"

327

"The thought occurred to me."

The door opened without a knock, and Lincoln Jones walked into the room, his gym bag in his hand. His dark face was cast in shadows by the pale lantern light.

"Lenny Moss. It's good to see you again." He stepped up to Cleopatra to give her a kiss. She turned away from him. He pulled back, looked down, saw a piece of white paper on the desk.

Cleopatra reached for the paper, but Lincoln was faster. He snatched it out from under her hand, held it up to the light. He saw his altered signature and knew the game was up.

Cool and confident as any surgeon with a scalpel approaching an intact stretch of skin, he placed his gym bag on the table and turned to her. "Sorry, baby. You know how it is."

"How could you, Lincoln? Helping that butcher!"

"You did a surgical rotation; you know the drill. In the OR the surgeon is God. You do what he tells you *when* he tells you. There's no room for debate."

"He was a racist butcher! He sterilized black women!"

"True. But he had great hands."

"Killing him was not the solution," said Cleopatra. "I was going to expose how the system *created* him. How the hospital *protected* him. I was gunning for bigger game."

"She'd be exposing how the hospital made millions of dollars in racist profits from Odom," said Lenny.

"So I took a shortcut. But I did it for us. For M-SOC."

"That is a lie," said Cleopatra. "You killed to protect yourself. *From me!*"

Moose picked up the receiver at the Seven South nursing station before the phone had completed its first ring. "Talk to me."

"It's me, Sandy. Lenny's car is still in the lot. There's no way he left the hospital."

"Shit," said Moose.

"Is my boy in trouble? What's going on?"

Moose quickly told him that Patience was supposed to meet Lenny at the end of the shift, but when she got to Seven South he wasn't there.

"Did you check the laundry?"

"Already called them."

"The housekeeping locker?"

"I went there first thing."

"What was the last thing he did?" asked Sandy.

"I know he was gonna argue with Freely in Human Resources over the laundry. I left word up here with Celeste that one of the M-SOC medical students was probably Odom's killer."

"Cleopatra Edwards?"

"No. Her friend, Lincoln Jones. Lincoln helped with the abortion that killed Charyse Desir. He didn't want anybody to know."

"No, shit," said Sandy. "Well if Lenny knew that, you got to believe he went to the student office."

"That's where I was going next."

"I'll meet you," said Sandy, and hung up.

Moose and Patience ran to the stairwell and hurried down. With their steps echoing in the hot, dim stairwell, it seemed as if the stairwell would go on forever. Both of them felt a growing panic, hoping that Lenny wasn't foolish enough to confront a killer alone.

As Cleopatra and Lincoln argued over Lincoln's guilt, Lenny began to inch for the door. He took another step, saw Lincoln nonchalantly unzip the gym bag. A stab of fear ripped through Lenny; his heart began beating madly. He took another step.

Reaching into the bag, Lincoln stepped between Lenny and the door. "You are a lot smarter than you look, Moss."

"Excuse me?"

"You put up a good façade. That simple custodian bit is very effective. But I knew as soon as I met you that you were smart as a whip. Nothing gets by you."

"That's very flattering," said Lenny. "But I'm really just a simple guy." He watched Lincoln's hand come out of the bag. "I eat peanut butter and jelly sandwiches." The hand held a stubby pistol. It was small and snug in his large hand. Lenny understood why Lincoln was planning on going into surgery. "I watch cartoons and The Three Stooges."

"Stop right there," said Lincoln." I don't want to shoot you in the office."

"I prefer a back alley, myself. Or a remote riverbank. You could always—"

"Lincoln Jones! Put that gun down."

"I can't do that, baby."

"But you can be a fool and go to prison for the rest of your life."

"Don't forget, we have the death penalty in Pennsylvania," said Lenny.

For reasons beyond his understanding, Lenny suddenly felt calm. The gun in Lincoln's hand would either kill him or stay silent. In a strange Kafkaesque way, he felt free to say and do whatever he wanted. The killer's inner demons would decide the outcome.

Lenny hoped it wouldn't hurt when the bullet struck him. Even as a kid he hated getting shots.

Chapter Fifty-Four

Staring at the pistol in Lincoln's hand, Lenny felt strangely calm. *This must be the Zen of dying,* he thought. He spoke in a matter-of-fact voice. "You know you might have gotten away with killing Odom, you had a pretty good alibi. And your fiancée was probably going to do the time. But are you sure you want to push your luck and make it a double nickel?"

"A what?"

"A double homicide. See, even with your confession to me, you have a shot at being found not guilty of Odom's murder, excuse the pun."

"He's right, Lincoln. Odom was a monster and that makes you a hero. But shooting an innocent hospital worker will not go down so well with a jury."

"It's all right, baby. I've got an escape plan. I've got an open ticket on a plane to Senegal. Once I get there, I'll disappear into the countryside. I'll practice medicine just like a certified physician. I'll make out like a bandit."

"Unless the police pick you up at the airport," said Lenny.

The door to the M-SOC office opened and Kate Palmer rushed in. She saw Lincoln holding a gun pointed at Lenny and Cleopatra standing beside Lincoln.

"Hi, Kate," said Lenny. "Did you bring the chips and dip?"

"Nobody told me it was a party."

"Lincoln," said Cleopatra, "are you going to shoot Kate as

well? Is that the kind of man you are? We're doctors. We save lives. We don't wipe them out."

"I don't want to shoot anybody," said Lincoln. "I just want to practice medicine somewhere."

Cleopatra stepped in front of Lincoln. "You'll have to kill me, too. I won't cover for you the way I did for Odom's murder. You'll be on your own."

"But baby . . ."

"Listen to her," said Lenny. "You ought to quit while you're ahead."

"What's that supposed to mean?"

"It's simple," said Lenny. "Right now you're a hero who killed a vicious racist. If you stay with that you'll be bigger than Mumia."

"You think?"

"Of course."

"I don't want to go to jail."

"Martin did," said Lenny.

"So did Malcolm," Cleopatra added.

"They faced the dogs and the water cannons and the cattle prods," said Lenny. "I know you can face the possibility of a little jail time. And you being a doctor, you'll end up in one of those country club joints that doesn't even have walls."

"Yeah, but if I go to jail, I won't get to finish my last year of med school."

"We'll start a campaign to let you study in jail," said Cleopatra. "You'll be in all the papers and on TV."

"All the students will support a petition," said Kate. "The school will have to give you credit. The fourth year is just electives, anyway."

"You can still come out a hero," said Cleopatra, her voice sweet and cajoling. "But only if you give me the gun."

She held out her hand, her long, slender fingers open, her eyes sparkling in the faint light.

"I might need it to get away."

"What will you do, rob a gas station on the way to the airport?" said Cleopatra. "Give—me—the—gun."

Lincoln looked into her eyes.

"It's all right, Linc," she said gently. "I'll be behind you the whole time."

"For real?"

"You know I will. We can get married before the trial, if you like."

"I'd like that." Slowly, he lowered his hand, pointing the gun at the floor. "I'd really like that."

Cleopatra stepped forward and pried his fingers apart, as though removing an instrument from a fresh corpse. She eased the gun out of his slack fingers and handed it to Lenny. Then she drew her hand back and slapped Lincoln hard across his face. The blow spun his head to the side. Tears formed in his eyes.

"You are without a doubt the most ignorant, selfish, useless piece of crap I have ever had the misfortune to know."

Lenny grinned as he held the gun pointed up at the ceiling. He felt a surge of anger at Lincoln for threatening to kill him, but decided it was better to let Cleopatra inflict a little street justice.

She grabbed his shirt and pulled him close to her. "I should have let the police have you when they interviewed me in the Dean's office. What a fool I was, feeling any loyalty toward you. Because you're a brother. Because you love me."

"I do love you, baby."

"You only love yourself and your high-stepping attitude. You can't fool me. As soon as you finished your residency, you were bound for a private practice and the big bucks. A new Lexus and a house in the suburbs. No more volunteering at Africa House. Uh-uh. You were bound for bigger things."

"Honest to God, Cleopatra, I'm not like that. I would have stuck with you through everything. The free clinics and all."

She released his shirt and pushed him backward. He struck the desk and stood paralyzed, not knowing what to do.

The door to the office opened. Sandy came through the entrance, followed by Moose and Patience. The little office was now crowded with people. Lincoln looked at them, dazed and confused.

"Give me your hands," said Sandy.

Like a little boy obeying a grown-up, Lincoln held his hands out in front of him. The old guard pulled the handcuffs from his belt and snapped them over Lincoln's wrists.

"Sorry, son. I got to arrest you for the murder of Leslie Odom. I'm glad as hell you killed the son of a bitch, but I still got to hand you over."

Lenny asked what he should do with the gun.

"Joe West likes guns, give it to him," said Sandy. He was leading his prisoner into the hall when the lights in the ceiling came back on.

"Glory hallelujah," he said. "It looks like PECO got their act together for once."

"Or the hospital has put another generator on line," said Moose.

"Either way, it sure makes our job a lot easier. I can't be running up and down those stairs with the elevator out of service. I'm way too old for that."

They walked to the elevator. Moose pushed the button. Everyone was relieved to see the button light up and hear the machinery start up as the elevator car began descending.

Once Sandy had Lincoln marching off to the security office, the others gathered outside the medical school.

"Jesus Christ!" said Lenny. "I am never, *never* getting mixed up in one of these investigations ever again."

Moose chuckled. "You love it. Don't kid me."

Patience put an arm around Lenny. "You are not bulletproof, you know that?"

"Aw, were you worried about me?"

"Yes, I was worried. You promised to take the kids to the movies on Friday."

"Do you hear this, Moose? Is this what I get for sticking my neck out?"

Moose just chuckled and looked at his friends, happy everyone was all right. "I don't know about you, but I could use something very cold to drink."

Without further argument they all left the hospital, crossed Germantown Avenue, and headed for the Cave.

Chapter Fifty-Five

Moose poured Lenny another beer from the pitcher. He raised his glass in a salute. Patience, Celeste and Birdie held up their glasses of Asti Spumante. Kate held up her Manhattan. Sandy lifted his whiskey and soda, Gary Tuttle, a Coke. Regis picked the wedge of lime from the mouth of his Corona and lofted the bottle.

"To us!" said Moose. "The heart and the soul of James Madison!"

Cheers rang out around the table.

Regis rubbed his arms with the wedge of lime. When Lenny asked him if he was using a new cologne, Regis explained that the formaldehyde smell in the morgue was the only down side to his work.

"It's a great job," he said. "Nobody bothers me down there, and the stiffs hardly ever complain."

"What do you mean, hardly ever?" asked Birdie.

"Sometimes, when we first manipulate the body, there's a rush of air from their stomach and lungs that rushes over their vocal cords. They make a weird sound, sort of an oooohh-ahhh. It's not really a complaint. We say it's a dead man talking."

"That is so gr-ross," said Patience.

"Yeah, I guess it is," said Regis.

With full electric power, the air-conditioning system in the bar had the room deliciously cool. The bartender had the evening news channel on the television. He called out, "Hey, guys, check this shit out!"

The headline read: JAMES MADISON MEDICAL STUDENT ARRESTED FOR KILLING RACIST DOCTOR. The announcer promised a full story at eleven, hinting that questions of guilt and innocence were complex and controversial.

"See, you were right," said Moose. "The media's gonna make him a hero."

"I don't know if a jury will let him walk on that," said Lenny.

"I believe the young man will do pretty good for himself on the stand," said Sandy. "The jury will buy his story that he did it for his people."

"Sandy's right," said Regis. "When the defense lawyer shows slides of the fetal remnants stuck to the womb, the jury will give Lincoln Jones a medal. No way they find him guilty."

"In that case, the DA might let him plead to a lesser offense," said Lenny.

"Are you sure you don't want to go to law school?" Kate held her glass out to Patience. "He would make a great lawyer, don't you think?" she said and clinked her glass with Patience's.

"Moss-sh for the defense!" said Patience. "Justice for all!"

"Are you loaded?" asked Lenny, leaning closer to Patience, his thick brows arching in delight.

"It's the boobles," explained Patience. "They go to my head."

Celeste poured the women more wine. "You think Lincoln Jones knew Odom was sterilizing his patients?"

"Remember, he volunteered at Africa House," said Kate. "He would have cared for several of Odom's victims."

337

"But he didn't know *how* Odom sterilized the women," said Lenny. "Kate found that out."

"The midwife pointed me in the right direction," said Kate. She sipped her Manhattan and reflected on the events. "Maybe we shouldn't have taken on the case. The cops would never have figured it out."

"Probably they would've arrested Cleopatra," said Moose.

"There was very little evidence against her," said Kate.

"That never stopped 'em before," Moose pointed out.

Celeste twisted her gold necklace around her finger. "Maybe Lincoln Jones had lots of good reasons to whack Odom, but it's all bull. He was afraid of a woman's anger, pure and simple. That's why he killed Odom."

"I agree with Celeste," said Birdie. "He was afraid his fiancée would find out he was helping kill black babies. If she did, *he* would have been the one with his balls cut off and not Odom."

"Lincoln Jones was a punk," said Patience.

"I agree," said Lenny. "Racial justice had nothing to do with it."

"I wonder if he knew about the altered due dates," said Kate.

All heads turned to look at her. She told them about her conversation with the OB resident at Women and Children's who'd quit the program at James Madison because he wouldn't agree to falsify the womens' due dates.

"That's what Mai Loo warned Odom about," said Lenny. "That was why he had her fired. He was pulling the same crap in Saudi Arabia, aborting fetuses that were viable, and she knew about it."

"That's something you never forget," said Birdie, looking at Moose and recalling the time that she'd miscarried their first baby. They had both worried she would never get another chance for a child.

"How is Mai Loo doing?" asked Patience.

"She has a temporary job with an agency," said Lenny. "And a lawyer. The hospital is going to be on the defensive when the whole Odom story comes out. I think they'll deal."

"I hope so," said Patience. "She's a nice kid."

"Hey!" said Lenny, turning to Patience. "I forgot to tell you. Mai Loo called and left a message on my answering machine. Remember when I got stuck with that needle on my floor last week?"

"Yeah," said Patience.

"She remembered where it came from. The night nurse used it to get air into an IV bottle."

"She was venting it to help the fluid run out," said Gary. "It's against hospital policy, but we do it all the time."

"Mai Loo remembered the night nurse had complained about giving the medication late because she couldn't get it to run until she stuck the needle in the bottle."

"Then the needle was never used on a patient," said Patience.

"That's right."

She leaned close to Lenny and kissed him on the cheek. "Then you might get lucky tonight," she said. "My sister took the kids."

Exclamations and whistles arose from around the table.

"There's one thing I don't understand," said Celeste. "Was it Odom or Lincoln Jones who contaminated the instruments in the delivery room with that killer bacteria?"

"It was Lincoln," said Kate. "He did an Infectious Disease rotation the month that the last case of E. coli o-one-five-seven was treated. He knew where the isolate was stored, and he knew the access code to the Microbiology Lab."

"Three, two, one," said Moose.

"Right."

Lenny held out his glass for another beer. "I don't think he wanted her to *die* from the infection. He probably planned on her becoming critically ill and coming to the hospital. That would make Odom's guilt even greater."

Lenny saw Cleopatra approach. She had a leather briefcase tucked under her arm.

"Hi," she said. "We retained a lawyer for Lincoln. He's depressed about being in jail, but they're treating him very well. He's already something of a celebrity."

"I told you the boy would make out all right," said Sandy.

"How are you doing?" asked Lenny. "Any fallout for you?"

"So far the hospital has left me alone. I'll be okay."

"Can you join us for a drink?" asked Patience. "I know you don't feel like celebrating, but . . ."

"No, thank, you. I have too much to do."

Cleopatra reached her hand out to Lenny. She let her fingers touch his rough cheek. "You're a good man, Lenny Moss," she said and winked at Patience.

"For a custodian?"

A smile lifted her lips. Then she bid the group good-bye.

Lenny suggested they order dinner. Cheese steaks and hamburgers were requested, the pitcher of beer and glasses of Asti Spumante refilled. Gary ordered a white wine, which drew a cheer from the others.

While they were waiting for dinner, Tyrell Hardy came sauntering into the Cave. He stepped up to the group, a bottle of beer in his hand, and told them how he escaped taking the breathalyzer test by convincing the guard that he was needed to check on the hospital's backup generator.

"You were born under a lucky star," said Lenny.

"Don't I know it," Tyrell replied, and went off to take his place at the bar.

Patience rested her head on Lenny's shoulder. "I'm so glad Lincoln didn't shoot you," she said.

"Me, too."

"You promised to oil the hinges on the doors. Half my doors squeak when you open them."

"That's my monitoring system to tell when the kids are moving about the house," said Lenny. "I need to know if they're approaching the bedroom."

He kissed the top of her head and took another swallow of beer. He was hungry and horny and happy, surrounded by friends and in love with a wonderful woman.

Chapter Fifty-Six

Lenny sat in a corner of the cafeteria, close to the vending machines, and watched as Kate Palmer strode up to him. He said nothing while she pulled out a chair and perched on the edge. He remained silent while she dug out a sheet of paper from her knapsack and slid it toward him.

"He wasn't involved in her delivery," Kate said. "The Attending was Dr. Basmajian. He was assisted by Dr. Rudder."

"Thank God," said Lenny, releasing a breath he hadn't realized he'd been holding.

"As far as the operative report and the physician's progress notes go, the delivery that Patience had for her last child was completely uneventful."

"Yeah, but she hasn't been able to get pregnant ever since. Coincidence?"

Kate looked into Lenny's eyes. With a reluctant hand she withdrew a second sheet of paper and slid it toward him.

"Because you told me that she hasn't been able to conceive ever since her last child was born, I got the midwife to pull the delivery records for the day that Patience delivered. And . . ."

Lenny felt a tightness in his chest. He was holding his breath again.

"The records show that Odom *did* deliver a baby that day. There's no evidence that he even went into her delivery room."

"But he was there. He could have injected that Doxy stuff into her."

"The times don't coincide perfectly, but he was in the hospital. That much we can say for certain."

"Shit." Lenny stared into his coffee cup.

"You're going to tell her, aren't you?"

"I don't know."

"I strongly urge you not to keep secrets. That's what killed my last relationship. And it was *me* keeping things from *him*."

"I guess . . ."

"There's no proof that he ever went near her," said Kate.

"I don't believe in coincidences. I've heard too many lies."

Kate put a hand gently on his. "There's still a lot we can do for her, even if she did receive the Doxycycline. Fallopian tubes can be repaired, eggs can be harvested and fertilized in vitro. There are many options."

"I know all that. And I'm actually very optimistic about her chances for conceiving. With *me*, which should produce a pretty weird kid. It's just the thought of that racist animal screwing with her insides that makes me sick."

"I know, Lenny. I know."

That afternoon, as Lenny drove Patience home, Malcolm and Takia in the backseat, several large, wet drops landed on the front windshield.

"Hey, it's raining," cried Takia. "Are we gonna wash the car?"

"Not today," said Lenny, laughing.

"But you always say we get a free rinse when it rains," said Malcolm.

"We're all going for a walk in the rain, instead."

"Mom, too?" asked Takia.

"Definitely," said Lenny.

"Yay!" the kids cried out in unison.

In the evening after the children were asleep, Lenny settled into bed beside Patience. He put his arm around her, kissed the top of her head. "I need to tell you about something," he said.

"Is something wrong?"

"Not exactly."

He took a minute to collect his thoughts. His throat was dry and constricted. He didn't know how to begin.

"If it's about marriage and commitment and all, you don't have to—"

"It's not that. I learned something today that's pretty . . . ugly."

She sat up. "Are you sick? Did the doctor find something?"

"It's not me. It's you. I had a friend check out the day you delivered Malcolm. The records were old and they had to dig back a long way, but I'll say one thing about the hospital, they keep very good records."

"What about Malcolm? Is there something wrong with him?"

His heart pounding in his chest, Lenny told her about the possibility that Odom may have been responsible for her inability to conceive. At first she was struck dumb. After a few seconds, she began to cry. The crying became deep sobs of sorrow and pain. He held her, stroking her hair, patting her shoulder, kissing her neck. After what seemed like hours, she fell asleep in his arms.

He turned out the light, pulled the sheet up to cover her from the air-conditioning. He lay awake a long time looking at her. Any doubts he once had about marrying her and adopting her children were washed away in the surge of love that he felt. He realized that after his wife's death he had floated aimlessly, until washing ashore on the island of this little home. Patience and the children offered everything he could ever want in a family. They welcomed him and loved him, and he felt the same way.

Yes, he would love to hold a little Lenny in his arms. But the secret of happiness was learning how to lose. There were losses ahead and losses behind. He knew he had to cherish what he had won and let the future happen—the good and the bad, the boring and the delightful.

He finally fell asleep in the arms of the woman he loved.

Acknowledgements

No words can fairly express my appreciation for the help given me in writing this book. First among the many who lent a hand is my union friend Dave, who tolerated my stealing from his life in fashioning Lenny Moss. Thank you. My crime writer friends Leah Robinson, Gordon Cotler, Bob Knightly, Reed Coleman and Eleanor Hyde slapped me around when I got lazy and let the writing sag—many thanks for keeping me focused. Without my sons, wonderful writers Matthew and Christopher, who discussed character and story line with me, the novel would still be in pieces all over my desk. And a special thanks to Denise Dietz, editor extraordinaire, who shaped and polished the manuscript until it was a thing of beauty.

Last but always first, thank you, Mary, for struggling with me to tell the truth and to write about the people and principles that inspire me.

About the Author

Timothy Sheard is a veteran critical care nurse with more than thirty-five years of hospital experience. He has published over 100 articles, short stories, plays and books. Sheard's crime novels are inspired by the real-life exploits of an 1199 hospital shop steward, as well as by his own experiences working in urban medical centers. He evokes the culture and inner workings of the hospital with a realism and truth rarely seen in fiction, showing the best and the worst of humanity, and the heartbreaking trials of critically-ill patients.